The Gen X

SCIENCE OLYMPIAD 6

Useful for Science Olympiads Conducted at School, National & International Levels

Authors
Shikha Gupta
Shikha Nautiyal

Peer Reviewer
P. Shyamla

Strictly According to the Latest Syllabus of Science Olympiad

Published by:

F-2/16, Ansari road, Daryaganj, New Delhi-110002
☎ 23240026, 23240027 • *Fax:* 011-23240028
Email: info@vspublishers.com • *Website:* www.vspublishers.com

Regional Office : Hyderabad
5-1-707/1, Brij Bhawan (Beside Central Bank of India Lane)
Bank Street, Koti, Hyderabad - 500 095
☎ 040-24737290
E-mail: vspublishershyd@gmail.com

Branch Office : Mumbai
Jaywant Industrial Estate, 1st Floor–108, Tardeo Road
Opposite Sobo Central Mall, Mumbai – 400 034
☎ 022-23510736
E-mail: vspublishersmum@gmail.com

Follow us on:

BUY OUR BOOKS FROM: AMAZON FLIPKART

© Copyright: V&S PUBLISHERS
ISBN 978-93-579404-5-0
New Edition

DISCLAIMER

While every attempt has been made to provide accurate and timely information in this book, neither the author nor the publisher assumes any responsibility for errors, unintended omissions or commissions detected therein. The author and publisher makes no representation or warranty with respect to the comprehensiveness or completeness of the contents provided.

All matters included have been simplified under professional guidance for general information only, without any warranty for applicability on an individual. Any mention of an organization or a website in the book, by way of citation or as a source of additional information, doesn't imply the endorsement of the content either by the author or the publisher. It is possible that websites cited may have changed or removed between the time of editing and publishing the book.

Results from using the expert opinion in this book will be totally dependent on individual circumstances and factors beyond the control of the author and the publisher.

It makes sense to elicit advice from well informed sources before implementing the ideas given in the book. The reader assumes full responsibility for the consequences arising out from reading this book.

For proper guidance, it is advisable to read the book under the watchful eyes of parents/guardian. The buyer of this book assumes all responsibility for the use of given materials and information.

The copyright of the entire content of this book rests with the author/publisher. Any infringement/transmission of the cover design, text or illustrations, in any form, by any means, by any entity will invite legal action and be responsible for consequences thereon.

Publisher's Note

The current decade has firmly established V&S Publishers as one of the Leading Publishers of General Trade Mass Appeal Books across popular genres along with Academic Books for school children. Having been in publishing trade for over 40 years we understand the need of the hour when it comes to Books. After successfully publishing over 600 titles in a rather short time span of 5 years and establishing a pan India network of booksellers & distributors including ecommerce platforms viz – Amazon, Flipkart etc; an extensive market research lead us to publishing our Bestselling Series ever – OLYMPIAD BOOKS.

The Olympiad Series launched 4 years back under our GEN X SERIES Imprint gained widespread popularity amongst students and teachers immediately owing to its rich, high quality content and unique presentation. Published for Classes 1-10 across subjects English, Maths, Science & Computers, these books are holistic in nature and unlike run of the mill workbooks in the market, which are mere replicas of one another, these books deal with the content in a much comprehensive manner. Recourse to the 'Principles of Applied Psychology of Student Learning' has been utilised to upgrade levels of conceptual understanding in all designated subjects among class 1 to 10 students.

Encouraged by this huge acceptability of our Olympiad Series among parents and students and after revolutionising the way Olympiad books were written and published, we at V&S Publishers decided to take this to the next level.

We present to you Brand New Edition of our book – **SCIENCE OLYMPIAD CLASS 6.**

Each book originally written by Subject Matter Expert, is now further Peer Reviewed by top School Teachers and HODs to eliminate the slightest of errors that were present earlier. Furthermore to ensure authenticity and accuracy of content the book is now completely revised and reformatted as per the guidelines of the examining body. The New and Revised Olympiad Book is now suited to Olympiad examinations conducted at School Level, National Level or International Level by any and all organisations/companies.

The New Edition of this Science Olympiad Class 6 is written in a Guide like pattern with images and illustrations at every step & is divided into different sections. Each chapter comes with Basic Theory and Solved Examples. Multiple Choice Questions with their Answer Keys and Solutions are liberally included.

Amalgamation of Technology with Content has always been at the forefront for V&S Publishers and our new Student Portal for Olympiad Practice–**www.vsexamprep.com** is further testimony to that. We recommend students logging in and using it to their benefit.

While every care has been taken to ensure correctness of content, if you come across any omission or mistake please notify us for immediate rectification in subsequent edition.

P.S. While every care has been taken to ensure correctness of content, if you come across any error, howsoever minor, anywhere in the book, do not hesitate to discuss with your teachers while pointing that out to us in no uncertain terms.

We wish you All The Best!

Contents

SECTION 1 : SCIENCE

1. Motion and Measurement of Distances 9
2. Light, Shadows and Reflections 17
3. Electricity and Circuits 25
4. Fun with Magnets 32
5. Air and Water 40
6. Sorting and Separation of Materials 50
7. Changes Around Us 60
8. Living Organisms and Their Surroundings 68
9. Food, Health and Hygiene 80
10. Fibre to Fabric 96
11. Body Movements in Animals 103

SECTION 2 : LOGICAL REASONING

1. Pattern 108
2. Analogy 113
3. Series Completion 118
4. Odd One Out 120
5. Coding – Decoding 123
6. Alphabet Test 127
7. Number and Ranking Test 131
8. Direction Sense Test 134
9. Essential Element 138
10. Mirror Images 141
11. Embedded Figure 147
12. Figure Puzzles 153

SECTION 3 : ACHIEVERS' SECTION

Higher Order Thinking Skills (HOTS) 158
SHORT ANSWER QUESTIONS 163
MODEL TEST PAPER – 1 169
MODEL TEST PAPER – 2 179
HINTS AND SOLUTIONS 187

SECTION 1
SCIENCE

Motion and Measurement of Distances

> **Learning Objectives**
> After reading the chapter, you will be able to:
> ☞ understand the science behind motion
> ☞ learn how to measure distances

Motion

We observe many objects in our daily life. Some of them move from one place to another, while others remain stationary.

> **Activity 1**
> On the way to your school, observe your surroundings and classify the objects under:
> **Objects in motion**   **Objects at rest**

From the above activity, we have learnt that some objects move and some remain stationary.

Can we find out whether an object is at rest or in motion only by observing them directly?

We can observe that some objects change their position with time. In some cases though, we cannot see the objects change their position; we come to know about their motion from the effects they make.

If an object does not change its position with respect to time, it is said to be stationary or at rest. If an object changes its position with respect to time, then it is said to be in motion. Hence, **motion** can be defined as the change of position of an object with respect to time.

For example, a car which stops at a traffic light is said to be at rest or stationary. Let us take our earth as an example. Do you think earth is stationary or in motion? Earth is constantly in motion. If the earth doesn't rotate, there will be no day or night.

Now let's try and understand another concept. When you are sitting inside a bus, the buildings, trees, road etc. are in motion or stationary? While your bus is in motion, you will feel that all objects outside the bus are in motion too, isn't it? But is that the truth or just an illusion?

Now consider this: will a person standing at a bus stop see the road, trees and buildings in motion too? The answer is no. An object may appear stationary to one observer and appear to be moving for other. In other words, an object is at rest in relation to a certain set of objects and moving in relation to another set of objects. This implies that *rest and motion are relative.*

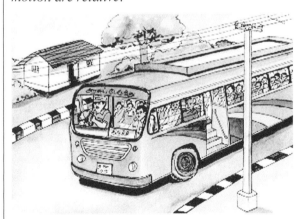

Different Types of Motion

Linear Motion

When an object moves along a straight line, it is said to be in a **linear motion** or **rectilinear motion**. For example, a lift in any building follows a linear path to transport people from one floor to another; a coconut falling from a tree falls in a straight line which is again linear motion; a car speeding along a straight road is again linear motion.

Circular Motion

Take a stone, tie a thread to it and whirl it with your hand and observe the motion of the stone. The stone is moving along a circular path, isn't it? In this motion, at any point in the circular path, the distance of the stone from the centre of the circle (hand) remains the same, doesn't it? When an object moves in a circular path, it is said to be in **circular motion**. Other examples include: fan on the ceiling, spinning of a top, child sitting on a merry-go-round.

Periodic Motion

When an object repeats the same type of motion at regular intervals of time, it is said to be in a **periodic motion**. Examples include: the motion of a child swinging; motion of a pendulum in a wall clock; motion of the earth revolving around the sun; motion of moon revolving around the earth.

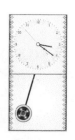

Random Motion

When an object moves at different speeds and in different directions, with no particular pattern, it is said to be in a **random motion**. Examples: fish swimming in a tank; movement of football on the field, motion of a butterfly.

Measurement

Sanchit went to the market with his father. He observed various weighing instruments that were used to measure different things. He had a doubt and asked his father, "Why are there so many different units of measurement?"

Before we answer Sanchit's question, let's first do the following activity.

Activity 2

Fill up the table given below with the help of daily basis examples:

Item	Quantity	Measuring Instrument

We know that measuring instruments like metre scale, balance, clock, measuring jar, etc. are necessary for measuring different items.

The comparison of an unknown quantity with a certain fixed quantity of the same kind is called **measurement**. Any quantity that can be measured is called a **physical quantity**. You might have noticed how a vegetable vendor uses weights to measure the weight of a particular commodity. He measures the commodities and then totals up the charges associated with each commodity based on the measurement taken.

Units of Measurement

Lengths, mass and time are called **fundamental quantities**, because they cannot be expressed in terms of any other physical quantity. The units used to measure these fundamental quantities are called fundamental units.

Different types of quantities need to be measured differently. Hence, we use different units of measurement for each. Let us attempt to understand the ways to conduct accurate measurement.

Measuring Length

The distance between two points is called the **length**. Let us try to measure the length of our classroom with the help of a meter scale. Suppose the length of the classroom is 2 meters. Here, **2 is the magnitude and meter is the unit of length**. Meter is the universal unit of measurement of length or distance, but the quantity or the magnitude has to be determined.

Precautions while measuring length:
(i) The scale should be placed in contact with the object along the length of the object
(ii) If the ends of the scale being used are broken, taking measurement from zero should be avoided. The measurement can be taken starting from 1.0 cm. Then the reading of this mark is subtracted from the reading at the other end.
(iii) Correct position of eye is equally important. Eyes should be exactly in front of the point where the scale is placed for measurement.

Measuring Weight
The amount of matter contained in a body is called **mass**. We can also measure your weight or mass using a weighing scale. Suppose, you weigh 58 kilograms. Here, again, **58 is the magnitude** and **kilogram is a unit of mass**. Kilogram, like, meter is a known constant unit of measurement for mass and weight.

Measuring Time
An interval between two events is called time. If it takes 20 minutes for you to reach your school, then **20 is the magnitude** and **minutes is a known unit to measure time**.

Any measurement that gives the same value for all is called **standard measurement**. Units used in standard measurement are called **standard unit**. Standard unit of measurement was given by the French and is known as the metric system. The system of units now used is called international system of units called SI units. Here are the most commonly used SI units:
(i) Length: meter
(ii) Mass: kilogram
(iii) Time: seconds
(iv) Temperature: Kelvin

Multiples and Submultiples of Length, Time and Mass
Lengths, mass and time are also measured by other units. However, kilometre, kilogram and seconds are used as standard units to make the conversions.

Length
The distance between two points is called **length**. Draw a straight line in your note book. Mark two points A and B on the line. Measure the distance between the two points using a scale. What you have measured now is the length. The SI unit of length is meter. To measure length, we use measuring tape, meter scale, etc.

Activity 3
Measure the length of the following and write them, using appropriate units.
Length of your pencil _____
Length of your thumb _____
Length of your eraser _____
Length of a leaf _____
Length of your pen nib _____
Length of the nail of your little finger

Multiples and Submultiples of Length
In the above activity, larger distances such as the distance between two places are expressed in kilometre. This is called **a multiple of length**. We express smaller lengths, such as length of a pencil, pen nib, etc. in centimetre and millimetre. These are called **submultiples of length**.

Subunits of length
1 centimetre (cm) = 10 millimetre
1 decimetre (dm) = 10 centimetre = 100 mm
1 metre (m) = 100 centimetre
1 metre (m) = 1000 millimetre
1 kilometre (km) = 1000 metre

Mass
The mass of a body is the amount of matter contained in it. The SI unit of mass is kilogram. We use beam balance, physical balance and electronic balance for measuring mass.

Subunits of mass
1 gram (g) = 1000 milligram
1 kilogram (kg) = 1000 gram
1 kilogram (kg) = 1000000 milligram
1 quintal = 100 kilogram
1 metric ton = 1000 kilogram

Motion and Measurement of Distances

Time

We perform many activities in our daily life, but the duration of each event/activity differs from one another. To understand it better, complete the following activity.

Activity 4

Look at the following activities. Discuss in small groups and tabulate the events/activities according to their duration. Use appropriate units of time. Then categorize them accordingly.

1. Time taken for bathing
2. Duration of sleep
3. Working hours of your school
4. Time taken to blink your eyes
5. Time taken for ripening of fruits
6. Time taken for a plant to grow into a tree
7. Time taken for curdling of milk
8. Time taken to weave a saree
9. Time interval between a new moon and a full moon
10. Time interval between the first term and the second term examination
11. Time taken by a coconut to fall from a tree
    a. **Events/activities occurring in seconds:**
    b. **Events/activities occurring in minutes:**
    c. **Events/activities occurring in hours:**
    d. **Events/activities occurring in days/months:**
    e. **Events/ activities occurring in years:**

Subunits of time

1 minute = 60 seconds   1 hour = 60 minutes
1 day = 24 hours   1 year = 365 ¼ days
1 century = 100 years

Multiple Choice Questions

1. Movement of a branch of a tree in air is an example of _____.
   (a) Random motion
   (b) Circular motion
   (c) Periodic motion
   (d) Rotational motion

2. Which of the following statements is correct?
   (a) A footstep can be used as a standard unit of measurement because its length is same for all the persons
   (b) A footstep cannot be used as a standard unit of measurement because its length is not same for all the persons
   (c) A footstep cannot be used as a standard unit of measurement because its length is 10 cm only for all the persons
   (d) A footstep cannot be used as a standard unit of measurement because it always remains constant

3. Who found that a pendulum of a given length always takes the same time to complete one oscillation?
   (a) Galileo Galilei   (b) Archimedes
   (c) Albert Einstein   (d) Newton

4. The scale should be kept _____ the length while measuring a length.
   (a) Perpendicular to   (b) Inclined to
   (c) Away from   (d) Along

5. When the bob of the pendulum is released after taking it slightly to one side, it:
   (a) Begins to move up and down
   (b) Begins to move to and fro
   (c) Becomes still and does not move
   (d) Comes to rest at the mean position

6. The motion of a rolling ball is an example of _____ motion.
   (a) Circular   (b) Linear
   (c) Rotational   (d) Random

7. Identify the types of motion from the images below.

   (a) Periodic, rotational, linear respectively
   (b) Periodic, rotational, circular respectively
   (c) Linear, rotational, periodic respectively
   (d) Rotational, linear, periodic respectively

8. Three cars are running on the road with three different speeds: 78 mph, 59 mph, and 65 mph respectively. Calculate the average of these three speeds.
   (a) 82.7 mph   (b) 74.5 mph
   (c) 67.3 mph   (d) 44.2 mph

9. What would be the best unit to use to measure the tip of your pencil?
   (a) Feet   (b) Kilometer
   (c) Millimeter   (d) Meter

10. Look at the following picture carefully.
    Now read the following paragraph carefully and fill the blank with correct sequence of words.

    A stone suspended with a non-stretchable thread makes a simple _____. When the pendulum is at rest, it is at position B. This is called the **rest position** or its _____.
    When it swings, it moves from B to A, back to B, from B to C and back to B. This completes one full swing of the pendulum. Each swing is called _____.
    (a) Mean position, one oscillation, pendulum
    (b) One oscillation, complete oscillation, pendulum
    (c) Mean position, pendulum, complete oscillation
    (d) Pendulum, mean position, one oscillation

11. Two athletes take part in two separate races and cover different distances in different times. Kavya runs 2 km in 10 minutes and Yamini runs 5 km in 20 minutes on two different tracks. Which of the following statements is correct?
    (a) Yamini runs faster than Kavya
    (b) Kavya runs faster than Yamini
    (c) Yamini runs faster than Kavya in one minute
    (d) Both a and c

Motion and Measurement of Distances

12. Which of the following is not a unit of speed?
    (a) km/min   (b) m/min
    (c) km/h   (d) kg/s

13. Look at the picture carefully: Fill in the blanks using words: stationary, moving.

    The potter at the railway station is _____ in relation to the train, but is _____ in relation to the bag on his head.
    (a) Moving, stationary
    (b) Stationary, moving
    (c) Stationary, stationary
    (d) Moving, moving

14. Why is measurement important to us?
    (a) It is required by students to learn mathematics and science
    (b) It is required only for advanced scientific calculations
    (c) It is required by every human being for their day-to-day living
    (d) It is required only to build satellites

15. Read the following two paragraphs. Analyze the situation and choose the correct options.
    1. A bus runs from Kolkata to Guwahati. It covers a distance of 400 km in 7 hours and then a distance of 550 km in the next 7 hours.
    2. Alisha takes part in a car race. She drives a distance of 70 km each in the first, second and third hours.
    (a) First statement is an example of uniform motion and second statement is an example of non-uniform motion
    (b) First statement is an example of non-uniform motion and second statement is an example of uniform motion
    (c) Both first and second are examples of uniform motion
    (d) Both first and second are examples of non-uniform motion

16. 1 cm = ………. m
    (a) 0.001   (b) 0.01
    (c) 10   (d) 0.1

17. The length of the blank card shown below is _____.

    (a) 1.6 inches   (b) 1.6 cm
    (c) 3.2 cm   (d) 2.5 inches

18. Which of the following objects cannot be used for measuring the length of a curved line?
    (a) Thread and ruler
    (b) Screw gauge
    (c) Set square
    (d) None of them

19. While reading an instrument, why is it important to place the eye in line with the reading?
    (a) To avoid parallax error
    (b) To see more clearly
    (c) To avoid reflections
    (d) To get a better view of the entire instrument

20. Look at the following graph. Observe it carefully.

    This graph shows:

    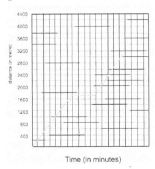

    Time (in minutes)

    (a) The motion of a school bus
    (b) The motion of Sanchit, who stops at the market on his way back home from school
    (c) The motion of an ant as it collects rice grains
    (d) The motion of an athlete running a 200 m race

21. A cyclist moves from a certain point X and goes round a circle of radius a and reaches Y, exactly at the other side of the point X as shown in the figure below. The displacement of the cyclist would be _____.

    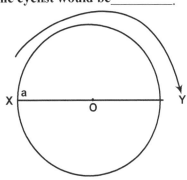

    (a) πa   (b) 2 πa
    (c) 2a   (d) 2 π/a

22. The unit of speed depends on the units of distance and time. Based on this statement, fill up the following table.

Units for distance	Units for time	Units for speed	
kilometers		kilometers per hour	Km/h
	second		
meter	minute		m/min

(a) Hour, meter, meters per second, m/sec, meter/minute
(b) Second, meter/minute, meter/second, m/sec
(c) Meter, meter/second, meter/minute, m/sec,
(d) Meter/minute, centimeter, minute, Km/h

23. In circular motion, the _____.
    (a) Acceleration is zero
    (b) Velocity is constant
    (c) Direction of the motion fixed
    (d) Direction of the motion changes continuously

24. Which of the following is false?
    (a) A ceiling fan shows rotatory motion
    (b) The motion of a swing is rectilinear as well as circular
    (c) A guitar shows vibratory motion
    (d) The pendulum of a clock shows oscillatory motion

Motion and Measurement of Distances

25. The picture here shows the position of the sun at different times of the day, if we were looking south. The picture also shows the shadow cast by the stick at 4 p.m.

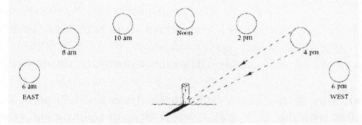

What time of the day would it be if the stick made shadows like these?

(a) 6 pm, noon, 8 am
(b) 10 am, noon, 4 pm
(c) 6 pm, noon, 10 am
(d) 8 am, noon, 6 pm

Light, Shadows and Reflection

Learning Objectives

After reading the chapter, you will be able to:
- learn about important characteristics of light
- explain luminous and non-luminous objects
- study opaque, transparent and translucent objects
- study the formation of shadows
- understand the features of a shadow
- learn about solar and lunar eclipses
- differentiate between an image and a shadow
- understand the formation of reflections

We *see* a lot of things around us: Trees, birds, cars, road, school building, etc. You might have also noticed shadows of some objects. Ever wondered how are shadows formed? What is reflection?

We shall aim to answer all these questions through this chapter.

Light

The natural agent that stimulates sight and makes things visible is called **light**. Objects that generate their own light are called **luminous objects**. For example, the sun is a luminous object. Candles and stars are also examples of luminous objects. On the other hand, all those objects which cannot generate their own light are called non-luminous objects. For example, your hand, balls, gloves, rubber, etc. are **non-luminous objects**.

Light has the ability to travel through various substances. Based on whether light can pass through them or not, objects are divided into three main categories:

(i) *Opaque objects:* Objects which do not allow the passage of light and through which one cannot see anything are called **opaque objects**. Examples include: wood, books, chair, shoes.

(ii) *Translucent objects:* Objects which allow light to pass through them partially and through which we are able to see but not clearly are called **translucent objects**. Umbrellas, coloured glass, wax paper, dirty water and certain kind of plastic objects, butter paper.

(iii) *Transparent objects:* Objects through which light can pass through easily and one can see clearly are called **transparent objects**. Glass, cellophane paper, air, diamonds are all transparent objects.

Please note that light always **travels in a straight line**. We have already learnt about rectilinear motion. Light is an example of rectilinear motion and this property of light is called **rectilinear propagation of light**. For the purpose of drawing a diagram to depict light, the path of light is represented by a straight line with an arrowhead depicting the direction of light. Such a straight line with an arrowhead is called the **ray of light**.

Shadow

The darkness that an object causes while preventing the light to pass through it is called a **shadow**. It is a dark region which doesn't contain any colour.

The size of a shadow is relative to the position of the object with respect to the source of light. The shadow of an object is formed only on another opaque object which is called a **screen** or **surface**. A shadow has the following characteristics:

(i) A shadow is formed only when the light is blocked by an opaque object.
(ii) A shadow is only a dark region which does not have any colour.
(iii) A shadow may or may not resemble the actual shape of an object.
(iv) A shadow can only be formed on a screen or surface.
(v) The size of a shadow is relative to the position of the light source with respect to the object.

Pinhole Camera
A pinhole camera is a small, light-tight can or box with a black interior and a tiny hole in the centre of one end. By using common household materials, you can make a camera that will produce pictures.

Mirrors and Images
We have learnt that opaque objects do not allow light to pass through them. So what happens to this light? It gets **scattered** in all directions. Every morning, when you get ready, do you see yourself in the mirror? What do you see? You see your own **image**.

Image 1

Image 2

In a dark room send a beam of light through a comb on to a mirror (as shown in Image 1). You will see a beautiful pattern getting formed (see Image 2). This pattern depicts that light travels in a straight line and also shows the **reflection** through the mirror.

A **mirror** is made of a thin glass, which is painted over with silver on one side. By polishing silver on one side, the mirror becomes an opaque object. When the light falls on the smooth surface of a mirror, it is sent out in a well-defined but different directions. This phenomenon is called **reflection**. A ray of light from an object falling onto a mirror is called an **incident ray**. The ray that is bounced back from the mirror is called a **reflected ray**. An image is formed only when a ray is reflected from a smooth and a shiny surface.

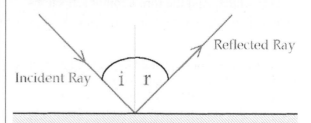

Plane Mirror

Eclipses
We know that the earth revolves around the sun and the moon revolves around the earth. Sometimes the earth, the sun and the moon come in a straight line. In such cases the light of the sun is blocked by either the earth or the moon. As a result, a shadow is formed. This phenomenon is called an **eclipse**. Following are the two types of eclipses:

Solar Eclipse
When the moon comes in between the sun and the earth, the moon acts like an opaque object blocking the light from the sun. The earth is the screen, such that the shadow of the moon falls on earth. When people from the shadowed part of the earth try to see the sun, it is blocked or partially visible. This phenomenon is called **solar eclipse**.

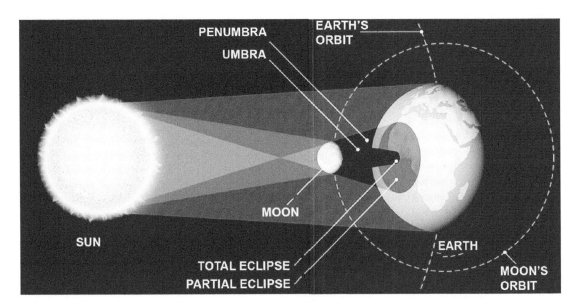

Lunar Eclipse

When the earth comes between the sun and the moon, it acts like the opaque object blocking the sun. The moon in this scenario is the screen. The shadow of the earth falls on the moon whose view gets partially or completely blocked for some time. This phenomenon is called **lunar eclipse**.

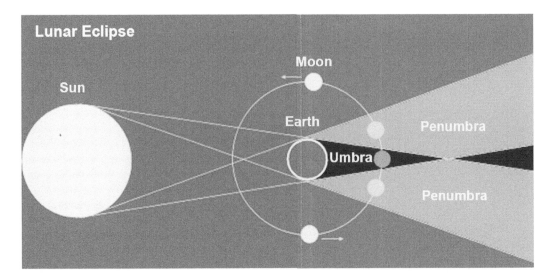

Differences between an Image and a Shadow

Here are some crucial differences between an image and a shadow:

1. A shadow does not show the details of an object whereas an image gives an exact replica of the object.
2. A shadow is formed by blocking the light by an opaque object. An image on the other hand is formed due to a reflection from an opaque smooth and shiny surface.
3. A shadow is always dark while the image shows the true colours of the object.

Light, Shadows and Reflection

Activity

Human eyes and light
Match the functions with the different parts of the eye that perform them.

1. cornea   sends messages to the brain
2. retina   protects the sensitive parts of the eye
3. pupil   controls the amount of light let in by the pupil
4. lens   lets in the correct amount of light
5. iris   focuses the light to give a sharp image
6. optic nerve   detects the light

Multiple Choice Questions

1. Why do the shadows made by the sun change in size during the course of the day?
   (a) Because the weather changes
   (b) Because the objects keep moving
   (c) Because the sun appears to move across the sky during the course of the day
   (d) Because the amount of light, emitted by the sun, keeps on changing

2. Light is a form of energy that is produced by a:
   (a) Transparent object
   (b) Luminous object
   (c) Non-luminous object
   (d) Opaque object

3. If a capital letter R is seen in an ordinary plane mirror, what does it look like?
   (a) R   (b) Я
   (c) ʁ   (d) ᴙ

4. The image of an object formed in the water is:
   (a) Diminished
   (b) Erect
   (c) Inverted
   (d) None of the above

5. Ishani saw the sun at different positions in the sky at different times of the day. Which one of the following is the cause for her observations?
   (a) Revolution of the earth
   (b) Rotation of the sun
   (c) Rotation of the earth
   (d) Movement of the earth around the moon

6. Which of the following will not form a circular shadow?
   (a) A CD
   (b) Shoe box
   (c) Ice-cream cone
   (d) A ball

7. When the moon comes in between the sun and the earth in a straight line, then a solar eclipse is formed. The eclipse occurs because of the _____.
   (a) Formation of a shadow of the earth on the moon
   (b) Formation of a shadow of the moon on the earth
   (c) Reflection of light by the earth
   (d) Reflection of light by the moon

8. In a completely dark room, if you hold up a mirror in front of you, you will see:
   (a) Your shadow
   (b) A sharp shadow
   (c) Your image
   (d) No image

9. Sanchit performed the following experiment:
   In a dark room, Sanchit took a flashlight, placed a cardboard in front of the flashlight and made a small hole at the centre of the cardboard. Then he switched on the flashlight.

   He observed that the light appears to come out from the small hole in a straight line.
   Conclusion of the above experiment could be:
   (a) Light travels in a straight line
   (b) This demonstrates the rectilinear propagation of light
   (c) A and B both
   (d) None of these

10. Butter paper is an example of _____ object.
    (a) A transparent
    (b) A translucent
    (c) An opaque
    (d) A luminous

Light, Shadows and Reflection

11. Deepti is a dentist. She uses a mirror to focus light on the tooth of a patient. Look at the following pictures and find out that what kind of mirror she uses?

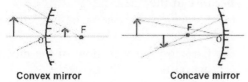

(a) Concave mirror
(b) Convex mirror
(c) Plane mirror
(d) Cylindrical mirror

12. If you stand before a plane mirror, your left hand appears right. This phenomenon is:
   (a) The reflection of light
   (b) The lateral inversion of light
   (c) The shadow formation
   (d) The diffusion of light

13. Shadow is formed due to:
   (a) The rectilinear propagation of light
   (b) The parallel propagation of light
   (c) The passing of light through object
   (d) All of these

14. Sanchit, Ananya, Ruhi and Rohit are discussing light, shadow and reflection. Choose the incorrect statement.
   (a) Sanchit: Light is a form of energy which cannot be seen
   (b) Ananya: The image formed by a pin-hole camera is inverted
   (c) Ruhi: We see the moon because it is a luminous body
   (d) Rohit: Plane mirror is used in periscope

15. Three identical towels of green, blue and red colours are hung on a clothesline in the sun. What would be the colour of shadows of these towels?
   (a) The colour of shadow does not depend on the colour of the object. The shadow is always black in colour. So, all three towels will form same colour shadow

(b) The colour of shadow depends on the colour of the object. So, all three towels will form same colour shadow as their original colours
(c) The colour of shadow does not depend on the colour of the object, it depends on the thickness of the object. The shadow is always black in colour. So, all three towels will form same colour shadow
(d) (a) and (c) both are correct

16.

Ambulance seen in a mirror

Look at the two pictures above and choose the correct statement given below.
(a) An image is a reflection of an object in the mirror. Mirrors generally change the direction of light which falls (incident) on them
(b) When an image of an object is formed in a plane mirror, some reversal of position takes place
(c) The reversal experienced by an image formed in a plane (flat) mirror is sideways
(d) All of them

17.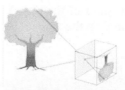

The image given above depicts:
(a) A pinhole camera
(b) A periscope
(c) An eclipse
(d) A and C both

18. The following picture is an example of a:
(a) Concave mirror
(b) Convex mirror
(c) Plane mirror
(d) Cylindrical mirror

19. There are two imaginary objects A and B. Object A reflects more than object B. Therefore, object A is likely to be _____ object B.
    (a) Made of the same material as
    (b) Smoother than
    (c) Just as smooth as
    (d) Rougher than

20. One night, Ahana was sleeping on her terrace. She looked up at the night sky and observed the things she could see. She made a list of the sources of light in night sky. What should she have written down on her list?
    (a) Moon
    (b) Clouds
    (c) Moon and stars
    (d) Clouds and moon

21. A girl is 2 m away from a plane mirror. If she moves away from the mirror by 0.5 m, what will be the new distance between the object and its image?
    (a) 2 m   (b) 1.5 m
    (c) 3 m   (d) 0.5 m

22. The focus of a concave mirror is _____.
    (a) Real   (b) Virtual
    (c) Undefined   (d) At the pole

23. When light falls on the following objects, which among them would show the darkest shadow?
    (a) A sheet of thin tissue paper
    (b) A glass window
    (c) A wooden chopping board
    (d) Water in a glass

24. A boy did the following experiment.
    He kept a wooden cube in front of a screen. He had three torches with him.

Without changing the position of the cube and the screen, he placed the other two torches one after the other, in the position of torch 1, and saw the shadow.

Which torch will make the largest shadow (umbra) on the screen?

(a) Torch 1
(b) Torch 2
(c) Torch 3
(d) The size of the shadow will be the same for all the three torches.

Answer the following questions based on the images below.

Natural light sources

Man-made sources of light

25. Natural light sources include sun, glowing rocks (lava from volcanoes), and _____.
    (a) Fire
    (b) Flame
    (c) Torch
    (d) Fire and flame

26. Are candles, light bulbs, flame, CFL's, tube-lights, kerosene lamps etc. man-made or natural sources of light?
    (a) Man-made sources of light
    (b) Natural light sources
    (c) Some are natural; some are man-made sources of light
    (d) None of them

27. Let us take these three objects (glass tumbler, coloured glass and wooden block). Keep them on the table. Now place a pencil box on the other side of these objects.

It was observed that in case of the glass tumbler, the pencil box on the other side can be seen clearly. In case of the coloured glass, the pencil box on the other side cannot be seen very clearly. In the third case, the pencil box is not seen at all from the other side of the wooden block.

So the conclusion can be:
(a) The first object is transparent, the second object is opaque, and the third one is translucent
(b) The first object is transparent, the second object is translucent, and the third one is opaque
(c) The first object is opaque, the second object is translucent, and the third one is transparent
(d) The first object is translucent, the second object is transparent, and the third one is opaque

28. When an object is placed at the focus of a concave mirror, the image will be formed at _____.
    (a) Infinity
    (b) The focus
    (c) The centre of curvature
    (d) The pole

29. In a lunar eclipse shadow of _____ falls on _____.
    (a) Sun, earth   (b) Earth, moon
    (c) Moon, sun   (d) Sun, moon

30. Place a lamp close to a mug and observe its shadow on a table. Notice that the shadow formed has two parts. The darker part of the shadow, is the _____ and the lighter part is the _____.
    (a) Umbra, penumbra
    (b) Penumbra, umbra
    (c) Thicker, thinner
    (d) Only Penumbra

Electricity and Circuits

Learning Objectives
After reading the chapter, you will be able to:
- understand the uses of electricity
- study the significance of electric circuits
- learn the concept behind an electric cell
- understand conductors and insulators

We use electricity on a daily basis. We use electricity to run the appliances at home such as fans, air conditioners, refrigerators, tube lights etc. Apart from these daily household usages, electricity is also used on a large scale. For example, electricity is used to draw water from the wells by using electric pumps. Electricity is also used in hospitals to run several diagnostic machines. So what is electricity? How is it used? How does it make machines work? This chapter will answer these and other similar questions.

Electricity

Electricity is a form of energy produced by the presence of charged particles, like electrons and protons. It is primarily derived from power stations and electric cells. Let us now try and understand electric cells in greater detail.

Electric Cell

When you turn the switch on, the bulb in your torch automatically lights up. How do you think that is possible? It is done through an electric cell. We use an electric cell in a number of devices including wrist watches, radio transistors, cameras and many other devices.

Fig 1

If you take an electric cell and notice it carefully, you will see that it has a metal disc on one side and a metal plate on the other. Both ends of a cell have a negative (−) and positive (+) sign. The metal cap is the positive terminal while the metal plate is the negative terminal. These two terminals are called the **positive terminal** and the **negative terminal** respectively.

The metal plates or the terminals are stored in a chemical called **electrolyte**. One of the chemicals is white in colour and is called **ammonium chloride** (NH_4Cl) and the other chemical is a black powder called **manganese dioxide** (MnO_2). These chemicals aid in the production of electricity within a cell. This cell in turn produces electricity and helps in the functioning of the appliance. This is how our wrist watches and radio transistors work. When the chemicals in the cell are used up the cell stops working. In that case the cell has to be replaced by a new one. The first cell was developed by a renowned scientist named **Luigi Galvani** and was improved by **Alessandro Volta**.

Electric Bulb

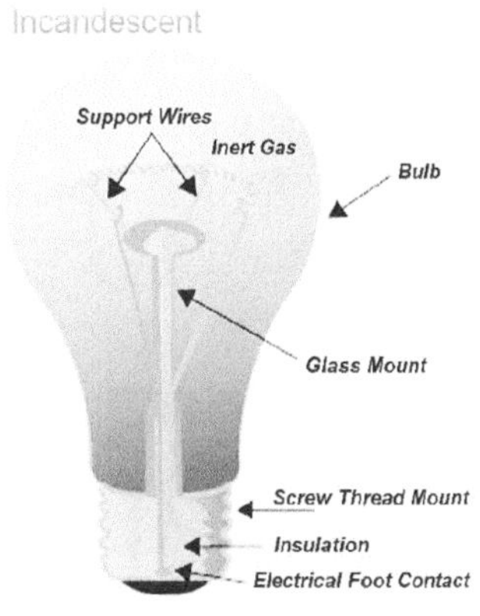

Fig 2

Take a bulb and look at it closely. You will notice a thin wire which gives out light. This thin wire is made of an element called **tungsten** and is called the **filament**. The filament is connected to two thick wires which also provide support to the filament. One of these wires is connected to the base of the bulb. The other thick wire is connected to the centre of the same base. Just like an electric cell, the base of the bulb and the metal tip of the base are the two terminals of the bulb. These two terminals are connected in such a way that they do not touch each other. When this bulb is connected to a power supply, the filament heats up and glows due to the passage of current. Hence, *electric energy* is converted into *light energy* when the current flows through the filament. Another thing to remember is that while the filament glows when the current passes through the bulb. Sometimes the filament may also be broken. In that case the bulb won't glow and the bulb said to be **fused**.

Electric Circuit

An **electric circuit** is a closed path along which an electric current flows from the positive terminal of the battery to the negative terminal. An **electric current** on the other hand is the flow of charge or electron. A cell is a source of electric current. An electric circuit consists of the following components:

(i) A source of electric current – a cell or battery (a group of cells makes a **battery**)
(ii) Connecting wires to carry the current
(iii) A device which uses the electricity – a bulb
(iv) A key or a switch – an entity which allows or stops the flow of the current.

When the switch is off and the current doesn't flow in the circuit, it is called an **open circuit**. When the switch is on and allows the flow of the current through the circuit, it is called a **closed circuit**.

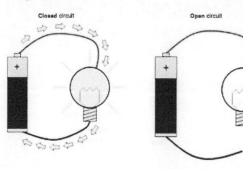

The connections made while trying to connect the bulb and the battery in the experiment above is an example of a circuit. The electric circuit makes a complete path for the flow of current through it. This electricity, in turn, lights up the bulb, as the current flows through the filament of the bulb.

Electric Conductors and Insulators

We have learnt about electricity and its flow. We have also learnt that a wire is required to allow the passage of electricity. However, not all materials allow the passage of current. Let's learn about these materials.

Conductors

Materials that allow electricity to pass through them are called **conductors**. Examples include water, copper, iron, steel, silver, aluminium amongst others. Conductors conduct electric current. Since metal is a good conductor of electricity, it is primarily used in the manufacturing of wires. Hence, the circuit shown above consist of wires to allow the passage of electricity. Sometimes we get an electric shock. This is because our bodies are good conductors of electricity.

Insulators

Materials that do not allow electricity to pass through them are called **insulators**. Insulators oppose the electric current and are hence used to protect oneself from coming into direct contact with electricity. Examples would include: glass, plastic, air, cotton, wood and rubber. Although water is a good conductor of electricity, its purest form called **distilled water** is an insulator.

We use various electrical appliances every day. Without the help of insulators, the use of electrical appliances would be impossible. The parts of the electric appliances that we touch are covered with insulating material. For example, plugs and switches are covered with an insulating material such as plastic, and the wire attached to the plug is a metal wire, which is a conductor. So conductors and insulators work hand in hand.

Activities

To show the heating effect of electric current

Activity 1
You will need

A cell, two bulbs

What to do?
1. Take two torch bulbs.
2. Make one of them glow using a cell as discussed previously.
3. Let the other bulb remain disconnected.
4. Touch both the bulbs one by one.
5. Which one feels hotter?

Record your observation here:

Activity 2
You will need

A cell, a rectangular piece of uncrushed aluminum foil of dimensions 7 cm × 1 cm

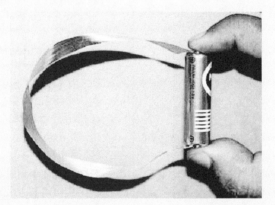

What to do
1. Tape the corners of the foil at the two terminals of the cell as shown.
2. Touch the foil after 30 seconds
3. What do you feel?
4. Disconnect the cell. Again, feel the foil.
5. Connect the cell again to the foil and touch it.

Record your observations:

Foil feels .... when connected to a cell and .... on disconnecting. This is because of the heating effect of the electric current.

Electricity and Circuits

Multiple Choice Questions

1. Moving an electron within an electric field would change the _____ the electron.
   (a) Weight of
   (b) Potential energy of
   (c) Amount of charge on
   (d) Mass of

2. Which one of the following statements is false?
   (a) Electricity can pass through copper, steel, iron, nichrome, brass, carbon and aluminium
   (b) Insulators are non-conductors of electricity and they prevent us from getting electrocuted
   (c) Silk, wool, leather and wood are materials that were once alive
   (d) None of the above

3. The diagram below shows an open circuit.

   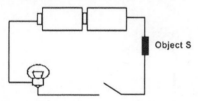

   When the circuit is closed, the light bulb does not light up at all.
   What could be the possible reasons?
   1. The light bulb has fused.
   2. Object S is a plastic ruler.
   3. The batteries are too strong.
   4. Object S is an insulator of electricity.
   5. The arrangement of batteries is incorrect.
   (a) 1, 2 and 4   (b) 2, 3 and 4
   (c) 1, 2, 4 and 5   (d) 1, 2, 3 and 5

4. Which of the following is the odd one in the group?
   (a) Silver   (b) Aluminium
   (c) Salt solution (d) Ceramic articles

5. The filament of a bulb is usually a:
   (a) Thick straight wire
   (b) Thin straight wire
   (c) Thin wire with many coils
   (d) Thick wire with many coils

6. The main function of a switch is to:
   (a) Make the bulb glow easily
   (b) Allow charges to flow
   (c) Complete or break a circuit
   (d) Prevent electric shocks

7. Look at the following circuit and read the following paragraph carefully.

   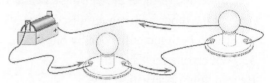

   All parts are connected one after another. Electrons flow from the negative terminal of the battery through the loop to the positive terminal.
   Which of the following statement is related to the circuit described in the paragraph above?
   (a) In a series circuit electricity has only one path to follow
   (b) If a light bulb is missing or broken in a series circuit, the other bulb will light
   (c) In a parallel circuit, electricity has only one path to follow
   (d) a and b both

8. If a light bulb is missing or broken in a parallel circuit, will the other bulb light? Explain.

   (a) Yes because the electricity can travel along a different path and avoid the broken bulb
   (b) No, because the path the electricity needs to follow is broken
   (c) Yes, because the path the electricity needs to follow is not broken
   (d) No, because the electricity cannot travel along a different path and avoid the broken bulb

9. Voltage _____ an electrical circuit.
   (a) Goes through
   (b) Is expressed across
   (c) Is constant throughout
   (d) Is the rate at which charges move through

10. If a battery provides a high voltage, it can _____.
    (a) Do a lot of work on each charge it encounters
    (b) Last a long time
    (c) Push a lot of charge through a circuit
    (d) Do a lot of work over the course of its lifetime

(For question 11 and 12) Alisha has a mobile phone. Energy is stored in the battery of the phone. The diagram below shows the battery being charged.

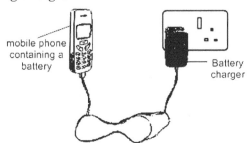

11. The main energy conversion in the battery as it is being charged?

    (a) Chemical potential energy ⟶ Electrical energy
    (b) Electrical energy potential energy
    (c) Electrical energy ⟶ Chemical energy
    (d) Potential energy ⟶ Electrical energy

12. When the phone is fully charged, Alisha unplugs the battery charger from the phone. State the energy conversion when the mobile phone rings.
    (a) Chemical energy ⟶ Electrical energy ⟶ Sound energy (+Kinetic energy + Heat energy + Sound energy)
    (b) Electrical energy ⟶ Chemical potential energy ⟶ Sound energy (+Kinetic energy + Heat energy
    (c) Sound energy ⟶ Electrical energy ⟶ Chemical energy
    (d) Sound energy (+Kinetic energy + Heat energy + Sound energy) ⟶ Electrical energy ⟶ Chemical energy

Use the following diagram for questions no. 13 and 14.

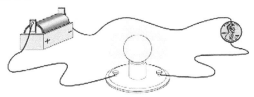

13. What supplies energy in an electric circuit?
    (a) Battery   (b) A conductor
    (c) Light bulb   (d) A wire

14. Which material is a conductor?
    (a) Glass   (b) Silver
    (c) Plastic   (d) Wood

15. Which of these could be used as a resistor in a circuit?
    (a) A rubber eraser
    (b) A pencil
    (c) An electric motor
    (d) A gas engine

16. Which statement is not correct about current electricity?
    (a) The type of electricity that is used to power things we use is called **current electricity**
    (b) Current electricity is electricity that flows through wires
    (c) Current electricity can flow in any circuit.
    (d) The path that electricity follows is called a circuit

17. In domestic wiring, the neutral wire has which of the following colors?
    (a) Red   (b) Black
    (c) Green   (d) White

18. In a circuit having one bulb, another bulb is added. The new bulb will:
    (a) Get fused
    (b) Not glow
    (c) Glow more brightly
    (d) Glow but less brightly

Electricity and Circuits

Direction (19 – 20): Study the circuit diagram below. The bulbs are labelled A, B, C and D. The switches are labeled 1, 2, 3 and 4. Use the diagram to solve questions 19 and 20.

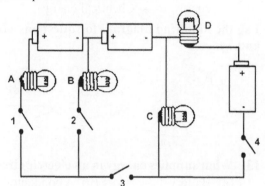

19. Which two switches should be closed so that only bulbs B and C would light up?
    (a) Switches 1 and 2
    (b) Switches 2 and 3
    (c) Switches 3 and 4
    (d) Switches 1 and 3

20. Which bulb(s) will remain lit if bulb D fuses and all the switches are closed?
    (a) Bulbs A, B and C
    (b) Bulbs A and B
    (c) Bulbs A and C
    (d) Bulb D

21. To determine whether an object is a conductor or an insulator, you can build a simple circuit with a battery, bulb, and three pieces of wire.

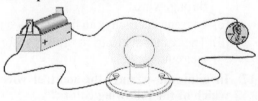

Touch the free ends of the wire to the object you are testing. If the bulb glows up, the object is a _____. If it does not, then the object is an _____.
    (a) Rubber, silver
    (b) Silver, rubber
    (c) Insulator, conductor
    (d) Conductor, insulator

22. Which part of the bulb is an insulator?

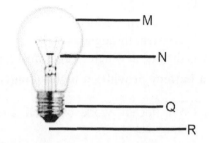

    (a) M   (b) N
    (c) R   (d) Q

23. The instrument that can measure current is called a/an:
    (a) Tester   (b) Ammeter
    (c) Resistor   (d) Voltameter

24. The path of electricity is called:
    (a) orbit   (b) filament
    (c) current   (d) circuit

25. Sanchit's mother warned him to avoid contact with electrical appliances or even electrical outlets when his hands are wet. This is because wet hands can alter _____.
    (a) The voltage of the circuit to be higher
    (b) The voltage of the circuit to be lower
    (c) Your resistance to be higher
    (d) Your resistance to be lower

26. Identify the A and B from the following diagram:

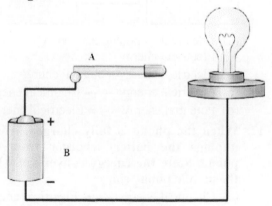

    (a) A = Circuit, B = Switch
    (b) A = Battery, B = Switch
    (c) A = Switch, B = Circuit
    (d) A = Switch, B = Battery

27. This wire is the filament of the bulb which becomes red hot and glows when the current is switched on. It is made of a metal called _____.
    (a) Tungsten
    (b) Needle
    (c) Insulator
    (d) Conductor
28. Combination of two or more cells is called a _____.
    (a) Circuit
    (b) Battery
    (c) Switch
    (d) None of these
29. The following diagram shows identical lamps X and Y connected in series with a battery. The lamps light with normal brightness. A third lamp Z is connected in parallel lamp X.

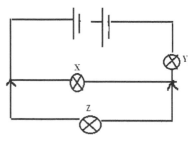

What happens to the brightness of lamp Y?
(a) Very dim
(b) Normal
(c) Brighter than normal
(d) Dimmer than normal

30. If we touch a naked current-carrying wire, we get a shock. This is because our body is a:
    (a) Source of electricity
    (b) Conductor of electricity
    (c) Insulator of electricity
    (d) (a) and (b) both

★★★

Electricity and Circuits

Fun with Magnets   4

Learning Objectives
☞ After reading the chapter, you will be able to:
☞ learn about how magnets were discovered
☞ learn the difference between magnetic and non-magnetic substances
☞ find out about the two magnetic poles
☞ learn about magnetic compass
☞ learn about natural and artificial magnets
☞ the reason behind attraction and repulsion of magnetic poles

You might have seen magnets. Have you ever enjoyed playing with them? We know that magnet attracts pins, iron pieces and iron particles in sand.

Why do the pins stick to the pin holder placed on headmaster's/headmistress's table?

Why does the door of the refrigerator get stuck automatically when it is very close to the refrigerator?

All these activities are possible because magnets are attached to the pin-holder and the refrigerator door.

How were Magnets Discovered?
There are several stories revolving around the discovery of magnets. The most popular legend is about an elderly shepherd named Magnes, who was herding his sheep in the northern Greece region about 4000 years ago. The nails in his shoe and the iron tip in his staff got stuck firmly to a large black rock on which he was standing. The rock was magnetite or lodestone which is a particular kind of iron ore that has the property of attracting small pieces of iron.

Magnetic and Non-magnetic Substances
Substances that are attracted by magnets are called **magnetic substances**. Iron, cobalt, nickel are **magnetic** substances.

Substances that do not get attracted by magnet are called **non-magnetic substances**. Paper, plastic are examples of non-magnetic substances.

Poles of a Magnet
Does magnet have poles?

Let's find out. To perform a simple experiment, it is sufficient to have iron filings and a magnet. When some iron filings are spread on a sheet of paper and a bar magnet is placed

over it, all the filings do not stick to the bar magnet uniformly, but we find more iron filings sticking to both ends of the magnet. Likewise, iron filings will stick to both ends of a horseshoe magnet.

The ends of a magnet have the strongest magnetic force. So, most of the iron filings cling to the ends of the magnet. They are called **poles** of the magnet.

North and South Poles

A magnet has two poles. They can be easily found by freely suspending the magnet as shown in the diagram below.

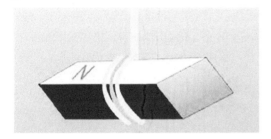

A freely suspended magnet always comes to rest in north-south direction. The North-seeking pole is called **North Pole**. The South-seeking pole is called **South Pole**. The Magnetic compass is designed by using this directive property of the magnet.

Magnetic Compass

A **magnetic compass** is a circular disc on which a small needle is pivoted at the centre. Different directions (North, South, East, and west) are marked on the compass. This needle can rotate freely and always points in the north-south direction.

Natural and Artificial Magnets

Magnets can be natural or artificial. **Magnetites** are natural magnets. They are called magnetic stones. **Natural magnets** do not have a definite shape. When a magnet is freely suspended, it always comes to rest in north-south direction. That is why they are called leading stones or **lode stones**.

After learning the method of changing the piece of iron into magnet (magnetization) we have been making and using several kinds of magnet. Such man-made magnets are called **artificial magnets**.

Here are some of the shapes of artificial magnets that we use in our daily life:

Make your Own Magnet

There are several methods of making artificial magnets. Let us learn the simplest one.

Take a nail/a piece of iron and place it on a table.

Now take a bar magnet and place one of its poles near one edge of the nail/piece of iron and rub from one end to another end without changing the direction of the pole of the magnet.

Repeat the process for 30 to 40 times.

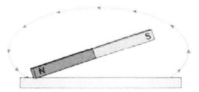

Bring a pin or some iron filings near a nail/a piece of iron to check whether it has become a magnet. If not, continue the same process for some more time.

Fun with Magnets

Attraction or Repulsion of Magnetic Poles

When we bring two north poles of two bar magnets closer as shown in the figure, they move away from each other. Similarly, when the south poles of two bar magnets are brought closer, they too move away from each other. When a north pole of one magnet and a south pole of another magnet are brought closer, they pull towards each other.

Like poles repel each other. Unlike poles attract each other.

When do magnets lose their properties?

Magnets lose their properties if they are heated or dropped from a height or hit with a hammer.

When they are heated

When they are dropped

When they are hammered

Storage of Magnets

Improper storage can also cause magnets to lose their properties. To keep them safe, bar magnets should be kept in pairs with their unlike poles on the same side. They must be separated by a piece of wood and two pieces of soft iron should be placed across their ends.

For a horse-shoe magnet, one should keep a piece of iron across the poles.

Activity

1. **Fill in the blanks, using the words in the box.**

NORTH	REPEL	FORCE	SOUTH	COBALT
IRON	ATTRACT	STEEL	POLES	NICKEL

   Magnetism is a .... that acts only between magnetic materials like ...., ..., ... and .... Magnets have two .... – a .... and a .... pole.

   If two magnets are put together, the poles that are the same will .... each other. If two magnets are put together, the poles that are different will .... each other.

2. **Label the poles on these magnets.**

   Magnets attracting each other

   Magnets repelling each other

3. **Draw the magnetic field around this magnet.**

   South   North

   a. Where is the strongest area of magnetism in the field?
   b. Where is the weakest area of magnetism?
   c. Draw the magnetic fields around the attracting and repelling magnets.

Fun with Magnets

Multiple Choice Questions

1. A magnet was placed on a steel table top. A force was exerted on the magnet to move it horizontally across the table from point A to point B as shown in the diagram below.

   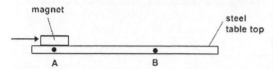

   Which of the following force(s) must the push overcome so that the magnet moves from point A to point B?
   (a) Frictional force only
   (b) Gravitational force only
   (c) Frictional force and magnetic force
   (d) Frictional force, magnetic force and gravitational force

2. Mini magnetized a metal rod, Y, using a strong magnet. She then put the magnetized rod Y close to a pile of pins and it attracted 12 pins. She wanted to repeat the experiment. However, Mini dropped rod Y three times.

   Mini then put rod Y close to the pile of pins again. Which of the following are possible observations she could get?
   1. Rod Y could attract less pins.
   2. Rod Y could attract more pins.
   3. Rod Y could not attract any pins.
   4. Rod Y could attract the same number of pins.
   (a) 1, 3 and 4   (b) 2 and 4
   (c) 1 and 4   (d) 1 and 3

3. Which of the following can be attracted by a magnet?
   (a) Wooden piece
   (b) Plain pins
   (c) Eraser
   (d) A piece of cloth

4. Freely suspended magnet always comes to rest in the _____ direction
   (a) North-east
   (b) South-west
   (c) East-west
   (d) North-south

5. The diagram below shows a simple pendulum facing a magnet XY. Attached to the pendulum is another magnet.

   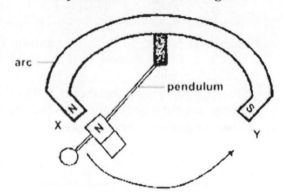

   What forces are involved when the pendulum swings from X to Y?
   (a) Gravitational force
   (b) Magnetic force
   (c) Frictional force between the magnet on the pendulum and the arc
   (d) Gravitational and magnetic force

6. Which of the following is used to make a permanent magnet?
   (a) Nickel   (b) Aluminium
   (c) Steel   (d) Iron

7. If the north poles of two magnets are placed near one another, there is a:
   (a) Repulsion between them
   (b) Attraction between them
   (c) No interaction between them
   (d) None of these

8. Look at the diagram carefully.

   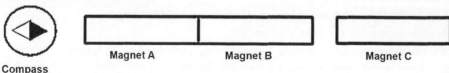

When the three bar magnets are placed near each other, magnet A and B are attracted to each other but magnet B and C repel each other.

Which of the following diagrams shows the correct poles for Magnet A and Magnet C?

(a) | S   N | | S   N |
     Magnet A   Magnet C

(b) | N   S | | N   S |
     Magnet A   Magnet C

(c) | S   N | | N   S |
     Magnet A   Magnet C

(d) | N   S | | S   N |
     Magnet A   Magnet C

9. A bar magnet is cut into four pieces. Which of the following observations would be true?
   (a) Each piece is a complete magnet
   (b) Each piece loses magnetism
   (c) Some pieces of them have only South Pole
   (d) Some pieces of them have only North Pole

10. A bar of steel can be permanently magnetized by:
    (a) Rubbing a bar magnet at its ends
    (b) Rubbing a bar magnet at its centre
    (c) Rubbing a bar magnet with it along the length
    (d) None of the above

11. An artificial magnet which is used for finding geographical directions is called:
    (a) Magnetic compass
    (b) Electromagnet
    (c) Bar magnet
    (d) Horseshoe

12. The acrurate test for magnetism is:
    (a) Attraction and repulsion
    (b) Attraction only
    (c) Repulsion only
    (d) None of the above

13. Shia had four magnets as shown below.

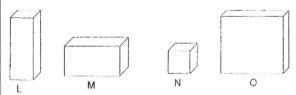

She placed the magnets near a pile of staples and recorded her observation in the table below.

Magnet	Distance between magnets and staples (cm)	Number of staples attracted
L	2	12
M	5	11
N	6	12
O	2	11

Which of the following about magnet is correct?
(a) Magnet L is stronger than magnet M
(b) Magnet N has the strongest magnetic strength
(c) The bigger the magnet, the stronger the magnetism
(d) Magnet M and magnet O have the same magnetic strength

14. Alisha found three objects and wanted to test if they were magnets. She bought a magnet from the school bookshop and placed it next to each of the objects. This is what she observed.

Object	Observation
Object A	No reaction
Object B	Repelled
Object C	Attracted

Which of the following object(s) is definitely a magnet?
(a) Object B
(b) Object C
(c) Objects A and C
(d) Objects B and A

Fun with Magnets

15. A student tries to magnetize a short steel rod. Which of the following tests will show that she has succeeded?
    (a) Both ends of a magnet attract the rod
    (b) One end of a magnet repels the rod
    (c) When freely suspended, the rod points in any direction
    (d) The rod picks up a small piece of paper

16. There are the following number of poles in a magnet:
    (a) One   (b) Four
    (c) Two   (d) Three

17. Loadstone is an example of:
    (a) A natural magnet
    (b) An artificial magnet
    (c) An electromagnet
    (d) None of these

18. The attraction of iron filings by the poles of a magnet is:
    (a) Minimum   (b) Maximum
    (c) Zero   (d) Medium

19. The presence of magnetism in a magnet is due to:
    (a) Its basic structural property
    (b) Due to the molecular arrangement in a particular order
    (c) Due to the molecular arrangement in the form of a closed chain
    (d) None of these

20. An effective length of a magnet is:
    (a) Either greater or smaller depending on the nature of the material
    (b) Equal to its geometric length
    (c) Smaller than its geometric length
    (d) Equal to its geometric length

21. The classification chart below shows how some things can be classified.

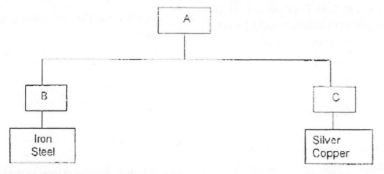

Which one of the following descriptions about A, B and C is correct?

	A	B	C
(a)	Magnets	Can be repelled by magnet	Cannot be repelled by a magnet
(b)	Metals	Can be made into magnets	Cannot be made into magnets
(c)	Metals	Non-conductor of heat	Conductor of heat
(d)	Materials	Non-conductor of electricity	Conductor of electricity

22. An object P is brought near a bar magnet and its end marked Z is attracted to the South Pole of the magnet as shown below.

Object P — Z | S   N — Bar magnet

Based on the information given, object P could be a _____.
(a) Copper rod and magnet
(b) Nickel rod and Copper rod
(c) Magnet and Nickel rod
(d) None of the above

23. Yuvi performed an experiment. He placed a sheet of plastic between two nails and a magnet as shown in the diagram below. The nails were attached to the magnet. Then Michael placed more and more similar sheets of plastic until the nails could no longer be attracted by the magnet.

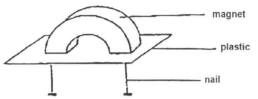

   What is the aim of Michael's experiment?
   (a) To find out if the plastic is magnetic
   (b) To find out if the nails are magnetic
   (c) To find out the strength of the magnet
   (d) To find out the part of the magnet that has the strongest pull

24. One day Sahil found an iron disc at the bottom of a heavy plastic tank half filled with oil as shown in the diagram below. He successfully removed the iron disc out of the tank with a magnet.

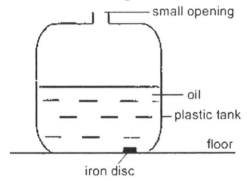

   Which one of the following statements is correct?
   (a) Oil was magnetised by the magnet
   (b) Magnetism can pass through iron disc
   (c) Oil and plastic tank were magnetised by the magnet
   (d) Magnetism can pass through the oil and plastic tank

25. A magnet can be made weaker by:
    (a) Playing with it
    (b) Keeping it wrapped in a cotton cloth
    (c) Using it as a hammer
    (d) Keeping it in a cool room

26. We should not store a floppy disc near a magnet. Why?
    (a) Because the magnet will break the disk
    (b) Because the magnet will rust
    (c) Because the magnet will become weaker
    (d) Because the information in the disk may be erased

27. In many houses we can find a magnet instead of a lock or a bolt in the doors. Magnets are used in such places mainly to:
    (a) Ensure safety
    (b) Make the articles look beautiful
    (c) Facilitate frequent usage
    (d) Make the articles airtight

28. Which of the following does not contain a magnet in it?
    (a) Radio   (b) Fan
    (c) Torch   (d) None

29. The best way to separate a mixture of sand and iron fillings is by:
    (a) Using compass
    (b) Filtration
    (c) Sedimentation
    (d) Magnetic separation

30. The people who made mariner's compass for the first time were:
    (a) Indians   (b) Europeans
    (c) Chinese   (d) Egyptians

Air and Water

5

Learning Objectives
Afer reading this chapter, you will be able to:
- understand the importance of water
- know the sources of water
- learn about the water cycle
- understand the effects of heavy or scanty rainfall
- understand the importance of water conservation
- learn about the composition of air and the uses of each component
- learn about the importance of air

Air and water are the basic necessities of life. We use water in our daily lives—whether it is to bathe, to wash clothes or to drink. It is a wonderful liquid. Three-fourth of the earth's surface is covered with water. Our body is composed of water by 70%. All living things require water for survival. Interestingly, a human being can survive without food for a longer period of time than without water.

Similarly, air is equally essential for life. Although invisible, air can be felt all around us. Sometimes, we can feel it when the wind blows: the trees sway, the hair ruffles; the kites fly. These are all examples of air in action. All living things breathe in air.

Air and water are extremely important for our planet's survival. Let us now try and understand each of these in detail.

How much water do we use?

Ever wondered as to what will happen if there is no water for your use, say, for two days? Can you imagine how this situation might affect your everyday routine? We have already learnt that water is used for several purposes in our daily lives. For example, bathing, flushing, drinking, cooking, washing, and even recreation.

Our bodies are also heavily dependent on water. More than half of our body weight is water! Like us, plants also need water to make their food. Seeds need water to germinate and to grow.

Now let us do an activity. First, make a list of all the activities that you or your families undertake, which require water, in the table given below. The activities may include bathing, cooking, watering the plants, washing clothes, etc. Then, note down the amount of water used against each activity. Can you calculate the amount of water used by your family on a monthly and a yearly basis?

Activities	Water Usage Details
Bathing	
Cooking	
Washing utensils	
Watering plants	
Washing clothes	

Sources of Water

We have learnt that three-fourth of the earth's surface is covered with water. Ponds, rivers, lakes, waterfalls, and wells are all sources of fresh water. You will notice that seas and oceans were not cited as fresh-water sources. Do you know why? Sea and ocean water is saline. It is saline because of the presence of dissolved salts (which come from the rivers) in these waters. This water cannot be used for our daily activities. However, seas and oceans play a pivotal role in supplying water. Why is it that the water in our wells and rivers is not saline, while the water in the seas and oceans is? Let's learn about it in the next chapter.

Water Cycle

The continuous circulation of water from the earth's surface to the air and from the air back to the earth's surface is called the **water cycle**.

Do You Know?

Have you ever wondered as to how common salt is made? We know that the sea water consists of huge amounts of salts. This water is stored in shallow pits dug into the ground. When the sun comes up, the water in these pits evaporates and leaves behind salt. This salt is then processed for our consumption.

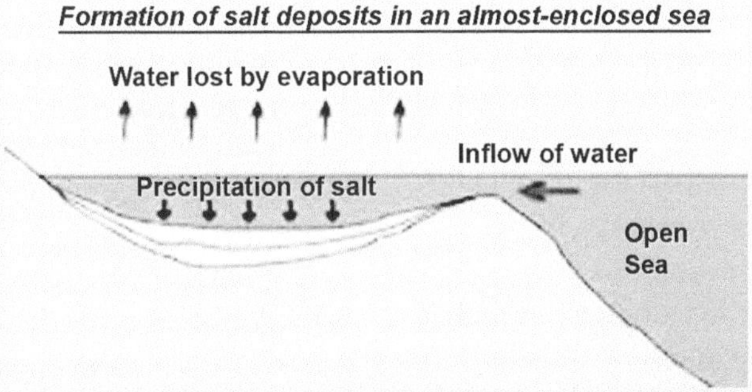

Fig 1: *Shallow Pits Filled with Water Contain Salt as a Residue*

The water from the seas, oceans, rivers, wells and ponds evaporates due to the heat of the sun. Please note that **although evaporation takes place at all temperatures, the rate of evaporation is faster when the water is heated**. Plants also lose water through their leaves. This process of loss of water by plants in the form of water vapour is called **transpiration**. Plants and animals also lose water during respiration. When water evaporates through any of these processes, it gets converted into water vapour and mixes with the air.

This water vapour rises up and as it rises, it cools down (the temperature decreases with altitude). This cooled water vapour then condenses into tiny droplets of water to form clouds in the sky. The tiny droplets combine with other small droplets to form larger droplets (bigger clouds). When the large water droplets become very heavy they fall down as rain. In very cold places, this rain gets converted into snow and comes down in the form of hail or snow.

The rain water fills the wells, lakes and rivers. The rivers in turn meet the seas and oceans and hence complete the water cycle.

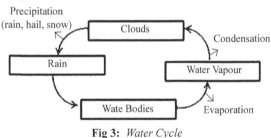

Fig 3: *Water Cycle*

What happens when the rainfall is heavy or scant?

When the rain falls heavily, it will cause the water level of lakes, ponds and rivers to rise, leading to a phenomenon called **floods**. Floods cause damage to crops, animals and human lives. They also lead to landslides, the spread of waterborne diseases, and also a scarcity of drinking water as it may get contaminated.

Air and Water

Alternately, if it does not rain for a long time, it can lead to a **drought**. Drought can lead to the following:
(i) The crop yield becomes less as the soil dries up due to loss of water;
(ii) Death of livestock and people;
(iii) Food and fodder become scarce which may lead to malnutrition;
(iv) Dehydration and related diseases may also occur.

Conservation of Water: Rainwater Harvesting

Water is precious and we must work towards its conservation. Some ways have been listed below:
(i) Use minimum amount of water for bathing.
(ii) Re-use water whenever possible.
(iii) Don't let the water run when you are brushing your teeth.
(iv) Make sure there are no leaky taps in your house.
(v) Avoid flushing unnecessarily.
(vi) Adopt rainwater harvesting.

The method of collection and storage of rainwater on rooftops or from land surfaces for future use is called **rainwater harvesting**. The rainwater harvesting can be done in the following ways:
(i) *Groundwater:* rainwater is allowed to go into the ground directly. This can be stored underground for later use.

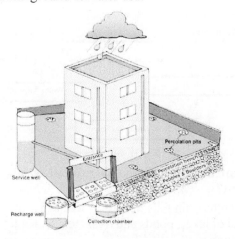

Fig 4: *Groundwater and Rooftop Harvesting*

(ii) *Rooftop rainwater harvesting:* the rainwater falling on the roof is collected in tanks with the help of pipes. This water needs to be cleaned before use as it may be dirty. The storage tank needs to be covered tightly to prevent contamination and breeding of mosquitoes. Open tanks are not recommended for collecting rain water.

Air

Now let us understand air. We know that air is present all around us. Although, we cannot see it, we can feel its presence around us. Our earth is surrounded by a thin layer of air called **atmosphere**. Air has many uses. Some of these have been listed below:
(i) Air contains gases like oxygen and carbon dioxide which are essential for sustaining life on earth.
(ii) The moving air is called **wind**. Wind moves the blade of a windmill which in turn is used to generate electricity, draw water from tube-wells and also run flour mills.
(iii) Air helps in winnowing.
(iv) Air also helps in the movement of aeroplanes, yachts and helicopters.
(v) Air helps birds fly.
(vi) Air is pumped into bicycle and car tyres which helps these run on roads.
(vii) Air is used by divers to float back to the ground.
(viii) Air helps in the dispersal of seeds and pollen grains for flowers.

Composition of Air

Air is a mixture of many gases including nitrogen, oxygen, carbon dioxide, noble gases, in addition to water vapour, smoke and dust particles. Let us now try and understand these components in detail.

Nitrogen

Nitrogen constitutes 78% of the air and is non-combustible, i.e., it doesn't help in burning of a substance. It is used to make fertilisers which, when added to the soil, help in the growth of plants and crops. Have you noticed a packet of chips? Aren't they inflated? The gas inside these packets is nitrogen. It helps to keep the chips fresh.

Oxygen

Oxygen constitutes 21% of the air. All living things including plants and animals require oxygen to breathe and stay alive. Even the aquatic plants and animals use the oxygen in water to survive. The fish use an organ called **gills** to inhale and exhale oxygen underwater. Hence, oxygen in the air is used for two primary purposes:

(i) *Respiration:* we know that all living organisms require oxygen to breathe. This oxygen then mixes with the food and releases carbon dioxide which the living things exhale. This process is called **respiration**.

(ii) *Burning:* unlike nitrogen, oxygen is a combustible substance. All fuels burn in the presence of oxygen and release carbon dioxide.

Ever wondered, if we are using oxygen so rapidly, what will happen if we use up all the oxygen in the atmosphere? Or rather, is oxygen getting replaced at all? The answer is that, oxygen is replaced by trees through *photosynthesis*. When green plants prepare their food, they use the carbon dioxide in the air, the sunlight and the green pigment present in the leaves to create food. This process of making food is called **photosynthesis** and oxygen is released as a by-product. Thus, *respiration* and *photosynthesis* play a pivotal role in maintaining oxygen in our atmosphere. However, as you go higher, the levels of oxygen in the air decrease., That is why mountaineers always carry oxygen cylinders while trekking.

Carbon Dioxide

Carbon dioxide makes up about 0.03% of air. Although, present in traces, carbon dioxide is an important gas. We have learnt that plants use carbon dioxide in photosynthesis. Animals also release carbon dioxide while exhaling. It is a non-combustible gas, i.e., it doesn't support burning. On the contrary, it is used to extinguish fires.

Water Vapour

The amount of water vapour in air is not fixed. It varies from place to place. In coastal regions, the level of water vapour in the air is higher as compared to that on plains.

Dust and Smoke

Dust and smoke are present all around us. Have you noticed the shiny particles in the beam of sunlight? That is dust. When we breathe in air, we also inhale dust particles. Our noses have fine hair and mucous which filter the air we breathe. Hence, the dust doesn't enter our bodies. However, when we breathe through our mouth, the dust enters our bodies and can cause harm. This is because our mouths cannot filter the air we breathe.

Have you noticed the smoke coming out of automobiles? When diesel and petrol burn, they release smoke. Several factories have tall chimneys which often spit out smoke in the air. This smoke is harmful.

Oxygen in the Soil

Oxygen is also present in the soil particles. If you take a lump of dry soil and add water to it, you will notice the release of bubbles from the soil. This is air, which is used by animals living underground to respire. Earthworms, for example, move in and out of the soil to create space for air. The excreta of these organisms provides nutrients to the soil for the plants to grow. However, if it rains heavily, earthworms come out to respire, as water fills up all spaces.

Activity

Make your own water cycle maze

You are provided with a word list. Use maximum words to fill in the maze.

Absorb; absorption; air; Arctic; atmosphere; breathing; burning; clouds; combustion; condensation; condense; dew; drought; energy; evaporation; excrete; excretion; porous; precipitation; rain; reservoir; respiration; respire; rivers; roots; sea; sleet; snow; stream; sun; transpiration

Multiple Choice Questions

1. **The pH of pure water is:**
   (a) 3 (b) 9
   (c) 7 (d) 4

2. **Plants regulate their temperature by:**
   (a) Respiration (b) Transpiration
   (c) Photosynthesis (d) Perspiration

3. **The rate of photosynthesis is very high during**
   (a) Day time (b) Midnight
   (c) Night (d) Evening

4. **Read the following information.**
   When water gains heat, it changes into water vapour.
   1 cm^3 of water forms more than 1000 cm^3 of water vapour but the amount of particles (matter) in water remains the same.
   What can you infer or conclude from the information given above?
   (i) The mass of water increases when water changes into water vapour.
   (ii) The spacing between the particles increases when water changes into water vapour.
   (iii) Water can exist in three interchangeable states.
   (iv) When water loses heat, it changes into ice.
   (a) (iii)
   (b) (ii) only
   (c) (iii) and (iv) only
   (d) (i), (ii), (iii) and (iv)

5. **A tank containing some aquatic plants is placed outdoors on a sunny day.**
   Identify the factors that will affect, directly or indirectly, the amount of oxygen in the water.

   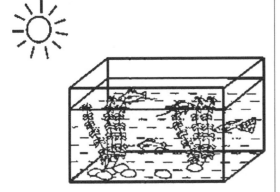

   (i) The intensity of light in the water
   (ii) The amount of plants in the tank
   (iii) The material used for making the tank
   (iv) The amount of carbon dioxide in the water
   (a) (i) and (iii) only
   (b) (ii) and (iv) only
   (c) (i), (iii) and (iv) only
   (d) (i), (ii), (iii) and (iv)

6. **The diagram below shows the water cycle.**

   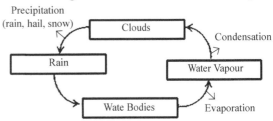

   Which of the following correctly shows heat gain or heat loss by water in Process A and Process B respectively?

	Process A	Process B
(a)	Heat gain	Heat loss
(b)	Heat loss	Heat gain
(c)	Heat gain	Heat gain
(d)	Heat loss	Heat loss

7. **The table below shows the melting and boiling points of substances P, Q, R and S.**
   Which substance(s) will change from gas to solid when there is a decrease in temperature from 200°C to 30°C?

Substance	Melting point (°C)	Boiling point (°C)
P	26	96
Q	8	120
R	95	195
S	60	150

   (a) R only (b) R and S
   (c) P and Q (d) Q, R and S

Air and Water

8. The glass bowl below contains some ice cream. The bowl is left on the kitchen table at room temperature. After two minute, droplets of water appear on the outside surface of the glass and the ice cream starts to melt.

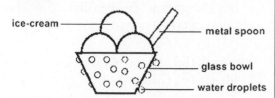

Which of the following explains the changes observed?
1. The glass bowl condenses to form water droplets.
2. The ice cream gains heat from the surroundings.
3. The glass bowl gains coldness from the ice cream.
4. The metal spoon conducts heat from the surroundings to the ice cream.
5. The surrounding water vapour loses heat to the cool surface of the glass bowl.
   (a) 1 and 2 only
   (b) 1 and 3 only
   (c) 2, 3 and 5 only
   (d) 2, 4 and 5 only

9. Pure and distilled water is not used for drinking, mainly because:
   (a) It is not available easily
   (b) It is not bacteria free
   (c) It has a very high solubility
   (d) It is poisonous

10. Saline water is useful for:
    (a) Agriculture
    (b) Washing clothes
    (c) Drinking
    (d) Medical purposes

11. All the plants require nitrogen for:
    (a) Transpiration
    (b) Reproduction
    (c) Photosynthesis
    (d) Growth

12. Who am I, if:
    1. I am present in the air
    2. A human body needs me to produce energy
    3. I enter your lungs when you breathe in
    (a) Nitrogen
    (b) Water Vapour
    (c) Carbon Dioxide
    (d) Oxygen

13. Study the classification chart below.

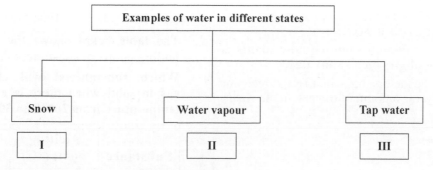

Which of the following is correctly classified?

	I	II	III
(a)	Hailstones	Dew	Mist
(b)	Steam	Mist	Icebergs
(c)	Hailstones	Steam	Dew
(d)	Icebergs	Dew	Mist

14. Abhilasha wanted to compare the time taken for different solutions to reach boiling point. She placed four beakers of different solutions over an electric stove and recorded the time taken for each of them to boil.

    Which of the following factors must she keep constant in order to carry out a fair test?
    (i) Size of the beaker
    (ii) Amount of solution
    (iii) Starting temperature of the solution
    (iv) Final temperature of the solution
    (a) (i) and (ii)
    (b) (ii) and (iii)
    (c) (i), (ii) and (iii)
    (d) (i), (ii), (iii) and (iv)

15. Which of the following about the water cycle is true?
    (a) Rain drops falling into the sea contain salt
    (b) The energy for the water cycle comes from the sun
    (c) Clouds are water in the gaseous state
    (d) Water condenses to form water vapour

16. Which of the following will change when water freezes?
    (i) State
    (ii) Mass
    (iii) Volume
    (iv) Temperature
    (a) (i), (ii) and (iii)
    (b) (i), (iii) and (iv)
    (c) (ii), (iii) and (iv)
    (d) (i), (ii), (iii) and (iv)

17. A bowl contained 400 g of water. A 30 g cube of sugar was placed in the bowl of water and stirred until it dissolved completely.

    After one day, it was found that only 400 g of the solution was left in the bowl. What would the remaining solution contain?
    (a) 420 g of sugar
    (b) 420 g of water
    (c) 370 g of water and 30 g of sugar
    (d) 400 g of water and 20 g of sugar

18. Chloe used the set-up below to study the property of air.

    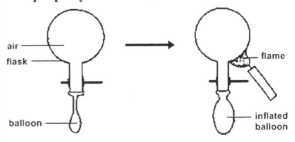

    What property/properties must the flask possess such that the balloon could be inflated quickly?
    (a) Transparent and painted silver
    (b) Painted silver
    (c) A good conductor of heat and painted silver
    (d) Transparent

19. The water vapour in air is due to:
    (a) The sweat of the animals evaporated due to the heat
    (b) The evaporation of water from oceans, rivers, lakes and streams
    (c) The water vapours released by plants through their leaves during transpiration
    (d) All of these

20. Hardness of water is due to the presence of:
    (a) Bicarbonates, chlorides of potassium and magnesium
    (b) Chlorides and sulphates of calcium and potassium
    (c) Bicarbonates, chlorides and sulphates of calcium, and magnesium
    (d) Chlorides and magnesium

Air and Water

21. Rachit pushed a balloon into a plastic bottle and stretched its mouthpiece over the opening for the bottle. Then he blew into the bottle but the balloon could not inflate fully as shown in the picture below.

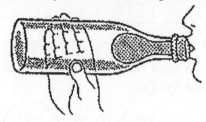

Which of the following actions could cause the balloon to inflate more fully within the bottle?
(a) Make a hole in the balloon
(b) Pour water into the balloon
(c) Make a hole in the bottle
(d) Use a glass bottle

22. Which statement is not correct?
(a) Water available for use is very limited
(b) Water evaporates from plants, animals and oceans
(c) There is no vegetation during droughts
(d) Animals living in the water are not harmed during floods

23. Lime water turns milky when exposed to air and stirred. This shows that air contains:
(a) Oxygen   (b) Carbon dioxide
(c) Hydrogen   (d) Nitrogen

24. This gas cause the harmful greenhouse effect:
(a) Oxygen   (b) Carbon dioxide
(c) Hydrogen   (d) Nitrogen

25. The water cycle can take place repeatedly because water _____.
(a) Freezes at 0°C and boils at 100°C
(b) Has volume and is not compressible
(c) Is essential for the survival of living things
(d) Can change from one state to another when it gains or loses heat

26. Sameer notices that when a paper wheel is held over a lighted candle as shown in the diagram below, it starts to turn quickly after some time.

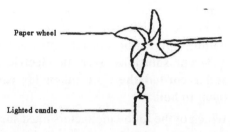

Which of the following can be the correct reason?
(a) The heat from the candle flame heats up the surrounding air. The hot air rises and the kinetic energy of the moving air causes the wheel to turn
(b) The heat from the candle flame heats up the surrounding air. The hot air rises and the potential energy of the moving air causes the wheel to turn
(c) Both (a) and (b)
(d) None of the above

27. Based on the following diagram about the gases present in the atmosphere, which of these is the most accurate description of air?

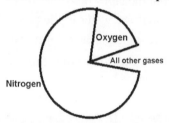

(a) One-fifth part is oxygen and four-fifths contains nitrogen and other gases
(b) Two-thirds part is nitrogen, one-tenth other gases
(c) Three-quarters part is oxygen and one-third nitrogen and other gases
(d) One-half part is nitrogen and one-half oxygen and other gases

28. Look at the following items:

(a)    (b)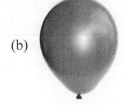

(c)  (d)

(e)

All these are filled with air. What is likely to happen when the same amount of air is pumped into each of the objects? [The air pumped in is not more than the holding capacity of these items.]

i. The gas cylinder and oxygen tank will not change their size but the air in them will be compressed.

ii. The two balloons will get bigger in size as more air gets in.

iii. The air-filled ball and tyre will also get bigger in size as more air is filled in.

(a) iii (b) i
(c) i and ii (d) all of the above

29. **Air pollution on the road can be reduced by** .
    (a) Encouraging the use of CNG in vehicles
    (b) Reducing the number of vehicles on the road
    (c) Planting trees on roadsides
    (d) All of them

30. **Which of the following happen because of the presence of air?**
    (a) Flying of birds
    (b) Dispersal of seeds
    (c) Generating electricity
    (d) All of them

★★★

Sorting and Separation of Materials

Learning Objectives
After reading this chapter, you will be able to:
- classify objects on the basis of the material's property
- collect and group things on the basis of appearance
- understand the significance of classification of objects
- understand the need to separate substances
- understand the various means of separating materials
- understand water as a solvent

Take a look around you. What do you see? Do you notice the different objects which surround you? You might see a table, a chair, pencils, pencil box, etc. Now make a list of all these objects and examine them more closely and try answering the following:

(i) What are these objects made of?
(ii) Are all objects made of the same material?
(iii) Do these objects have the same colour, size and shape?
(iv) Is there a need to separate materials?
(v) What are the methods used to separate materials?
(vi) How can two liquids be separated?
(vii) Can solids be separated from liquids?

This chapter aims to provide answers to all these and several other questions.

Materials
All objects are made of different *materials*. Some objects maybe made of plastic, some of wood and others of mud or soil. Examples of materials include: wood, metal, fibre, steel, paper, leather amongst many others.

A single object may be made of various materials. For example, the body of the television may be made of plastic. However, when you open the television set, you will find metal, wires and even glass.

Different Materials

Classification of Materials
Materials are broadly divided into two main groups:

(i) *Natural materials:* Materials obtained directly from living things, including plants and animals are called **natural materials**. Examples include leather, rubber, wood, metal, clay.

(ii) *Man-made materials:* Materials obtained from natural materials through chemical processes are called **man-made materials**. For instance, nylon, plastic, rayon, polyester are all man-made materials.

Properties of Materials
Ever wondered, why a tumbler is not made of paper but only glass or plastic? This is because paper is not strong enough to withstand the weight of the contents to be put inside the tumbler. Similarly, why

do you think a cooking vessel is not made of cloth but aluminium or steel? This is because aluminium or steel can retain the heat and cook the food faster; while a cloth will catch fire if exposed.

Different materials have different properties. Hence, in order to decide which materials need to be used to make an object, one must be aware of the properties of the materials. Up till now you have classified the objects based on shape, size and type of materials. Now, we'll learn about grouping different materials into different categories based on the following properties. These include:

(i) Appearance
(ii) Texture
(iii) Solubility
(iv) Ability to float or sink in water
(v) Transparency

Appearance

Every object looks different. This is because the materials used to make objects are different from each other. For instance, wood is different from rubber. Copper is different from gold, silver or aluminium. But, note how substances like copper, silver or gold shine, whereas wood and rubber don't. Based on this property, materials are categorised as:

(i) *Lustrous:* Objects that shine are called **lustrous objects**.
(ii) *Non-lustrous:* Objects which don't shine are called **non-lustrous objects**.

Hardness

While, some objects squeeze easily, others feel hard to touch. Take a nail and try scratching the surface of a table, a chair, a candle, a tumbler, a chalk etc. You will notice that while some surfaces are easier to scratch, some prove difficult. Any material which can be compressed or scratched easily is called **soft material**. On the other hand, any material which is difficult to press and scratch is called **hard material**. For example, cotton or sponges are soft materials whereas iron is a hard material.

Cotton Balls

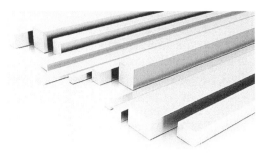
Iron Bars

Soluble and Insoluble Materials

Although a large number of materials can get dissolved in water, some materials cannot. Materials can also be classified on the basis of their ability to dissolve in water:

(i). *Soluble materials:* Materials which get dissolved in water are called **soluble materials**. Examples include: sugar, salt, baking powder, vinegar, etc.

(ii) *Insoluble materials:* Materials which do not get dissolved in water are called **insoluble materials**. Examples include: oil, wax, sand, flour, clay, steel, pencil, rocks etc.

Additionally, some gases are also soluble in water, while some are not. For example, water consists of some quantity of oxygen. Aquatic plants and animals use this gas to survive underwater. Another gas which is soluble in water is carbon dioxide. Aquatic plants use carbon dioxide to prepare their food underwater. Nitrogen gas, however, is insoluble in water.

Ability to Float or Sink

Materials can also be grouped based on their ability to **float** or **sink** in water. For example, objects such as dried leaves, oil, paper, rubber band, plastic balls, etc. float in water.

Whereas, objects such as a key, a rock, coins, etc. sink in water.

Transparency

Those substances or materials through which things can be seen are called **transparent materials**. Glass, water, air and certain types of plastic are examples of transparent materials. Materials can be grouped into the following categories based on their property of transparency:

Sorting and Separation of Materials

(i) *Opaque objects:* Objects through which one cannot see anything are called **opaque objects**. Examples include: wood, books, chair, toys, and shoes.
(ii) *Translucent objects:* Objects through which we are able to see a little but not clearly are called **translucent objects**. For example, umbrellas, coloured glass, waxed paper, dirty water and certain types of plastics.
(iii) *Transparent objects:* Objects through which one can see clearly are called **transparent objects**. Glass, cellophane paper, air, diamonds are all transparent objects.

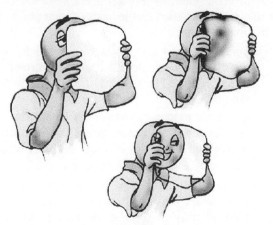

Opaque, Translucent and Transparent Objects

Separation of Materials

Many things that we see or use in our daily lives are a mixture of several components. For example, soil is a mixture of clay, pebbles and sand; a rock is a mixture of vital minerals and the air is a mixture of several gases, including oxygen, nitrogen amongst others. The substances that make up a mixture are called **components**. For example, the components of soil would be rocks, clay, sand, etc.

The components/constituents of a mixture can be separated getting separated from a mixture. For instance, the tea leaves are separated from the beverage by the use of a strainer. Seeds are separated from the fruit while eating; milk is churned to separate butter and so on.

Need for Separation

So, why do we need to separate the components from a mixture? There are several reasons for this:

1. To derive two different but useful components (for example, separating milk from butter);
2. To remove harmful components or impurities from a mixture (for example, husk is removed from rice or dal before cooking);
3. To remove useless components from a mixture (for example, removal of tea leaves from tea).

Methods of Separation

There exist several methods by means of which components from a mixture can be separated easily and effectively. Let's discuss some of them in detail.

Handpicking

As the term suggests, the method of separating the components of a mixture by hand is called **handpicking**. For example, a mixture of different-coloured lentils can be separated by the use of hand. Please note that this method is useful only under following conditions:

(i) When the components of a mixture are present in small quantities;
(ii) When the components can easily be removed by hand;
(iii) When the components have different shapes, colours and sizes.

Handpicking

Threshing

In agriculture, after the harvesting is complete, the farmers use a special technique to separate seeds from the stalk. In order to do this, the farmers thresh the stalk on a wooden platform which enables the separation effectively. Machines and bullock carts are also used to segregate seeds from the stalks. This technique of separating seeds from the stalk(s) is called **threshing**.

Threshing

Winnowing

Most often threshing results in a mixture comprising seeds and husk. In order to remove the husk from the seeds, the farmers use a technique called *winnowing*. The process of separating grain seeds from husk by the use of wind is called **winnowing**. In this method the mixture of seeds and husk is taken into a winnowing basket. The farmer stands on a raised platform and raises the basket to his/her shoulder height. He/she then tilts the basket allowing the mixture to fall slowly to the ground. The lighter husk particles are carried away by the wind, while the seeds being heavier, fall to the ground.

Winnowing

Sieving

The method of separating components from the mixture by the use of a suitable sieve is called **sieving**. For example, you might have noticed one of your parents using a sieve to separate flour from impurities. The process is called sieving. At a construction site, labourers often use a big sieve to separate sand from pebbles. Please note that this technique is applicable only when the size of one component is bigger than the other. Let's take the construction site example again. What if the size of the pebbles is same as that of the sand? Both the components will pass through the sieve. Hence, this technique can only be used if the sizes of the components are different.

Sieving

Separation of Insoluble Solids from Liquids

The techniques we have discussed so far help in separating solids from a solid mixture. Now let's learn about a number of techniques that are used to separate insoluble solids from liquids. You have already learnt about insoluble substances. This section will provide an overview of the techniques used to separate insoluble solids from liquids. Let us look at each of these closely.

Sedimentation

When the heavier component of a mixture settles at the bottom of a container, after water is added to the mixture, it is called **sedimentation**. Let us take an example. If you mix chalk and water in a transparent vessel, after sometime, chalk will settle down at the bottom of the vessel. This is primarily because chalk does not dissolve in water. It is an insoluble solid.

Sorting and Separation of Materials

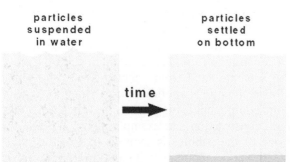

Decantation

Decantation involves letting the mixture settle for a while. The heavier insoluble substances will settle at the bottom of the liquid, while a clear liquid will be left at the top. Once the clear liquid is poured out, you will be left with the *decanted* substance. Let us take the example of sand and water in a container. When you allow such a mixture to stand for a while, the sand will settle down at the bottom of the glass, with clear water left at the top. When you remove the water, you are left with the decanted substance, in this case, sand.

Separating Funnel: It is used to separate two immiscible liquids like oil and water. Oil being lighter floats on water and water forms the bottom layer. By opening the cork water is collected first and then oil is collected in another container.

Filtration

Filtration is another technique used to separate insoluble solids from liquids. A *filter paper* is placed on a glass funnel and a container is put underneath. The mixture of solid and liquid is poured on to the filter paper. The liquid flows through the filter paper into the container, whereas, the solid remains on the filter paper. The solid left behind is called **residue**. The liquid in the container is called **filtrate**. Let us take an example. When your parents make *paneer*, they put a few drops of lemon juice in boiled milk. This leads to the formation of *paneer* which floats on the milk surface. Thereafter, they *filter* the *paneer* by the means of a strainer or sieve.

Do You Know?

A centrifuge is a spinning machine, a bit like a clothes dryer, that separates materials. A mixture of liquids and solids is spun at a high speed in a tube. The larger, denser particles sink and collect at the bottom. Light particles collect at the top. Blood cells are separated from plasma (the liquid part of blood) by this method.

Separation of Soluble Solids from Mixtures

Let us now look at separating soluble solids from liquids.

Evaporation

The process of converting water into water vapour is called **evaporation**. It is primarily used to separate soluble solids from water or any other liquid. For example: sea water. You know that sea water consists of high quantities of salt. What will you do if you want to separate salt from this water? Very simple: take some sea water into a container and put it in the sun. You will notice that due to sun's heat, all the water will *evaporate* from the container. Towards the end, you will be left with a solid residue behind, which is salt.

Evaporation

Condensation

The process by which water vapours are converted into water is called **condensation**. During summer, when you feel extremely thirsty, you take a water bottle out of the refrigerator and drink the water. However, if you leave the water bottle outside for some time, you will notice small droplets of water forming on the surface of the water. How is this possible? The chilled water bottle has a frosted appearance. This frost is nothing but vapours. When this bottle is left outside, the water vapour present in air comes in contact with the cool surface of the bottle and it changes to water droplets.

Condensation

Water as a Solvent

Water can dissolve many substances including solids, liquids and gases. Hence, it is termed as the **universal solvent**.

Solution

A mixture of a solute and solvent is called a **solution**. For example, the mixture of salt (solute) and water (solvent) is called a solution. To this solution if you continue to add salt, there will come a stage when no more salt is dissolved in water. This solution is called **saturated solution**.

In other words, a solution in which no more solute can be dissolved at a given temperature is called **saturated solution**.

However, if you heat the saturated solution of water and salt, you will notice that the salt will get dissolved.

Activity

Take some water in a beaker and mix salt in it until it cannot dissolve any more salt. This will give you a saturated solution of salt in water.

Now, add a small quantity of salt to this saturated solution and heat it. What do you find? What happens to the undissolved salt at the bottom of the beaker? Does it get dissolved? If yes, can some more salt be dissolved in this solution by heating it?

Let this hot solution cool. Does the salt appear to settle at the bottom of the beaker again?

The activity suggests that larger quantity of salt can be dissolved in water on heating.

Does water dissolve equal amounts of different soluble substances? Let us find out.

Multiple Choice Questions

1. The rate of sedimentation is increased by adding _____ to the water.
   (a) Salt (b) Sugar
   (c) Alum (d) Soap

2. The process followed to separate grains from the stalks is called
   (a) Winnowing (b) Threshing
   (c) Sieving (d) Handpicking

3. Look at the picture below and find out the method by which components in the mixture are separated.

   (a) Handpicking (b) Winnowing
   (c) Threshing (d) Sieving

4. When a bottle of soda water is opened, carbon dioxide escapes, producing a fizz. This is due to:
   (a) A decrease in the solubility with a decrease in temperature
   (b) A decrease in the solubility on decreasing pressure and temperature
   (c) A decrease in the solubility on increasing the quantity
   (d) A decrease in the solubility on decreasing the quantity

5. Butter is separated from curd by the process of:
   (a) Filtration (b) Heating
   (c) Churning (d) Sieving

6. Which of the following is not characteristic of solids?
   (a) High rigidity
   (b) Regular shape
   (c) High density
   (d) High compressibility

7. When we blow air into the balloon, it inflates because:
   (a) Air particles diffuse into the balloon
   (b) Air particles collide with the walls of the balloon and exert pressure on them
   (c) Rubber is elastic in nature
   (d) The temperature of air in the balloon increases

8. Select a good conductor of heat among the following options.
   (a) Glass (b) Graphite
   (c) Rubber (d) Wood

9. The process in which particles of a solid settle down in a liquid is known as:
   (a) Sublimation (b) Precipitation
   (c) Decantation (d) Sedimentation

10. Which of the following is essential to perform winnowing activity?
    (a) Soil
    (b) Wind
    (c) Water
    (d) None of these

11. Handpicking method is effective in:
    (a) Solid mixtures
    (b) Liquid mixtures
    (c) Gaseous mixtures
    (d) None of these

12. Which of the following is an example of irreversible change?
    (a) Freezing water to make ice
    (b) Boiling an egg
    (c) Baking a cake
    (d) Breaking glass

13. The picture below shows a mixture of beads and flour in a bowl.

    Rehan wants to separate the beads from the flour in the bowl. What separation method can he use?
    (a) Handpicking
    (b) Threshing
    (c) Winnowing
    (d) Sieving

14. Saimaa is making herself a cup of coffee. She adds in sugar to her coffee. What will happen if she continues adding more coffee powder to her drink?
    (a) The coffee powder will continue dissolving in the water
    (b) The coffee powder will not dissolve in the water. The coffee solution will reach a stage where no more solid (coffee powder) can dissolve. The solution will become saturated
    (c) The solution will become unsaturated
    (d) None of these

15. Which of the following is incorrect?
    (a) Solids that can dissolve in a liquid are said to be soluble in that liquid
    (b) When a solid dissolves in a liquid, the resulting mixture is known as a solution
    (c) When a solid is added to a liquid and the liquid changes colour, it means that the solid is soluble
    (d) It is impossible to change the rate at which a solid dissolves in a liquid

16. Study the picture below and answer the questions that follow.

    What is the name of the process taking place in the picture?
    (a) Loading   (b) Filtration
    (c) Sedimentation   (d) Evaporation

17. The picture below shows a teabag in a glass of water. What is the function of the teabag?
    (a) The teabag acts as a sieve which allows water to pass through, but keeps the tea leaves in the bag
    (b) The teabag acts as a filter which allows water to pass through, but keeps the tea leaves in the bag
    (c) The teabag acts as a filter which allows water to pass through, but sediment the tea leaves in the bag
    (d) The teabag acts as a decanter which allows water to pass through

18. Fill in the blanks below, using the helping words provided in the box. Each word can be used only once.

    filtration, soluble, permanent, substance, reversible, temporary

    1. When a sliced apple turns brown, a new _____ has formed.
    2. Burning plastic is a _____ change.
    3. We can separate insoluble solids from liquids by _____.
    4. A _____ change takes place when a material that has undergone a change can return to its original form.
    5. When a solid is able to dissolve in water, we say that it is _____ in water.
    6. A change is _____ when no new substances are formed.

    Choose the correct sequence:
    (a) Permanent, filtration, substance, reversible, soluble, temporary
    (b) Substance, permanent, filtration, reversible, soluble, temporary
    (c) Permanent, filtration, reversible, substance, soluble, temporary
    (d) Soluble, temporary, permanent, filtration, reversible, substance

Sorting and Separation of Materials

19. Samarth mixed the following things in a bowl, then carried out the following steps.

Which two steps are not in a correct sequence?

Step 1: Remove the pencils by sorting them by hand.

Step 2: Use a magnet to separate the iron nails.

Step 3: Pour water into the mixture of sand and sugar.

Step 4: Remove the copper nails by sorting by hand, or by using a sieve.

Step 5: Use filtration to separate the sand.

Step 6: Use evaporation to obtain the sugar.

(a) 1 and 2 (b) 2 and 3
(c) 5 and 6 (d) 3 and 4

20. Match the objects given below with the materials from which they could be made. Remember, an object could be made from more than one material and a given material could be used for making many objects.

Objects	Materials
1. Book	Plastic
2. Shoes	Wood
3. Toy	Glass
4. Chair	Leather
5. Tumbler	Paper

Choose the correct sequence
(a) Wood, leather, plastic, paper, glass
(b) Paper, leather, wood, plastic, glass
(c) Wood, plastic, glass, paper, leather
(d) Leather, wood, plastic, paper, glass

21. Select the correct option.
(a) Stone is transparent, while glass is opaque
(b) A notebook has lustre while an eraser does not
(c) A piece of wood floats on water
(d) Chalk dissolves in water

22. A pure substance is one which _____.
(a) Is made up of only one type of particles
(b) Has a uniform texture throughout
(c) Has a fixed boiling point or melting point
(d) All of these

23. Salt is obtained from sea water by using which of the following processes?
(a) Centrifugation
(b) Condensation
(c) Sedimentation
(d) Evaporation

24. Two solids are separated by winnowing depending on _____.
(a) Difference in their colours
(b) Difference in their sizes
(c) Difference in their weights
(d) Difference in their odours

25. A mixture of wheat and husk can be separated by _____.
(a) Filtration (b) Decantation
(c) Winnowing (d) Evaporation

26. Mariam is a housewife. She lives in a small town. She has gone to visit her village house. Prior to her departure, she kept her utensils, crockeries, chopper, spoons, etc. under lock and key. She returned home after a few days. She saw that there was deposition of brown colour on her chopper. The cooking pots, spoons, remained the same as they were. Of the crockeries, some are made of metal and some are of non-metals.

What is the name of brown coloured coating on the chopper and knife?
(a) Soil (b) Rust
(c) Iron (d) Both b and c

27. The sequence of steps for separating a mixture of salt, sand and camphor is _____.
(a) Adding water, filtration, evaporation, sublimation

(b) Adding water, filtration, sublimation, evaporation
(c) Sublimation, adding water, filtration, evaporation
(d) Sublimation, adding water, evaporation, filtration

28. **A solution which cannot dissolve more of a given substance at a given temperature is** _____.

(a) A saturated solution
(b) A filtrate
(c) A solution
(d) An unsaturated solution

29. **Sam's father prepared *paneer* from curdled milk. Which method did he use to separate paneer from curdled milk?**
(a) Condensation (b) Filtration
(c) Evaporation (d) Sedimentation

30. Study the following flowchart and find out what X, Y and Z could be.

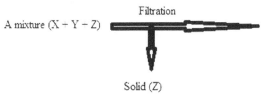
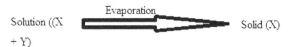

(a) Sugar, water, sawdust
(b) Sawdust water, sugar
(c) Chalk powder, water, sawdust
(d) Salt, water, sugar

Changes Around Us

Learning Objectives
After reading this chapter, you will be able to:
☞ understand the difference between reversible and irreversible changes
☞ understand physical and chemical changes
☞ learn about the changes when different substances are mixed

Everything in this universe undergoes a change. In our daily life, we observe many changes around us—at school, home, playground, garden or any other place. For example, sudden changes in the weather, flowering of plants, melting of ice, ripening of fruits, drying of clothes, milk changing into curd, germination of seeds, cooking of food, rusting of iron, burning of firecracker, etc. are the common changes that occur in day-to-day life. Some of the changes are permanent in nature, and hence, cannot be reversed. However, some changes, brought about in position, shape, size or state of the things, are temporary in nature, and hence, can be reversed.

Do you know why these changes occur? There is always a reason behind every change, for example, changes in weather occur due to the position of the earth in relation to the sun. The day and night occur because of the rotation of the earth.

Can we put some of the changes together in a group? Yes, changes which take place in nature are known as **natural changes**. Examples: weather, rainfall, etc.

Summer Season

Winter Season

Changes can be classified into various categories. A few of them are:
(i) Reversible and irreversible changes
(ii) Physical and chemical changes
(iii) Changes when different substances are mixed

Let's learn more about different categories of changes grouped together:

Reversible and Irreversible Changes

Changes take place around us all the time. However, in some cases, we can get the original substance back by reversing the process, but not in others.

A **reversible** change is a change that can be undone or reversed. Such a change can be reversed easily to obtain a substance in its original or previous form. Melting, boiling, evaporation and condensation are all examples of reversible changes.

Let's perform an activity to show an example of a reversible change.

Take a spring and suspend it from a support.

Hang a weight to the lower end of the spring. The spring gets stretched and its length increases.

When the weight is removed, the spring comes back to its original length.

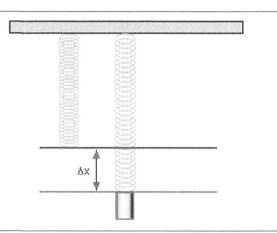

Some more examples of reversible changes:
(i) A balloon comes back to its original shape when we let the air escape the balloon.
(ii) The molten wax becomes solid again when cooled.
(iii) A blacksmith can change the shape of a piece of iron into any desired shape. For that, the piece of iron is heated until it's red hot. It is then beaten into the desired shape.

In most reversible changes, the internal structure of the substances involved does not change. In other words, the molecules that make up the substance do not change.

An **irreversible change** is a change in which the substances involved cannot be obtained back in the same form. Examples:
(i) When a piece of paper is burnt, it changes to ash and smoke. From ash and smoke, we cannot get the paper back. Thus, the change is irreversible.

Burning Paper

(ii) A candle, on burning, forms carbon dioxide gas and water vapour. These products cannot be converted back into the candle. But the wax that melts can be obtained back.
(iii) When a cracker is set on fire, it burns with a bright flame and a loud noise. However, on cooling it, it cannot be changed back into the cracker.

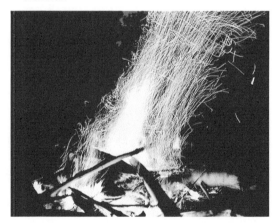

In most of the irreversible changes there is a change in the internal structure of the molecules. However, in some irreversible changes the internal structure of the substances does not change.

For example, when balloon bursts, there is no change in the molecules of the rubber. But it still can't be restored to its original shape.

Physical and Chemical Changes

The process in which a substance undergoes a change in shape, size or state is called a **physical change**. The new substance has the same properties as the old one. No new substances are produced.

Changes Around Us

Evidence of Physical Changes

A substance is described or identified by its properties. The physical properties are the observable properties, such as: size, colour, odour, shape, melting point, boiling point.

Physical changes can be brought about with forces like motion, temperature and pressure.

If a chalk piece is broken, it loses its original size and shape. This causes a change in some of its physical properties, but there is no change in the identity of the substance that makes up the chalk.

The following are a few of the observable evidence of a physical change:
(i) Change of shape: modeling clay is moulded into different shapes.
(ii) Change in size: a sheet of paper cut into many pieces of different sizes.
(iii) Change of state: butter melts on toast.

In all the above examples, the identity of the matter does not change; therefore, the change is a physical change.

A change in which one or more new substances are formed is called a **chemical change**. The new substance formed is different from the original. It has properties that are different than those of the original materials.

For example, as a log of wood burns, it produces ashes and releases gases, which have different properties than the log of wood. Thus, it is a chemical change.

Evidence of Chemical Changes
Heating lead nitrate
Materials required: lead nitrate powder, a test tube, a test-tube holder, litmus paper, Bunsen burner
Method:
(i) Take a small amount of lead nitrate in a dry test tube. Hold the test tube with a test tube holder.
(ii) Heat the test tube over the flame of the burner.
(iii) Observe the colour of the gas evolved.
(iv) Put a strip of moist blue litmus paper above the mouth of the test tube to test the nature of the gas evolved.
(v) Bring a glowing splint near the mouth of the test tube.

Expected observations:
(i) On heating lead nitrate, a crackling sound is heard. A brown gas is produced which has an irritating smell. The gas turns blue litmus red.
(ii) A yellow solid residue remains in the test tube.
(iii) The glowing splinter rekindles.

Conclusions:
(i) The brown gas was nitrogen dioxide which is acidic in nature.
(ii) The residue was yellow solid of lead oxide.
(iii) The splint rekindles because another gas produced during the reaction is oxygen.

The above reaction is an example of a chemical change which could be identified by the colour of the gas (brown), the odour (pungent smell), the formation of a yellow residue, and the sound (crackling).

A chemical change is usually accompanied by:
(i) *Change in colour:* for example, a fresh slice of apple, if kept in the open, becomes a brown in colour.
(ii) *Release or absorption of energy in the form of light, heat or any other radiation (uV):* for example, burning of magnesium ribbon.
(iii) *Evolution of a gas:* for example, when metal zinc reacts with hydrochloric acid, hydrogen gas is evolved.
(iv) *Production of sound:* for example, when hydrogen gas burns, a pop sound is heard.
(v) *Change in odor:* It only takes one experience with a rotten egg to learn that they smell different than fresh eggs. When eggs and food spoil, they undergo a chemical change. The change in odor is a clue that the food has undergone a chemical change and must be avoided.

Do You Know?
When maple leaves change colour in autumn, it is an example of a chemical change.

Changes When Different Substances React

Till now, we have seen the kind of changes that occur in an object or the material it is made of. Let us see what kind of changes occur when two different substances are mixed. It can result in chemical or physical or both the changes.

Experiment:
(The reaction should be carried out under an elder's supervision in a well-ventilated area, under a hood or near a window.)
(i) Take two 100 mL beakers (beaker A and beaker B), 100 mL of granulated sugar, and concentrated sulphuric acid
(ii) Fill each beaker half full with sugar.
(iii) Add 40 mL of water to the first beaker and 40 mL of concentrated acid to the second. Stir and allow them to stand for some time.

In which beaker do the reactants still have the same properties?

In the first beaker, the sugar and water are simply mixed together illustrating a physical change. The components of the mixture still retain their physical properties and could be separated back out of the mixture using those properties.

However, in the second beaker, the sugar and the acid did not merely mix together. A chemical change took place, resulting in products that are completely different from the original sugar and acid. A gas (SO_2) is produced along with water vapor forcing a mass of charcoal to expand out of the beaker. The reaction cannot be reversed.

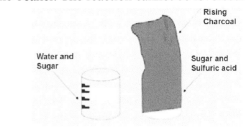

Activity
Fill up this table

	Changes in materials when heated	
Material	Will it change? Your prediction	How does it change?
1. Jelly		
2. Candle		
3. Bread		
4. Chocolate		
5. Water		
6. Paper		

Changes Around Us

Multiple Choice Questions

1. Which of the following is a reversible change?
   (a) Melting of ice
   (b) Burning of matchstick
   (c) Changing of milk into curd
   (d) Germination of seed

2. In a chemical change _____.
   (a) The molecules of the substance do not change
   (b) The molecules of the substance change
   (c) The substance remains same
   (d) Change is reversible

3. Which of the following is an example of physical change?
   (a) A bud turning into a flower
   (b) Rusting of iron
   (c) Ripening of fruit
   (d) Boiling of water

4. In a chemical change _____.
   (a) Energy is either absorbed or given out
   (b) Energy is always absorbed
   (c) Energy is given out
   (d) Energy changes do not occur

5. While making a wooden wheel, the iron rim is made slightly smaller than wooden wheel. Why? Choose the correct option.
   (a) Because on heating the rim, the iron expands. The wooden wheel is then put in the rim in its expanded state. On cooling, the iron rim contracts and fits tightly with the wooden wheel
   (b) Because the iron expands on cooling
   (c) Because the wooden wheel contracts on heating
   (d) All of them

6. Electric wires or telephone wires become tight during winter but sag a little during summer, because they are made of metal which _____.
   (a) Expands on heating
   (b) Remains the same on heating
   (c) Contracts on heating
   (d) Changes shape on heating

7. Which of the following is not an example of the changes that occur by mixing two substances?
   (a) Salt dissolved in water
   (b) Mixing sand and water
   (c) Burning of a matchstick
   (d) Sugar dissolved in water

8. The changes which are not useful to us and may cause harm are called undesirable changes. Which of the following is/are example(s) of undesirable changes?
   (a) Eruption of volcano
   (b) Rusting of iron
   (c) Melting of ice
   (d) Both (a) and (b)

9. Which of the following are true?
   (a) Cooking rice is a physical change
   (b) Rotation of a fan is a fast change
   (c) Heat is absorbed or liberated during a change involving energy
   (d) (b) and (c) are true

10. Read the activity carefully.
    i. Take two flasks, flask A and flask B.
    ii. In both of the flasks, take some lemon juice.
    iii. In flask A, add washing soda in the lemon juice.
    iv. In flask B, add salt in the lemon juice.

    Which could be the observation of this experiment?
    (a) Lots of bubbles will be formed in flask B because a chemical change takes place
    (b) Lots of bubbles will be formed in flask A because a chemical change takes place
    (c) Lots of bubbles will be formed in flask A because a physical change takes
    (d) Lots of bubbles will be observed in flask B because a physical change takes place

11. Physical changes can be generally reversed. Which of the following is an example of a physical change?

i. Zinc oxide, on heating, changes to yellow colour. However, on cooling, its colour changes to white.
ii. When a piece of iron is stroked with a permanent magnet, it gets magnetized. However, if the magnetized iron is hammered, it loses its magnetism.
iii. Wax, on being heated, changes into its liquid state. However, liquid wax changes into solid on cooling.
   (a) i and ii both
   (b) Only iii
   (c) i, ii and iii
   (d) None of these

12. Look at the following graph. It represents the energy consumption of a reaction. What kind of a change is it?

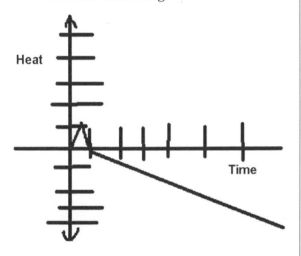

   (a) Physical change
   (b) Exothermic change
   (c) Endothermic change
   (d) Periodic change

13. Shahna took a small amount of lead nitrate in a dry test tube, holding the test tube with a test-tube holder. She put the test tube over the flame of the burner, and heated it. Soon a brown gas with a pungent smell is produced. The gas turns blue litmus red. She also observes a yellow solid residue remains in the test tube.

    Conclusion of the above experiment may be:
   (a) The brown gas evolved was nitrogen dioxide which is acidic in nature. The residue was yellow solid of lead oxide
   (b) The brown gas evolved was lead oxide which is acidic in nature. The residue was the yellow solid of nitrogen dioxide
   (c) The brown gas evolved was acidic in nature. The residue was the yellow solid of nitrogen dioxide
   (d) None of these

14. In which of the following statements is it proven that energy keeps on moving from one source to another and that it is not static?
   (a) Glowing of a light bulb
   (b) Burning of candle
   (c) Baking of cake
   (d) All of these

15. What property remains the same during physical or chemical changes?
   (a) Density
   (b) Shape
   (c) Mass
   (d) Arrangement of particles

16. Which of the following does not indicate a chemical change?
   (a) Change in colour
   (b) Change in shape
   (c) Change in energy
   (d) Change in odour

17. What is common among the following phenomena?
   i. A slice of apple, if kept in the open, develops a brown colour.
   ii. Burning of magnesium ribbon.
   iii. A new substance is formed during this change.
   (a) All are examples of periodic changes
   (b) All are examples of undesirable changes
   (c) All are examples of chemical changes
   (d) All are examples of irreversible changes

Changes Around Us

18. Look at the flowchart and study it carefully.

```
           P                                    Q
No new substance is formed during this change.  A new substance is formed during this change.
           ↓                                    ↓
Composition of the substance does not change.   Composition of the substance changes.
           ↓                                    ↓
```

Which of the following is correct?

(a) P: Reversible	Q: Irreversible
(b) P: Physical	Q: Chemical
(c) P: Reversible	Q: Reversible
(d) P: Chemical	Q: Physical

19. Which statement is not correct?
    (a) Rust is an iron compound which is formed due to the reaction between iron, water and oxygen
    (b) The reactions which are accompanied by release of heat are called exothermic reactions
    (c) When the temperature of a solid is increased, the thermal energy of its particles increases
    (d) When the temperature of a solid is increased, the kinetic energy of its particles increases

20. A teacher kept a beaker of water on a hot plate. The beaker is shown before and after the hot plate is turned on.

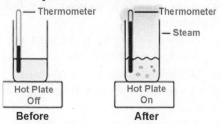

    What evidence points to the fact that water is changing state?
    (a) The hot plate is turned on
    (b) The temperature increases
    (c) The water bubbles and the steam is visible
    (d) The mass of the water in the beaker increases

21. 10 gm of solid wax on melting will form _____ gm of molten wax.
    (a) 20 gm   (b) 5 gm
    (c) 10 gm   (d) 2.5 gm

22. Which of the following is an example of a periodic change?
    (a) Landslide
    (b) A car accident
    (c) Heartbeat
    (d) Eruption of volcano

23. A chunk of cement lying in the open gets wet due to rain during the night. The next day the sun shines brightly. What do you think happened to the cement? Could the change have been reversed?

    (a) Due to the rainwater, the cement hardens and its composition changes. It is a chemical change and hence, cannot be reversed
    (b) It is an irreversible change
    (c) Yes, it is a reversible change
    (d) Yes, it is a physical change and physical changes are usually reversible

24. **If you pour a few drops of petrol on your palm, it will feel cool as the drops evaporate. This change is a/an _____.**
    (a) Chemical change
    (b) Exothermic change
    (c) Slow reaction
    (d) Endothermic change

25. **What are these examples of: the motion of planets around the sun, the motion of fans blades, and the blinking of traffic light?**
    (a) Undesirable changes
    (b) Periodic changes
    (c) Reversible change
    (d) Chemical changes

26. **In an endothermic reaction _____.**
    (a) Energy is not required
    (b) Energy is absorbed
    (c) Energy is neither released nor absorbed
    (d) Energy is released

27. **Medicines and food articles are labelled "store in a cool and dry place" to preserve them, because _____.**
    (a) Chemical reactions slow down in a cool environment
    (b) Bacteria are frozen in a cool environment
    (c) Microorganisms cannot survive in a cool environment
    (d) Both (a) and (c)

28. **The product formed by dissolving a substance into another is called _____.**
    (a) A compound   (b) A solution
    (c) A solvent   (d) A solute

29. **Atoms combine through the _____.**
    (a) Rise in temperature
    (b) Interaction of protons
    (c) Interaction of electrons
    (d) Presence of a catalyst

30. **Substances react with each other and form chemical bonds to _____.**
    (a) Form newer compounds
    (b) Increase their energy
    (c) Decrease their energy
    (d) Become stable compounds

Living Organisms and Their Surroundings

Learning Objectives
After reading this chapter, you will be able to:
- understand your surroundings
- learn the characteristics of living and non-living things
- know the differences between living and non-living things
- learn about organisms and their surroundings
- understand the meaning of habitat and adaptation
- define different types of habitats
- explain biotic and abiotic components of a habitat

If you look closely around you, you will notice various objects, which we often tend to take for granted in life. Things such as plants outside your home, puppies on the street, the clothes you wear, the pencils or pens you use to write in your notebooks at school and many others. All these objects are of different *shapes, sizes and colours*.

But have you ever wondered as to why is it that a plant grows into a tree? Why a puppy grows into a dog? Why is it that a pen or a pencil never grows? Why do your clothes don't comply with your own physical growth?

This chapter will aim to provide clarity on these questions as well as many others.

Living and Non-living Things
Based on the power of our keen observation, we understood that some objects grow and move while some objects don't. Based on these characteristics of movement and growth, objects around us are divided into two main categories:
1. *Living things:* Thing that show the characteristics of life is called a **living thing**. For example: plants and animals.
2. *Non-living things:* Objects that do not display the characteristics of life is called a **non-living thing**. For example: rock, water, sun etc.

Characteristics of Living Things
Living things are called organisms. All organisms have certain common characteristics based on which they are differentiated from non-living things. Following are the typical characteristics of living things:

1. *Definite shape and size:* All organisms of one kind have a definite shape and size. For example, a cat is different from a tiger; a fly is different from a crab. Similarly, a banyan tree is different from a eucalyptus trees, and a *neem* tree is different from a peepal tree. Living things or organisms also exhibit differences in shapes. For example, a *neem* tree or a banyan tree is bigger than a cactus, while a cactus plant is larger than grass. Similarly, an elephant is way bigger than an ant.

2. *All living things are made of cells:* All living things are made of tiny structures called cells. Cells are the basic unit of life and are the smallest unit of function and structure. While most organisms are made up of multiple cells (such organisms are called **multicellular**); some organisms comprise just one cell (such organisms are called **unicellular**). Unicellular organisms cannot be seen with the naked eye. They can only be

seen under a microscope. Examples include bacteria, yeast and amoeba.

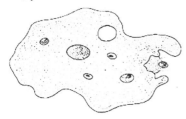

Amoeba

3. *Living things can adapt:* Organisms have the ability to adapt to the changes in their surroundings. Changes include: shortage of food, oxygen; excessive heat or cold; damage to the body, etc. The ability of a living organism to adjust to changes in its surroundings or environment is called **adaptation**. Living things have the ability to repair damages caused to their bodies. For example, when you cut off a branch of a tree, the branch grows back. This is because the cells of the trees grow back. Take yourself as an example. When you cut your finger, you wrap a band-aid around it. After a few days the skin grows back. Why? This is because the cells of your skin regenerate and grow back.

4. *Living things can move:* Most organisms show movement. Any change in position of a body is called **movement**. When an organism moves from one place to another is called **locomotion**. All animals exhibit locomotion (by moving from one place to another) as well as movement (movement their body parts); plants exhibit only movement. Animals move from place to place in search of food or a comfortable home. For example, a squirrel moves around to find nuts; a lizard moves around to find insects; while fish swims to find food. Although, plants do not show movement explicitly, they do move towards a stimulus. For example, the shoot of a plant will grow upwards toward sunlight (phototropic); while the roots grow downwards to draw water from the earth. ???(Geobropism)

Fig. 2: *Adaptation by Animals*

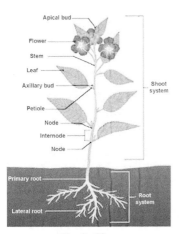

Fig. 3: *Plant*

5. *Living things need food and energy:* All organisms need energy to survive. Energy is derived from food. Animals move from place to place in search of food. Ever wondered, how plants prepare their food, considering they are fixed? Plants make their food with the help of sunlight and carbon dioxide. This process of preparing food by the use of sunlight and carbon dioxide by green plants is called **photosynthesis**. This process also releases oxygen which is vital for all living things' to survive. Only green plants have the ability to make food from solar energy and carbon dioxide. They are called **autotrophs**. Green plants are a source of food for animals on earth. Non-green plants and animals cannot make their own food. They are dependent on other plants and animals for their energy. These organisms are called **heterotrophs**.

6. *Living things respire:* The process of oxidation or burning of food to release energy is called respiration. Respiration helps in release of energy which is used by living organisms to stay alive. For example: we inhale oxygen into our lungs and exhale carbon dioxide. This carbon dioxide is in turn used by plants to prepare their own food; the oxygen so created through photosynthesis helps us inhale and stay alive. At night, plants too take in oxygen and give out carbon dioxide, just like animals. All animals including birds, snakes, etc. breathe through lungs. Fish breathe through gills and insects through air tubes.

7. *Living things excrete:* The process of removal of waste and other harmful substances formed in the body is called **excretion**. In animals the waste produced includes undigested food, carbon dioxide, urea and excess of salt and water. Animals expel undigested food in the form of faeces; carbon dioxide is expelled by the process of respiration; urea is expelled through the process of urination; excessive salt and water is expelled through sweat or as urine. Plants on the other hand produce oxygen during the day and carbon dioxide during the night. The process of removal of wastes from animals is called **excretion**, while in plants the process is called **secretion**.

8. *Living things respond to stimulus:* All living things respond to changes in their environment. For examples, on a sunny day, when you feel hot, what do you do? You go take a bath and wear loose, comfortable clothes. Similarly, on a cold day, you would wear thick woollens or cover yourself in a quilt to save yourself from the cold. The change in the environment which evokes a reaction from the organism is called **stimulus**. The reaction to the stimulus is called **response**. The ability of an organism to react to changes in its environment is called **responsiveness**. For example: when you touch a hot pan, you immediately withdraw your hand. In this case, the hot pot is the stimulus and the withdrawal of your hand is the response. How do plants respond to stimulus? Plants respond to touch, temperature, moisture, etc. For example: the shoot of a plant will always grow towards light and the root will grow downwards to secure water. Similarly, if you touch a touch-me-not plant, its leaves will fold.

9. *Living things reproduce:* The ability of living organisms to produce their own kind is called **reproduction**. It is unique to *only* living organisms.  Although, both animals and plants reproduce, the methods of reproduction vary. Animals including fish, frog, snakes, lizards, cockroaches, etc. lay eggs which hatch into young ones. Animals such as dogs, cats and human beings give birth to babies. In plants, new plants grow from stems, roots or leaves. For example, rose, jasmine and sugarcane grow from stem cuttings; ginger and potato multiply from underground stems.

10. *Living things grow:* Growth is an increase in size of a living organism. Growth is an *irreversible* and *permanent* process. A kitten grows into a cat and a baby grows into an adult human being. While plants grow all through their life span, animals stop growing after a while. For living things growth is internal, i.e., the cells multiply. For non-living things growth is external which means that these things can only grow in size if extra matter is added to them.

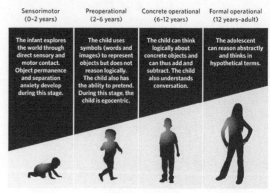

Growth

Fig 4: *Growth*

11. *Living things have a definite life span:* The life span of an organism is the period for which it remains alive. In other words, it is the time period starting from the birth till the death of an organism. Although all organisms have a definite life span, some organisms live longer than others. For example: a tortoise lives an average of 100 years, while a bacterium survives for 20–30 minutes.

SUMMARY: DIFFERENCES BETWEEN LIVING AND NON-LIVING THINGS	
Living Things	**Non-living Things**
Living things have a definite shape and size.	Non-living things don't have a definite shape and size.
Living things are made up of cells.	Non-living things are not made up of cells.
Living things can repair the damage caused to their bodies.	Non-living things cannot repair the damage caused to their bodies.
Living things can adapt.	Non-living things cannot adapt.
Living things show movement.	Non-living things cannot move.
Living things need food for growth, energy and repair.	Non-living things don't need food.
Living things respire.	Non-living things don't respire.
Living things excrete.	Non-living things don't excrete.
Living things respond to stimulus.	Non-living things don't respond to stimulus.
Living things reproduce.	Non-living things don't reproduce.
Living things grow.	Non-living things don't grow.
Living things show a definite life span.	Non-living things don't have a definite life span.

We have learnt that we derive our food from our surroundings. The immediate surroundings of an organism is the environment. It consists of the physical surroundings (air, water, soil) as well as other living organisms.

Habitat

The natural dwelling of an organism is called habitat. In other words, the place where an organism lives in nature is called habitat. For example, desert is the habitat of the camel and the cactus plant; mountains are inhabited by yaks and the pine trees; a forest is the habitat of several animals, including tigers and a variety of plants and trees. A habitat has abundant food, water and climatic conditions which favour the survival and reproduction of the organisms living in a particular area/region.

Natural Habitat

Types of Habitat
There are two types of habitat: aquatic and terrestrial.

1. *Aquatic Habitat:* The organisms that live in water are called **aquatic animals** or **aquatic organisms**, and their habitat is called **aquatic habitat** or **water habitat**. This includes: oceans, rivers, ponds, seas lakes, etc. Fish, sharks, whales, seals are all examples of aquatic animals who live in an aquatic habitat. Please note that plants living in water are called **hydrophytes**.

2. *Terrestrial Habitat:* The organisms that live on land are called **terrestrial animals** or **terrestrial organisms**, and their habitat is called **terrestrial habitat** or **land habitat**. Examples include: birds, snakes, elephants, human beings, lizards, etc. There are several types of terrestrial habitats. These include:

   a. *Desert habitat:* Deserts are extremely hot/cold and dry, and get scanty rainfall. About one-fifth of the earth's surface is desert. Animals such as camels and gerbil live in the desert, while plants such as cacti, date palms, etc. form the desert's vegetation.

   Adaptations of animals living in desert:
   (i) Animals like rats and snake stay in burrows deep in the sand during the day due to intense heat.
   (ii) Camel is called ship of the desert. It can live without water for many days. The fat gets stored in the hump of the camel. It makes use of this fat for energy. It drinks upto 32 gallons of water (46 litres) in one go. Camel has very thick lips to eat the prickly desert plants without pain. They have padded feet which enables them to walk easily on sand without sinking into it. The color of the body of a camel blends with the surroundings.

Desert Habitat

   Adaptations of desert plants:
   (i) They lose very little water through transpiration.
   (ii) The leaves are either missing or they are very small in the form of spines to reduce the water loss in transpiration.
   (iii) The leaf like structure of cactus is actually stem. Photosynthesis is carried out by the stem in desert plants.
   (iv) The stem has a waxy covering which helps in retaining water.
   (v) Roots of desert plants are usually tap roots penetrating deep into the soil to absorb water.

   b. *Mountain habitat:* Mountain habitats are cold, rocky and dry. Snowfall is common at higher altitudes, followed by chilly winds. The trees on mountains have needle-like leaves and produce a cone-shaped fruit. These trees are called pine trees. Animals such as snow leopard and goats are commonly found here.

   Adaptations of mountain plants:
   (i) Trees of hilly regions are usually cone shaped and have sloping branches. This helps the snow to slide of easily.

(ii) The leaves of some trees are needle-like. They also cannot hold back the snow falling on them & it slides off easily.

Mountain Habitat

Adaptations of mountain animals:
(i) Animals have thick skin or fur to protect them from cold. For example, yaks can be seen with long hair that keeps them warm.
(ii) Snow leopard has thick fur on its body including feet and toes. This protects its feet from cold when it walks on the snow.
(iii) Mountain goats have strong hooves for running up the rocky slopes of mountains.

c. *Grasslands:* Grasslands are hot and partly dry areas with very few trees and mostly covered with grass. Grasslands are home to both herbivores and carnivores. Buffaloes, giraffes, goats, sheep, elephants are herbivores which live in grasslands; while tigers, foxes and hyenas are the carnivores found in grasslands.

Grassland Animal Adaptations:
(i) Animals like lions have long claws in their front legs that can be withdrawn inside the toes.
(ii) It is light brown in colour and can easily hide in dry grasslands when it goes hunting for its prey.
(iii) The eyes in the front of the face allow it to have a correct idea about the location of its prey.
(iv) Deer has strong teeth for chewing hard plant stems in the forest/grasslands.
(v) Deer has long ears to hear movements of predators.
(vi) The eyes on the side of its head allow it to look in all directions for any danger sensed.
(vii) The speed of a deer helps in an easy escape from predators.

Those animals which live on land as well as in water are called **amphibians**. Examples would include frogs, crocodiles, alligators, etc.

Adaptations of Aquatic Plants:

Aquatic plants are of three types – floating, partially submerged and fully submerged.

Floating plants like lotus have long and hollow stems which are very light. The stems grow upto the surface of water while leaves and flowers float on the surface of water.

Fully submerged plants grow completely under the water. All parts are seen under the water. Leaves of these plants are narrow and thin **ribbon-like. They can easily bend in flowing** water.

The partially submerged plants have highly divided leaves through which water passes without tearing or causing any kind of damage to them.

Adaptations of Aquatic Animals:
(i) Aquatic animals usually have a streamlined body that facilitates their easy movement.
(ii) These animals have gills that help them to take dissolved oxygen from water.
(iii) Whales and Dolphins have blowholes instead of gills on the upper part of their head. This helps them to breathe in air when they swim near the surface of water. They can stay inside the water for a long time without breathing.

Components of a Habitat
(i) Our surroundings comprise living and non-living things. The living things in our environment such as plants, animals etc. constitute the **biotic component** of the environment.
(ii) The non-living things in our environment such as air, water, sunlight, etc. form the **abiotic component** of the environment.

Living Organisms and Their Surroundings

Activity

There are five rows of different words. Use the words from each row and make 5 meaningful sentences.
HINT: Cross through the word when you have used it.

1. Woodland   Weather   Sustainable   Species
2. Soil   Savannah   Rainforest   Producer
3. Plants   Herbivore   Forest   Foodweb
4. Extinct   Environment   Ecosystem   Desert
5. Decomposer   Deciduous   Coniferous   Carnivore

Multiple Choice Questions

1. Which among these children made a correct statement?
   (a) Saumya: Global warming increases the concentration of carbon dioxide in the atmosphere
   (b) Sumit: Global warming increases the concentration of nitrogen in the atmosphere
   (c) Sanchit: Global warming increases the concentration of oxygen in the atmosphere
   (d) Ashi: Global warming increases the concentration of ozone in the atmosphere

2. Which of the following characteristics of a glass of water reason that it cannot be considered alive?
   (a) It has no heart
   (b) It has no arms or legs
   (c) It has no cells
   (d) It has no tissues

3. Some yeast, sugar and water are mixed in a test-tube. The diagrams show the test-tube at the start and after one hour.

   Which process causes this change?
   (a) Growth
   (b) Irritability
   (c) Reproduction
   (d) Respiration

4. Excretion, irritability and reproduction are characteristics of _____.
   (a) All animals and plants
   (b) Animals only
   (c) Plants only
   (d) All animals and some plants only

5. Look at the following picture carefully. Which of the following characteristic of living organisms is it showing?

   Venus Flytrap

   (a) Living things are made of cells
   (b) Living things obtain and use energy
   (c) Living things grow and develop
   (d) Living things require food for energy

6. One of the characteristics of living organisms is that they all respire by _____.
   (a) Obtaining oxygen by breathing
   (b) Obtaining energy from sunlight
   (c) Obtaining energy by chemically breaking down food
   (d) Breaking down large molecules to smaller molecules by digestion

7. The following picture is an example of _____ in plants. The picture is of _____.

   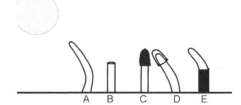

   (a) Sensitivity, germination of seeds
   (b) Locomotion, seed dispersal
   (c) Locomotion, wilting
   (d) Sensitivity, phototropism

8. Which of the following organisms is not ultimately dependent on the sun as a source of energy?
   (a) A night-blooming flower is pollinated by night-flying bats
   (b) An underground earthworm avoids the sun
   (c) A cave fish feeds on debris that washes down to it
   (d) No, all the organisms are ultimately dependent on the sun

9. What is the term which refers to all the chemical energy transformations that occur within a cell?
   (a) Evolution   (b) Metabolism
   (c) Adaptation   (d) Homeostasis

10. Soham set up two small aquariums at home. He placed three rainbow fish in each aquarium but he put hydrilla plants in aquarium A only. After some time he observed that that the fish swam freely in aquarium A but the fish in aquarium B swam near the water surface.

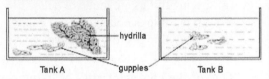

   He concluded that the hydrilla plants _____.
   (a) Help to beautify the aquarium
   (b) Provide shade for the fish
   (c) Provide oxygen for the fish to breathe during photosynthesis
   (d) Are the main source of food for the fish

11. Study the diagram as shown below.

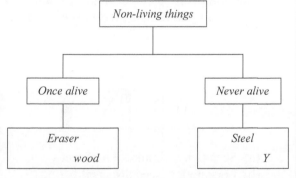

   Which one of the following is an example of Y?
   (a) Glass bottle   (b) Cotton shirt
   (c) Exercise book   (d) Dried flower

12. Study the diagram below:

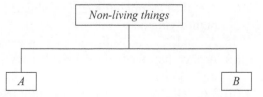

   Which group of items can you put into box A?
   (a) Glass bottle, paper clip, cotton shirt
   (b) Paper plate, plastic fork and spoon
   (c) Leather sofa, rubber boots, bamboo cane
   (d) Rubber balls, plastic cup, metal spoon

13. John set up two tanks. He placed three guppies in each tank but he put hydrilla plants in Tank A only. John found that the fish swam freely in Tank A but the fish in Tank B swam near the water surface.

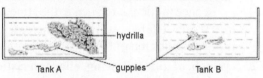

   In the night, both the guppies and the hydrilla plants take in _____ and give out _____.
   (a) Oxygen; oxygen
   (b) Carbon dioxide; oxygen
   (c) Oxygen; carbon dioxide
   (d) Carbon dioxide; carbon dioxide

14. Some green beans were placed on some damp cotton wool in a dish and placed in a dark corner. A few days later, the beans started to grow into seedlings. The beans get their food for growth from the _____.
   (a) Air
   (b) Cotton wool
   (c) Seed-leaves
   (d) Water used to damp the cotton wool

15. Which of the following describes respiration?
   Ananya: Animals take in carbon dioxide and give off oxygen.
   Sanchit: Animals take in oxygen and give off carbon dioxide.
   Saumya: Plants take in carbon dioxide and give off oxygen.
   Ranchit: Plants take in oxygen and give off carbon dioxide.
   (a) Ananya and Ranchit
   (b) Sanchit and Saumya
   (c) Sanchit and Ranchit
   (d) Ranchit only

16. Animals have structural and behavioural adaptations which enable them to survive in their natural habitats.

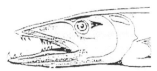

By looking at the picture of the head of the fish, which of the following is true of how this organism survives in its natural habitat?
(a) It is a herbivore
(b) It has sharp teeth to feed on other animals
(c) It uses its eyes to scare away predators
(d) It is able to hold its breath underwater for a long time

17. The following aquatic animals are grouped according to their breathing adaptations. Which group of animals does not breathe in the same way?
(a) Water stick insect, water scorpion
(b) Tubifex worm, tadpole
(c) Crab, wood louse
(d) Water spider, great diving beetle

18. Which of the following animals have the correct form of adaptation?
(a) Camel: bristles on his feet
(b) Whale: blow holes in its head
(c) Mudskipper: lungs for breathing
(d) Birds: compact bones

19. Animals use different parts of their bodies to move around.

In the following table, the body parts used by the corresponding animals are matched. Which animal is matched incorrectly?

Animal	Legs	Wings	Fins	Flippers	Body
Snake					Y
Penguin		Y			
Cheetah	Y				
Dolphin			Y	Y	

(a) Snake
(b) Penguin
(c) Cheetah
(d) Dolphin

20. Based on the diagrams of the dolphin and the fish (not drawn to scale), which characteristic they share in common?

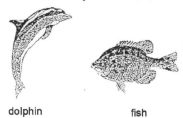

dolphin   fish

i. They both have whiskers.
ii. Each has a tail to propel itself forward in the water.
iii. Both have gills to breath.
iv. Both are warm blooded.
(a) Only ii (b) i and iv only
(c) ii and iii only (d) iii and iv only

21. Mike had a glass tank containing some earthworms, dead leaves and maize seeds. He added another animal into the tank. He observed the tank for a few hours. Then he drew a graph to show his observations.

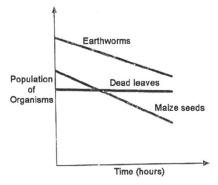

By looking at the graph, we can tell that the animal that Mike put in was a _____.
(a) Snail (b) Chick
(c) Toad (d) Grasshopper

Living Organisms and Their Surroundings

22. Samantha found a healthy plant with red leaves in her garden. She said that the plant is not able to make food because its leaves are not green. Is Samantha correct?
    (a) Yes. The plant does not have green leaves. Hence, it will not make its own food but gets its food from the ground
    (b) Yes. The plant does not have green leaves. Hence, it does not have chlorophyll to absorb sunlight to make food
    (c) No. Even though the plant has no green leaves, it can still make food through its underground stem
    (d) No. The green pigment, chlorophyll, is hidden under the red pigment in the leaves. Hence, the plant can still make food

23. Study the flowchart below carefully.

    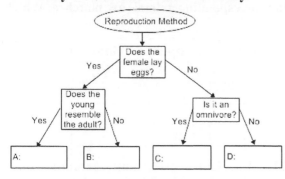

    Put the following animals: lizard, zebra, man and dragonfly on the boxes above.
    (a) A: Lizard; B: Dragonfly; C: Man; D: Zebra
    (b) A: Zebra; B: Dragonfly; C: Man; D: Lizard
    (c) A: Dragonfly; B: Dragonfly; C: Man; D: Lizard
    (d) A: Man; B: Dragonfly; C: Lizard; D: Zebra

24. Based on the information below, answer the following questions:

    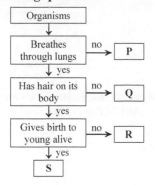

    Identify the characteristic(s) that is/are common for both organisms R and S.
    (a) They breathe through gills and have hair on their body
    (b) They breathe through lungs and have hair on their body
    (c) They breathe through nose and have hair on their body
    (d) They breathe through lungs

25. Look at the following pictures carefully.

    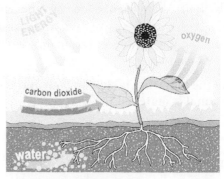

    The two living organisms in these pictures are _____ and the common life process that occurs in both the living organism is _____.
    (a) Plant and mushroom, respiration
    (b) Plant and animal, photosynthesis
    (c) Plant and snail, mobility
    (d) Plant and snail, excretion

26. Which living organisms excrete uric acid?
    (a) Birds and lizards
    (b) Birds and reptiles
    (c) Birds
    (d) a and b both

27. When plants grow in dark, they become tall, yellowish and weak, and the leaves are very small.

    This happens because of _____.
    (a) Lack of sunlight
    (b) Lack of photosynthesis
    (c) Lack of photosynthesis due to no sunlight
    (d) Lack of air

28. Read the features of a plant as given below:
    i. They have waxy upper surface.
    ii. Leaves are large and flat.
    iii. Roots are much reduced in size.
    iv. Stems are generally long and narrow.

    To which of the following habitats does this plant belong?
    (a) Polar region
    (b) Desert
    (c) Aquatic
    (d) Tropical rainforest

29. What is a common character among the following animals?

    (a) They all lack backbone
    (b) They all live in water
    (c) They all lay eggs to reproduce
    (d) They all have scales on their body

30. Four groups of mice were taken for an experiment. One group was control group and other three were test groups. The test groups consume different amounts of sweetener in their food. The control group is the one that receives _____.
    (a) 10 mg/day of sweetener
    (b) 50 mg/day of sweetener
    (c) No sweetener
    (d) Extra food

Food, Health and Hygiene

Learning Objectives
After reading the chapter, you will be able to discuss:
- food and its necessity
- functions of food
- autotrophs and heterotrophs
- herbivores, carnivores and omnivores
- food items that come from plants and animals
- components of food
- health and hygiene

There is an old saying, "You are what you eat". But what exactly do we eat?

The material or substance which we eat is called food. Why do we need food? Let us compare our body to a car. What happens to a car if there is no petrol in its tank? It stops running. Petrol is the fuel which runs the car. Similarly food is the fuel which living organisms require to keep functioning. Organisms require food for the following purposes:

(i) To provide energy for various activities of the body
(ii) For growth and development of the body
(iii) To protect the body from diseases and keep it healthy
(iv) For repairing injured body parts
(v) For reproduction

Functions of Food
Why do we need food?

Food contains materials which provide us energy required for:
(i) various activities to stay alive;
(ii) growth and development;
(iii) protection from diseases;
(iv) body repair and reproduction.

Autotrophs and Hetrotrophs
Food has chemical energy stored in the form of organic molecules. Food provides both the energy to do work and the carbon to build bodies. Green plants make their own food from carbon dioxide and water in the presence of sunlight. We call this process **photosynthesis**.

Animals, including human beings, and non-green plants eat plants and other animals that eat plants as food. Hence, green plants are called **autotrophs** and animals are called **heterotrophs**.

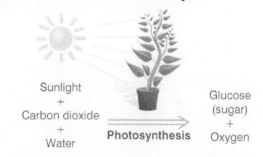

Types of Animals Based on Food Habit
Different animals eat different types of food. They depend directly or indirectly on plants for their food. Their body parts are designed to the kind of food they eat.

Herbivores

Herbivores are consumers that eat only plants. Since plants, trees, and shrubs make their own food, herbivores get energy from eating these producers. In a forest ecosystem, deer and rabbits are common herbivores. In a savannah ecosystem in Africa, zebras and elephants are common herbivores.

Carnivores

Carnivores are consumers that eat only other animals. In marine ecosystems, sharks, walruses, seals, and octopuses are common carnivores. In land ecosystems, lions, wolves, hawks and eagles are common carnivores. Some carnivores are called scavengers. These carnivores eat animals that are already dead. Most of the time, scavengers eat leftovers from other carnivores. One example of a scavenger is a vulture.

Omnivores

Omnivores are consumers that eat both plants and animals. Since they can eat a variety of organisms, omnivores can easily adapt to changing environments. Pigs, bears, raccoons and humans are examples of omnivores.

Food, Health and Hygiene

Decomposers

Organisms such as fungi and bacteria get energy in a different way than producers or consumers. These organisms, called **decomposers**, get energy by breaking down nutrients in dead organisms. As they break down the nutrients, decomposers produce simple products such as water and carbon dioxide. These products are returned to the ecosystem for other organisms to use. Decomposers are very important because they return nutrients and products back to the ecosystem. One way to think of decomposers is as recyclers. Termites and earthworms are examples of decomposers.

Sources of Food

Food is obtained by living things from both plants and animals.

Plants as Source of Food

You know that green plants can prepare their own food. For this reason, they are known as producers. They prepare more food than what they need themselves. This extra food is stored in different parts of the plant body.

The different plant parts from which food is obtained are the roots, stems, leaves, flowers, seeds and fruits.

Do you know which part of the plant you are eating when you eat potato, cabbage, onion, radish, carrot or mango?

The plant parts which are eaten are called **edible parts**. For example, the edible part in a mango is the fruit; in onion and potato, it is the stem; while in radish and carrot, it is the root; and leaf is the edible part in cabbage.

Food items obtained from plants
(i) Cereals (wheat, rice, maize)
(ii) Pulses (pea, bean, soyabean, gram, groundnut)

(iii) Vegetables (carrot, radish, potato, onion, spinach, cabbage, tomato)
(iv) Fruits (banana, apple, mango, grape, orange, pineapple)
(v) Sugar (sugarcane)
(vi) Oils (mustard, groundnut, coconut, soyabean, cotton seed, sunflower)
(vii) Spices (turmeric, chilli, ginger, saunf or fennel, elaichi or cardamom)

Let us find out which plant parts provide us these food items

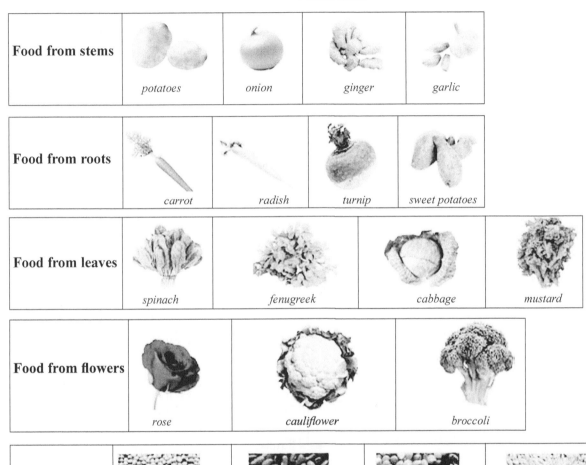

Food, Health and Hygiene

Animals as Source of Food

A variety of food products are obtained from animals. These include milk and milk products, eggs, meat and honey.

Dairy products are made from milk. Some examples of dairy products are paneer, cheese, butter, ghee and curd. Animals which provide meat and egg are called **poultry**. Poultry products are rich in proteins.

Honey is a sweet liquid produced by honeybees from the nectar (sweet juice produced by flowers). It consists of sugar, water, minerals and enzymes. Honey is stored in beehives.

Food Ingredients

Food items which we eat may consist of a single ingredient or many ingredients. For example, fruits like banana, apple or mango consist of single material. Think of food items like rice, dal, chapati/roti, kheer and idli. These food items consist of two or more items. Different items which are used to prepare food items are called **ingredients**.

No.	Food Item	Ingredients
1.	Chapati/Roti	Atta (flour) and water
2.	Rice	Rice grains and water
3.	Dal	Pulses, water, salt, oil/ghee and spices
4.	Vegetable curry	Vegetables, salt, oil, spices and water
5.	Kheer	Milk, rice and sugar
6.	Idli	Rice, urad dal, salt and water
7.	Chicken curry	Chicken, oil/ghee, spices, vegetables and water

Components of Food

The components of food are certain organic substances and minerals found in food. They are called **nutrients**. Nutrients provide the body with energy and enable it to grow, repair and maintain itself. Hence it is important that we understand the exact role of nutrients in our food and recognize the various foods that provide these nutrients.

Nutrients are essential for good health, so it is important that our food includes all these nutrients in sufficient quantities. Besides these nutrients, dietary fibers and water are also important components of food. Dietary fibers form the roughage part of our food. They help in maintaining regular bowel movements.

Water helps our body in absorbing nutrients from the food. It also helps in removing the waste from the body.

Carbohydrates

Carbohydrates are the primary source of energy for your body. Carbohydrates help in the proper functioning of every system in your body, including your brain, heart, muscles and internal organs. Carbohydrates can be simple (table sugar, corn syrup) or complex (whole grain). Simple carbohydrates enter your bloodstream very quickly. Carbohydrates contain carbon, hydrogen & oxygen. Complex carbohydrates are processed more slowly.

Types of carbohydrates

Carbohydrates are of three types: sugars, starch and cellulose. Starch and sugars make up major part of our food.

Sugar

Sugars are simple carbohydrates with sweet taste. These are soluble in water. Glucose, lactose, fructose and sucrose are examples of sugar.

Sources of sugar:

Fruits, they are sweet because of glucose or fructose.

Table sugar, which contains sucrose.

Honey also contains sucrose and fructose.

Lactose, is found in milk.

Honey

Sugar

Starch

Starch is a complex carbohydrate present in our food. A starch molecule is made up of a large number of glucose molecules joined together to form a long chain. Starch is tasteless, odorless and like a white powder. It is insoluble in water. Major sources of starch are wheat, rice, maize and potatoes.

Rice

Maize

Potatoes

Activity 1: Test for Starch

Take a small quantity of a food item or a raw ingredient. Put 2–3 drops of dilute iodine solution on it. Observe if there is any change in the colour of the food item. Did it turn blue-black?

A blue-black colour indicates that it contains starch.

Cellulose

Cellulose is also a complex carbohydrate. Like starch, it is also tasteless and white in colour. It is found in the cell wall of plant cells, wood, cotton and jute in the form of fibers. Cellulose fibers are made up of 1000–3000 glucose molecules joined together.

Do You Know?

How are carbohydrates digested?

Carbohydrates are your body's preferred energy source and are found in the forms of starch, sugar and fiber. The process of digestion begins in your mouth where the process of chewing mechanically breaks food into small pieces. The enzymes in the saliva initiate chemical digestion. When you swallow, partially digested carbs travel down your oesophagus to the stomach with little additional digestion. From there, carbohydrates move into the small intestine where enzymes released by the pancreas break them into simple forms to be absorbed into the bloodstream. Fiber is indigestible and passes through your gastrointestinal tract without being broken down.

Fats

Fat is a concentrated source of energy (1 g of fat provides 9 kcal). It is insoluble in water but soluble in organic solvents. Fats occur in both plant and animals. Mustard oil, coconut oil, sunflower oil and other vegetable oil are obtained from plants. Dry fruits like almonds and cashew nuts are also good source of plant fats. Butter and ghee are animal fats. Meat, fish, egg-yolk and cheese are also sources of animal fats.

Fats are divided into two categories, according to their structure.

(i) Fats of plant origin are called unsaturated fats. They are liquid at room temperature. E.g., sunflower oil. They are considered healthy for humans.

Sunflower Oil

(ii) Fats of animal origin are called saturated fats. They are solids at room temperature. E.g. ghee, butter.

Ghee

Food, Health and Hygiene

Proteins

One-fifth of an adult's total body weight is protein. Protein is found in every cell of our body.

All the tissues in our body, such as muscle, blood, bone, skin and hair are made up of proteins. Protein is thus essential to maintain cellular integrity and function, and for health and reproduction.

Proteins contain carbon, hydrogen, oxygen and nitrogen. They are distinguished from carbohydrates and fats by the presence of nitrogen. Protein is synthesized from basic units called **amino acids**. Protein molecules, which contain up to hundred aminoacids, are much larger than carbohydrates or lipid molecule. Some proteins also contain sulphur, phosphorous or a metal.

Twenty different kinds of amino acids join in a specific manner in order to make a single protein molecule. A combination of 3 amino acids makes one protein.

Biological value of protein is the percentage of nitrogen that is absorbed and is available for use by the body for growth and maintenance.

The quality of a protein is determined by the kind and proportion of amino acid it contains. Proteins that contain all essential amino acids in proportion capable of promoting growth are described as **complete protein, good quality protein**, or **proteins of high biological value**. A good quality protein is digested and utilized well. Egg protein is a complete protein and is considered as a reference protein with the highest biological value. The quality of other proteins is determined in relation to their comparison with egg protein.

Activity 2: Test for Protein

Take a small quantity of a food item for testing. If the food you want to test is a solid, you first need to make a paste of it or powder it. Grind or mash a small quantity of the food item. Put some of it in a clean test tube, add 10 drops of water to it, and shake the test tube.

Now, using a dropper, add two drops of solution of copper sulphate and ten drops of solution of caustic soda to the test tube. Shake well and let the test tube stand for a few minutes. What do you see? Did the contents of the test tube turn violet? A violet colour indicates presence of proteins in the food item.

Vitamins

Vitamins are a group of nutrients that our body requires in small quantities. They are essential for the proper working of the body. If our diet is lacking in any vitamin, we suffer from certain diseases called **deficiency diseases**.

Vitamins are classified based on their solubility as fat-soluble and water-soluble vitamins.

Fat soluble	Water soluble
Vitamin A, D, E, K	Vitamin B1, B2, B6, B12 (Niacin), Nicotinic Acid, Folic acid and Vitamin C

Water-soluble vitamins are not accumulated in the body, but are readily excreted while fat-soluble vitamins are stored in the body. For this reason excessive intake of fat-soluble vitamins, especially Vitamin A and D, can prove toxic. Excessive intake leads to the condition called **hypervitaminosis**.

Minerals

Minerals are nutrients that contain certain elements. All of them perform particular functions in the body. They are required by our body in small quantities in the diet to maintain good health. Inadequate amount of minerals in our diet can also lead to deficiency diseases.

Essential minerals, which are inorganic substances, are classified as macro and micro, based on the amount needed by humans per day.

Macrominerals are those which are vital to health and are required in the diet by more than 100 mg per day;those required less than 20 mg in the diet per day are called **microminerals** or trace minerals.

The essential microminerals are calcium, phosphorous, magnesium, sulphur, potassium and chloride. Important microminerals of relevance in human nutrition are iron, zinc, copper, sodium, cobalt, fluoride, manganese, chromium, iodine and molybdenum.

Water

Water makes up almost 70% of our body weight. Most of this water is present in the cells of our body.

Water is colourless, calorie-less compound of hydrogen and oxygen that virtually every cell in the body needs to survive. Water is closer to being a universal solvent than any other liquid.

Functions of water

(i) It is an essential constituent of all the cells of the body and the internal environment.
(ii) It serves as a transport medium by which most of the nutrients pass into the cells; it also helps remove excretory products.
(iii) Water is a medium for most biochemical reactions within the body.
(iv) It is a valuable solvent in which various substances, such as electrolytes, non-electrolytes, hormones, enzymes, vitamins are carried from one place to another.
(v) It plays a vital role in the maintenance of body temperature. Heat is produced when food is burnt for energy. Body temperature must be kept at 80°–108° Fahrenheit, for higher or lower body temperature can cause death. Body heat is lost through the skin, lungs, urine and faeces.
(vi) It is a constituent of the fluids in body tissues; (e.g.) the amniotic fluid which surrounds and protects the foetus during pregnancy.
(vii) Saliva is about 99.5 percent water. It makes swallowing easier by moistening the food.
(viii) Water helps in maintaining the form and texture of the tissues.
(ix) Water is essential for the maintenance of acid base and electrolyte balance. It should be noted that pure water consists of hydrogen ion (H+) and hydroxyl ion (OH–).

Roughage

Plant foods, such as fruits and vegetables, contain a carbohydrate that cannot be digested by the body. It is called **roughage**. It should form an important part of our diet because of the following reasons:

(i) Roughage adds bulk to our food. Since it is not digested, it passes down the entire digestive tract from the mouth to the anus. The muscles of the digestive tract need this bulk to push against, like squeezing toothpaste out of a tube.
(ii) It prevents constipation and ensures proper bowl movement.

Do You Know?

What would the world look like without decomposers (bacteria and fungi?)

Without bacteria there would be no life as we know it, no plants, no animals, not even protists could live on this planet. Because:

1. Most bacteria live in soil and water where they multiply to staggering numbers provided their living requirements are met. A single drop of pond water can contain millions, a water sample taken near some decomposing aquatic vegetation can contain billions of these.
2. Bacterial decomposition allows the nutrient molecules, that would otherwise remain locked up in dead bodies, to be recycled in the living world.
3. Bacteria have played key role in this evolutionary drama. They were among the first cells to appear on earth.

Activity 3

Test the food usually eaten by cattle or a pet to find out which nutrients are present in animal food.

Health and Hygiene

Health is a state of complete physical, mental and social well-being. We take health as being free from diseases but it is much more than just the absence of a disease.

To keep ourselves free from diseases and to have good health, we should be careful about hygiene. The various practices that help in maintaining good health are called **hygiene**. Thus, health and hygiene go hand in hand or they are interrelated.

Proper nutrition, physical exercise, rest and sleep, cleanliness, and medical care are essential parts of maintaining good health. Health includes both personal and community health.

Healthy Lifestyle

Our lifestyles today are very busy. We have family, school, sports, leisure and social commitments to fit into a limited time. We need to be healthy to cope with the demands of daily life. But what does it mean to have a healthy lifestyle?

To have a healthy lifestyle, we need to:
(i) eat a balanced diet most of the time.
(ii) do regular exercise.
(iii) have time to relax.
(iv) get adequate sleep so that our body recuperates and feels fresh.

Benefits of exercise

Exercise improves the body in many ways.
(i) The lungs take in more air, giving us more oxygen.
(ii) The heart works hard to supply more blood and oxygen to different parts of the body that are working.
(iii) The muscles become strong and fit.
(iv) Weight-bearing exercises like running, skipping and hopping help to develop strong bones.
(v) Food is processed more efficiently and waste products are more quickly removed, leaving the body feeling more comfortable.
(vi) The skin, hair and eyes look better because the "inside" is healthy.
(vii) Toned muscles gives the body a better shape and posture.
(viii) Chemicals are released into the brain which make us feel happy. These are called endorphins. They make us feel more confident and improve our self-esteem.
(ix) We sleep better.

Strength, stamina and suppleness are improved. Some important points related to personal health are enlisted below:
(i) Balanced diet
(ii) Personal hygiene
    a. Regular toilet habits
    b. Washing hands before eating
    c. Bathing regularly and wearing clean clothes
    d. Cleaning teeth and gums
(iii) Domestic hygiene
(iv) Clean food and water
(v) Cooking with care
(vi) Brushing teeth twice a day & massage to gums

Diseases

A **disease** is defined as any deviation from health or any state when body is not at ease. Diseases can be categorised as communicable and non-communicable diseases.

Non-communicable diseases do not spread from an infected person to another. Pathogens are not involved. These diseases may be caused due to dietary deficiency (rickets, scurvy, kwashiorkor), genetic defects, hormonal imbalances, allergy, etc.

Diseases that spread from one person to another by the entry of pathogens are called infectious or transmissible or **communicable** diseases. They are directly related to hygiene and cleanliness. Let's learn more about it.

Communicable diseases are caused by microorganisms commonly called germs. Microbes or germs that cause diseases are of the following types:
(i) Bacteria   (ii) Viruses
(iii) Protozoa   (iv) Fungi

The diseases caused by these germs are given below:

Germ	Diseases caused
Bacteria	Typhoid, Cholera, Plague, Pneumonia, Tuberculosis, Meningitis
Viruses	Common cold, Flu, Chicken pox, Measles, Polio, AIDS, Rabies
Protozoa	Amoebic dysentery, Malaria
Fungi	Ringworm, Athlete's foot

> **Do You Know?**
> **What is community health?**
> Activities, undertaken at the government or local organisation level to maintain health of the people (for controlling diseases) are known as community health.
> There are several organisations working towards good community health.
> Some of these are listed below.
> 1. Government hospitals, and dispensaries
> 2. The National Malaria Eradication Programme
> 3. The Tuberculosis (T. B.) Eradication Programme
> 4. National Immunization Programme
> 5. National Pulse Polio Programme

Spread of Diseases

The disease-causing germs or microbes travel from the sick person through air, food and water, insects or direct contact with the sick person.

Through air: Many communicable diseases spread through air. A person suffering from common cold or whooping cough when sneezes or coughs in front of a healthy person, germs enter into the healthy person's body through the droplets carried by the air. The germs of diphtheria, viral fever, measles, chicken pox, etc. travel through air and infect healthy persons.

Through food and water: Some diseases are spread by dirty food and water, such as typhoid, diarrhea, cholera, jaundice. Food and water get infected with germs when they are not stored properly.

Through insects: Malaria and dengue are spread through mosquito bite. When a female anopheles mosquito bites a sick person, it picks up the germs. Next when it bites a healthy person, the germ (protozoa) enters into the blood of the healthy person. Thus, a healthy person gets infected by the mosquito and falls sick. Aedes mosquitoes spread a disease called dengue in the same manner.

Through direct contact: Some diseases spread when a healthy person comes in direct contact with the sick person or use the articles, such as towels, clothes, soap, etc., used by the sick person. Chicken pox, measles, whooping cough, ringworms, etc. spread in this manner.

Spreading of Diseases

Prevention of communicable diseases

Communicable diseases can be checked by bringing awareness amongst the common people. Common preventive steps include:

1. **Education:** People should be educated about the communicable diseases. Education will bring awareness and people will learn how to protect themselves from these diseases.
2. **Isolation:** A person who is suffering from chicken pox/measles should be kept in a separate room so that others do not catch infection from him or her.
3. **Sanitation:** We should keep our surroundings clean because garbage heaps, open drains, polluted water, food exposed to dust, flies, etc. carry lot of germs that cause diseases. We should drink clean and germ-free water. We can remain healthy in clean and green environment.
4. **Vaccination:** Vaccination is a technique to develop ability of the body to fight against

Food, Health and Hygiene

disease. When a vaccine of a particular disease is given to a healthy person, the person develops an ability to fight against the germs of the disease. This ability of fighting against germs is called **immunity**. Today, vaccines are available against many diseases, such as polio, mumps, small pox, cholera, rabies, measles, etc. **DPT** vaccine is given to prevent diphtheria, tetanus and pertussis. **Polio** vaccine is given to prevent polio. **MMR** vaccine is given to prevent measles, mumps and rubella.

Environmental Hygiene

You can keep your body clean but what will happen if you live in dirty surroundings? If so, you are sure to fall sick. Thus, to have a healthy living one must live in clean surroundings. Unclean surroundings may become breeding ground for flies and germs, thus, leading to spread of diseases.

Environmental hygiene includes environmental sanitation or keeping the surroundings clean.

To keep the environment healthy, we should be careful about the disposal of the garbage. Some of the practices for disposing the garbage are:

(i) **Keeping the house clean:** The house must be cleaned every day. We must sweep and mop the house to remove dirt from every nook and corner of the house. The furniture must also be wiped clean. The cobwebs from the walls and roof should be cleared at least once a week.

(ii) **Throwing garbage in dustbins:** Do not throw your household garbage on the roadside. This makes street dirty and allows flies, mosquitoes and other animals to breed. This garbage not only looks dirty, but also produces foul smell. Garbage should be thrown inside the dustbins. The bins should also be cleaned after emptying the garbage.

(iii) **Keeping dustbins covered:** To prevent entry of insects and other animals inside the house, dustbins should be kept covered.

Dealing with Garbage

Safai karamcharis collect the garbage in trucks and take it to a low lying open area. It is called a landfill.

There the part of garbage that can be reused is separated out from the one that cannot be used as such. So, garbage has both useful and non-useful components. The non-useful component is separated out. It is then spread over the landfill and covered with a layer of soil. Once the landfill is completely full, it is usually converted into a park or playground.

Compost: The useful components of the garbage are used in the making of compost. Certain things in the garbage rot. They form manure which is used for plants. The rotting and conversion of some materials into manure is called composting.

Vermicomposting: The method of preparing a compost by using redworms is called vermicomposting.

Vermicompost can be prepared by digging a pit in the backyard where there is no direct sunlight. The pit should be about 30 cm deep. 1–2 cm thick layer of sand should be spread in the pit. Then some vegetable wastes & peeds of fruits can be added to the layer of sand. Dried animal dung, green leaves, dried stalks of plants are all added. Some water is sprinkled to make it wet slightly. The layer waste should not be pressed very hard. It should remain loose.

Then the redworms are added into the pit and covered loosely with a gunny bag or an old cloth, or even a layer of grass. After few days the layers should be gently mixed.

Redworms do not have teeth. They have a structure caused gizzard. It helps them to grind their food. Redworms need moisture & dampness to survive.

In about 3–4 weeks the contents of the pit will turn to soil-like material. This soil like material serves as a good manure for crops or vegetable garden of a house.

Multiple Choice Questions

1. Read the following statements about diseases.
   i. They are caused by germs.
   ii. They are caused due to lack of nutrients in our diet.
   iii. They can be passed on to another person through contact.
   iv. They can be prevented by taking a balanced diet.

   Which pair of statements best describe a deficiency disease?
   (a) i and ii   (b) ii and iii
   (c) ii and iv   (d) i and iii

2. Calcium, iron, potassium, iodine and common salt are examples of _____.
   (a) Proteins   (b) Vitamins
   (c) Minerals   (d) Fats

3. Mosquitoes live on blood that they suck from humans and other animals. Mosquitoes and flies both come from the insect group. To which of the following categories do the mosquitoes and flies belong?
   (a) Omnivores, scavenger
   (b) Scavenger, parasite
   (c) Parasite, scavenger
   (d) Parasite, omnivores

4. Which vitamin is synthesised by bacteria in the intestine?
   (a) Vitamin E   (b) Vitamin K
   (c) Vitamin D   (d) Vitamin A

5. Green plants are known as producers. They prepare more food than they need. The extra food is stored in different parts of the plant. Identify the parts of the plant from which the following food items (W, X, Y and Z) are obtained and select the correct option.

Onion, potatoes	Spinach, Cabbage
W	X
Broccoli and Cauliflower	Rice and wheat flour
Y	Z

	W	X	Y	Z
(a)	Stem	Leaf	Flower	Seed
(b)	Fruit	Leaf	Flower	Seed
(c)	Leaf	Flower	Seed	Stem
(d)	Stem	Fruit	Leaf	Flower

6. The diagram below shows a simple food web. Which animal is classified as an omnivore?

   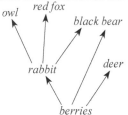

   (a) Red fox
   (b) Deer
   (c) Black bear
   (d) Rabbit

7. It is a form of malnutrition in which nutrients are oversupplied relative to the amounts required for normal growth, development and metabolism.
   I. What is this condition called?
   II. This condition will lead to _____.

	I	II
(a)	Malnutrition	Rickets
(b)	Overnutrition	Obesity
(c)	Overnutrition	Scurvy
(d)	Malnutrition	Kwashiorkor

8. Some beetles break down the remains of dead animals. Some mushrooms breakdown the remains of dead trees. How do these actions most benefit plants?
   (a) By returning nutrients to the soil
   (b) By releasing oxygen into the air
   (c) By making space for new animals
   (d) By decreasing the population of herbivores

Food, Health and Hygiene

9. The diagram below shows a simple food chain.

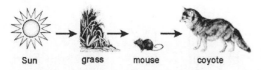

Which of the following animals might compete with the coyote in this food chain?

(a)   (b)   (c)   (d)

10. Which of the following food turns blue-black with iodine solution?
    (a) Onion   (b) Sugar
    (c) Potato   (d) Groundnut

12. Name the following:
    i. The nutrients which mainly give energy to our body.
    ii. The nutrients that are needed for the growth and maintenance of our body.
    iii. A vitamin required for maintaining good eyesight.
    iv. A mineral that is required for keeping our bones healthy.
    (a) (i) Proteins and fats, (ii) Proteins and minerals, (3) Vitamin A, (iv) Calcium
    (b) (i) Proteins and minerals, (ii) Vitamin A, (iii) Calcium, (iv) carbohydrates
    (c) (i) Fats, (ii) Proteins and minerals, (iii) Vitamin A, (iv) Calcium
    (d) (i) Carbohydrates and fats, (ii) Proteins and minerals, (iii) Vitamin A, (iv) Calcium

13. Basu lives in Delhi. One day Basu went to his ancestral village with his grandfather. He saw some people whose throats were somewhat swollen.
    I. What is the name of this disease?
    II. Which nutrient is lacking in the diets of the people who were suffering from the disease?

	I	II
(a)	Goitre	Iodine
(b)	PEM	Protein
(c)	Anemia	Iron
(d)	Scurvy	Vitamin

14. Read the following steps carefully.
    i. Take few leaves of spinach.
    ii. Let a spinach leaf stand in the air for two days.
    iii. You will see that the spinach will wilt and grow smaller as the water in it dries up.
    What does the above experiment show?
    (a) Food is mostly fat
    (b) Food is mostly carbohydrates
    (c) Food is mostly water
    (d) Food is mostly proteins

15. When two drops of iodine solution are put on a substance, we get a blue-black colour. This indicates the presence of _____.
    (a) Carbohydrates   (b) Starch
    (c) Fat   (d) Protein

16. It is said that water is vital for our body. Which of the following statements does not justify this statement?
    (a) It helps our body absorb nutrients from food
    (b) It serves as a solvent in which all chemical reactions take place in our body
    (c) It provides energy to our body
    (d) It transports nutrients throughout the body

17. The following parts of banana plant are used as food _____.
    (a) Flower, leaf, stem
    (b) Fruit, stem, flower
    (c) Leaf, stem, fruit
    (d) Root, fruit, flower

18. An oily translucent patch on the paper shows that the food item contains _____.
    (a) Minerals   (b) Carbohydrates
    (c) Proteins   (d) Fat

19. Match Column I with Column II, and choose the correct option.

	Column I	Column II
i.	Herbivores	a. Are animal product
ii.	Lions and tigers	b. Are vegetables
iii.	Milk, curd, paneer, ghee	c. Eat other animals
iv.	Spinach, cauliflower, carrot	d. Eat plants and plant products

(a) i-b, ii-a, iii-d, iv-c
(b) i-d, ii-c, iii-a, iv-b
(c) i-c, ii-a, iii-d, iv-b
(d) i-b, ii-d-iii- a, iv-c

20. The colour of an egg is dependent on the _____.
    (a) Breed of the hen
    (b) Diet of the hen
    (c) Shape of the egg
    (d) Variety of the egg

21. The food items shown in the figure are rich in nutrient X.

Read the given statements regarding the nutrient X.
i. When we grow, our body needs X to make new cells.
ii. X is also needed to replace old and damaged cells.
iii. Growing children and sick people require less amount of X in their diet.
iv. The total requirement of X for an adult is about 100–103 grams per day.

Which of the above statements are incorrect?
(a) i and iv   (b) iii and iv
(c) ii and iii   (d) I and ii

22. Reeta eats following foods in her diet.

In her diet which of the following food category and nutrient is she is lacking in?
(a) Protective foods, mineral
(b) Protective foods, vitamins
(c) Protective foods, vitamins and minerals
(d) Body building, vitamins and minerals

Direction for question 23.
Coyotes, willows, squirrels and snowshoe hares are all part of a particular forest ecosystem.

23. Which of the following food chains is possible for the organisms in this forest?
    (a) Sun → Coyote → Snowshoe hare → Willow
    (b) Sun → Willow → Snowshoe hare → Coyote
    (c) Sun → Squirrel → Snowshoe hare → Coyote
    (d) Sun → Willow → Snowshoe hare → Squirrel

Food, Health and Hygiene

24. What does the arrow represent in the question no. 23)?
    (a) Energy cycle
    (b) Energy flow
    (c) Food flow
    (d) Food cycle

24. Identify a food product that has a micronutrient added to it.

Food	Micronutrient(s) added
(a) Sweet porridge	Folic acid, other B vitamins, and calcium
(b) Mango shake	Vitamin D, Vitamin A
(c) Salty khichdi	Iodine
(d) Some juices	Calcium

25. My favourite food is chocolate. If I eat only chocolates for a long period of time, _____. [Children are encouraged to incorporate a wide variety of foods in their diet to make sure that they get adequate nutrition.]

    Which of the following sentence is correct for completing above sentence?
    (a) I may become deficient in several macronutrients
    (b) I may become deficient in several macro and micronutrients
    (c) I may become deficient in several micronutrients
    (d) I may become deficient in protein

26. Choose the correct option:
    I. Name the nutrient which mainly gives energy to our body.
    II. Name the vitamin required for maintaining good eye sight.

	I	II
(a)	Fat	Vitamin B
(b)	Proteins	Vitamin A
(c)	Vitamins	Vitamin A
(d)	Fats	Vitamin A

27. Which one of the following food items is likely to contain the MOST bacteria?
    (a) Frozen raw chicken
    (b) Recently cooked chicken
    (c) An opened can of a fizzy drink
    (d) Bottled mayonnaise

28. What are the basic steps for washing hands?
    (a) Wash thoroughly with water and dry
    (b) Apply soap, wash thoroughly, rinse and use paper towels
    (c) Apply soap, wash thoroughly
    (d) Wash thoroughly with water

29. Choose the correct option:
    i. Rice alone is sufficient to provide all nutrients to the body.
    ii. Deficiency diseases can be prevented by eating a balanced diet.
    iii. Balanced diet for the body should contain a variety of food items.
    iv. Meat alone is sufficient to provide all nutrients to the body.
    (a) i and ii   (b) ii and iii
    (c) iii only   (d) i and iv

30. The food items shown in the figure are sources of mainly _____.

(a) Fats (b) Carbohydrates
(c) Vitamins (d) Proteins

Food, Health and Hygiene

Fiber to Fabric

Learning Objectives
After reading the chapter, you will be able to:
- describe and classify different types of fibres
- state the characteristics of different types of fibres
- describe the ways in which fibres are extracted from plants and animals
- learn about the history of clothing material

There exists a deep-rooted relationship between us and the nature. Take for instance, the three basic necessities of life – food, shelter and clothes. We need food to survive and to remain strong; a house to protect ourselves from natural elements. But why does one need clothes? We wear clothes to protect ourselves from the weather, the natural elements and also for aesthetic reasons. The material used to make clothes is called *fabric*.

Ever wondered, what fabric is made of? How do you get a host of variety in fabrics? Why are some fabrics warm, while others are soft or rough? Why do some fabrics go bad after a wash, while the others remain unaffected?

This chapter aims to provide an answer to all these questions.

What is Fibre?
A fibre is a thread which can be spun into strings, ropes and clothes. In other words, the clothes you wear or the fabric you use to make clothes is made of fibre. Try an experiment. Take a cloth and pull out a thread; untwist to loosen this thread. You will notice that the cloth is made of smaller thread or hair like strands. This single hair-like strand is called fibre.

> A fibre is a hair-like strand which is the fundamental substance used to create a fabric.

Types of Fibres
Fibres are classified into two categories:
(i) Natural fibres
(ii) Manmade fibres

Natural Fibres
Fibres obtained from natural sources such as plants and animals are called *natural fibres*. Examples of natural fibres include: cotton, jute, silk, wool and linen. Cotton comes from the cotton plant, jute from the jute plant, silk from silkworms, wool from sheep and linen from flax plant.

Cotton   *Jute*

Silk

Wool

Cotton

Cotton by far is the most commonly used natural fibre. It is used to manufacture t-shirts, bed sheets, pillow covers, socks, shirts, trousers amongst many others. Cotton is derived from the cotton plant and wrinkles easily as well as absorbs moisture. It is strong, durable, accepts dyes easily, and is comfortable to be worn in summers. Although cotton creases easily, it can also be ironed at the highest temperature to remove the same.

Cotton Clothes

Where is cotton grown in India?

Cotton is grown in Maharashtra, Madhya Pradesh, Tamil Nadu, Karnataka, Gujarat, Uttar Pradesh (UP), Andhra Pradesh, Haryana and Punjab. The cotton plant requires high temperature, light rainfall, lots of bright sunlight and no frost.

How is cotton obtained?

As mentioned above, cotton is obtained from cotton plants. The fruit of a cotton plant is called a **cotton boll** which is a protective capsule around the cotton seed. A cotton boll is white in colour, fluffy and spherical in shape. When a cotton boll matures, it opens and one can see the cotton fibre inside. The seeds with cotton fibres are removed by hand from the cotton boll. Thereafter, the seeds are taken to the *ginning plant* where the seeds are separated from the cotton fibre by a process called **combing**. The process of separating seeds from the cotton fibre by means of combing is called **ginning**.

Cotton Boll

Previously, ginning was done by hand, however, now it is done using machines called **cotton gins**. Cotton gin is a short form for cotton engine and is used to separate seeds from cotton fibre effectively and easily. The seeds so collected can be sowed again to grow the cotton plant. However, the damaged seeds are discarded

Cotton Gins

Jute

Jute is a long, soft and shiny fibre which can be spun into strong threads. It is extracted from the jute plant. It is the second most affordable fibre, second only to cotton in terms of amount produced. Jute is also called 'golden fibre' due to its high cash value and colour. Jute is primarily used to make ropes, bags, matting material and is also woven into curtains and carpets.

Jute Carpets

Where is jute grown in India?

Jute is primarily grown in Meghalaya, Assam, West Bengal, Orissa and Bihar. A jute plant thrives

Fiber to Fabric

in hot and humid climate. The soil should be well-drained and fertile. High temperature also favours the growth of a jute plant.

Jute Plants

How is jute obtained?
Jute is extracted from the stem of the jute plant and is harvested during the flowering season. After the harvest, the jute stems are cut and left in water for a few days. Eventually, the stems rot and the jute fibre is extracted from the stem by hand.

Silk
Silk is a long and shiny natural fibre. It is used to make a variety of textiles, including sarees, shirts, ties, scarves, etc. Silk is an absorbent of heat which keeps us warm during the winters. Silk is obtained from the cocoon that the larvae of a silkworm spins around itself. The process of rearing silkworms for the production of silk is called **sericulture**.

Silk Cocoons

Wool
Wool is another natural fibre derived from sheep. Like silk, wool is also a heat absorbent and hence, protects us from the cold. Wool captures the air between its fibres and doesn't allow the heat from our bodies to escape. Wool is used to manufacture sweaters, gloves, suites, scarves, blankets, etc.

Yarns of Wool

Wool Mill

Man-made Fibres
Man-made fibres, as the name suggests, are artificially created by man. Man-made fibres are also called **synthetic fibres**. Examples of man-made fibres include nylon, rayon, polyester and acrylic. These fibres are created in factories. Man-made fibres have the following characteristics:
1. They are wrinkle-free.
2. They can be easily cleaned.
3. They are very strong.
4. They can catch fire easily.
5. They do not absorb sweat.
6. They dry quickly.
7. They need little or no ironing.

Now let's revise the various types of fibres we have learnt so far:

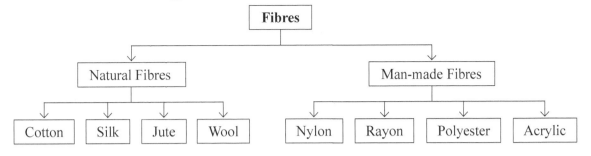

Do You Know?

Textile fabrics made by weaving, stitch bonding or knitting often lack special characteristics wanted by the user. The colours don't look bright enough. They do not have a smooth surface or resistance against later wears or environmental impacts. The clothes have to be treated mechanically or chemically. The necessary measures are called "textile conditioning". The logistic sequence is divided into pre-treatment – patterning – after-treatment.

Fibres and Fabrics

The material used to make clothes is called **fabric** which in turn comprises *fibres*. Proper clothes protect us from the climate. People living in different parts of India, wear different types of clothes. For example, people living Himachal Pradesh wear woollen clothes whereas, people living in Tamil Nadu wear cotton clothes.

History of clothing material

It is not known when humans began wearing clothes. In the pre-historic era the early man used animal skin and leaves to protect their bodies against any extreme climate. Gradually, the early man realized that fibres can be extracted from cotton plant or jute stem. These fibres could then be weaved to manufacture clothes.

Early Indians grew cotton on the banks of river Ganga, while Egyptians grew cotton on the banks of river Nile. Ancient Egyptians also grew a plant called flax plant to produce a natural fibre called **linen**. Linen is comfortable and cool to wear. It dries fast, is absorbent and durable. The use of linen by Egyptians date back as far as 8000 BC. India, China, Holland and Belgium are the major flax-producing countries in the world.

Activity

Observe the image carefully. Can you guess what these symbols used on fabric labels stand for? Check to see how many you got right.

Quick guide to fabric care symbols

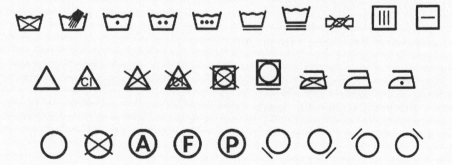

Fiber to Fabric

Multiple Choice Questions

1. Cotton is the most desirable fabric for making undergarments because it is _____.
   (a) Absorbent (b) Dull
   (c) Shining (d) Strong
2. Which fabric has a dull surface?
   (a) Nylon (b) Polyester
   (c) Silk (d) Wool
3. Which of the following fabrics does not take stains easily?
   (a) Cotton (b) Nylon
   (c) Wool (d) Silk
4. The natural fibres are obtained from _____.
   (a) Plants
   (b) Animals
   (c) Plants and animals both
   (d) Neither from plants nor animals
5. Nylon and polyester are obtained from _____.
   (a) Plants
   (b) Animals
   (c) Both
   (d) From chemical substances
6. An experiment that tests dye fixation on a 100% cotton-woven fabric would examine which of the following properties?
   (a) Easily washable
   (b) Water repellence
   (c) Abrasion resistance
   (d) Moisture absorption
7. Which of the following does not yield wool?
   (a) Yak (b) Camel
   (c) Goat (d) Woolly dog
8. The rearing of silkworms to obtain silk is called _____.
   (a) Sericulture (b) Horticulture
   (c) Agriculture (d) Aqua-culture
9. Cotton bolls are developed from the _____.
   (a) Seeds (b) Leaves
   (c) Flowers (d) None of these
10. Silk fibre obtained from silk moth is _____.
    (a) Carbohydrate (b) Fat
    (c) Protein (d) Sugars
11. Silkworms are reared on _____.
    (a) Mulberry plants
    (b) Mango plants
    (c) Money plants
    (d) None of these
12. Part of the jute plant that is used to make cloth is the _____.
    (a) Stem (b) Root
    (c) Leaf (d) Flower
13. Which fabric is made of staple fibre?
    (a) Cotton (b) Nylon
    (c) Polyester (d) Silk
14. Which of these is not a property of jute?
    (a) Biodegradability
    (b) Durability
    (c) Smoothness
    (d) Strength
15. Which of these do you think traps the most air?
    (a) Nylon (b) Cotton
    (c) Wool (d) Polyester
16. Ananya, Ranchit, Sanchit and Soni are talking about wool and silk. Who among them is correct?
    (a) Ananya: Silk doesn't need to be detangled like wool because silk is obtained directly as thread from cocoon
    (b) Ranchit: Silk doesn't need to be detangled like wool because thread from a single cocoon can be used as yarn directly
    (c) Sanchit: Silk doesn't need to be detangled like wool because silk fibre is stronger than wool
    (d) Soni: Ananya and Ranchit are correct
17. Can all the fleece of a sheep be used to make wool?
    (a) Yes
    (b) No, sheep stays dirty which makes some fleece useless
    (c) Yes, it can be done in case of a few sheep
    (d) No, sheep has hair of different thicknesses and quality like us. Only some of them can be used to make wool

18. Identify P in the given Venn diagram _____.

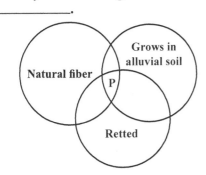

(a) Jute (b) Silk
(c) Wool (d) Nylon

19. The harvesting of which natural fiber includes rippling, retting, and scutching _____.
(a) Cotton (b) Linen
(c) Wool (d) Silk

20. What does filament mean?
(a) A process to add bulk to a fiber
(b) Fibrous chemical found in all plants
(c) Long, continuous strands measured in yards or meters
(d) The main component of plants

21. Which of the following is a correct difference between weaving and knitting?
(a) Weaving is the process of interlacing two sets of yarns at right angles to each other to form a fabric while knitting is inter looping of one or more set of yarns
(b) Weaving is done for silk only while knitting is done for wools only
(c) Weaving is done with machines while knitting is done by hand
(d) All of them

22. Refer to the following Venn diagram. Which of these characteristics can be represented by P?

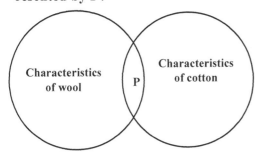

(a) Comfortable to wear in hot and humid weather
(b) Ability to trap and retain water
(c) Fluffy texture
(d) Natural fibers

23. Cotton is stronger when it is wet. This is because of _____.
(a) Crystalline fiber
(b) Hydrophilic in nature
(c) Cellulose layer
(d) All of them

24. Satin weave fabrics are _____.
(a) Durable
(b) Cheap
(c) Expensive
(d) Dull

25. Rehan wants to check the fiber type of a piece of cloth to find out if it's a natural or synthetic one. He performed burn test to solve that purpose in the following steps:
i. Rehan pulled a small snippet from the seam allowance or the end of yarn.
ii. He held it with a pair of tweezers, put a flame to the end and then pulled it away.
iii. He saw that it continued to burn after the flame was removed.

Identify the fiber now:
(a) Wool
(b) Synthetic
(c) Cotton
(d) Silk

26. Select the correct statement from the following
(a) Jute is obtained from stem of the jute plant
(b) Coir obtained from cotton is a weak fiber
(c) The process of making yarn from fiber is called weaving
(d) Both (a) and (b)

27. Which of the following can be used as an unstitched piece of fabric?
(a) Dhoti
(b) Turban
(c) Skirt
(d) Both (a) and (b)

Fiber to Fabric

28. I am sometimes referred to as the "workhorse" fiber of the industry. My strength reinforces the cotton fibers. Who am I?
    (a) Synthetic fiber
    (b) Polyester fiber
    (c) Flax fiber
    (d) Jute fiber

29. In case of man-made fibres, this process is done by three different methods (wet, dry, melt).
    (a) Washing
    (b) Cleaning
    (c) Spinning
    (d) Both (a) and (b)

30. Look at the picture below. He is a football player named Lionel Messi. Which fiber-made clothing he wears while playing football?

    (a) Asbestos clothing
    (b) Fur
    (c) Protective padding
    (d) Robes

Body Movements in Animals

Humans move from one place to another place by using their legs. Legs are used for walkin, running, climbing, jumping, hopping. Physical activities like swimming, basket ball (playing) make use of both hand and legs.

We can rotate or bend our body only at those places where there is a joint. The place where two parts of our body are joined together is called a **joint**.

There are different types of joints in the human body that are useful to carry out different types of movements and activities. The various types of joints are:

i. Ball & Socket joint
ii. Hinge joint
iii. Pivotal joint
iv. Fixed joints

Ball & Socket Joint: In these joints the rounded end of one bone perfectly fits into the cavity (hollow space) of the other bone. This type of joint allows movement in all directions. For example, our shoulder joint is an example of Ball & Socket joint. We can move our arm in all directions 360°.

Hinge Joint: This joint permits movement just like the hinge of a door. These joints allow back & forth movement only. Unlike the ball & socket joint this joint allows movement in one direction only. For example, elbow joint and knee joint.

Pivotal Joint: The joint between our neck and head is called a Pivotal Joint. This joint allows us to bend our head forward and backward and also turn the head to our right and left. In this type of joint a cylindrical bone rotates in a ring.

Ball and Socket joint, Pivotal joint & Hinge joint are all examples of **movable joints**.

Fixed Joint: Not all joints are movable. Some joints in our body are fixed. The joints between the bones in our head cannot be moved. Such joints are called fixed joints. The lower jaw is movable. But the upper jaw is fixed to the rest of the head. It is fixed joint.

All the bones of our body form a framework that gives a shape to our body. This framework of bones is called SKELETON.

Rib Cage: The bones that join the chest bone and backbone together and form a box like structure called Rib cage. Some important internal parts of our body are protected by the rib cage.

Our backbone is made up of small bones due to which we can easily bend. The rib cage is joined to these small bones of the backbone.

The pelvic bones enclose the portion of our body below our stomach. This is the region on which we sit.

The skull of humans is made up of many bones that are joined together. It encloses and protects an important part called Brain.

Cartilage: Certain regions of the skeleton are not as hard as bones but they are flexible and can be easily bent or folded. This is called cartilage. Cartilage is found in the external ear (pinna) and our nose. Our ear (external) has no bones. It is only made up of cartilage.

So, we can say that our skeleton is made up of many bones, joints, and cartilage.

In addition to all this the bones also have muscles attached to them. On contraction the muscles become short, stiff & thick. It helps to pull the bone.

Muscles work in pairs. When one of the muscle contract, the bone is pulled in that direction. The other muscle of the pair relaxes. To move the bone in the opposite direction, the relaxed muscle contracts to pull the bone towards its original position, while the first relaxes. A muscle can only pull. It cannot push. Thus, two muscles have to work together to move a bone.

Movement in Animals

Gait: The manner of movement of an organism is called Gait.

Movement of Earthworm: The body of an earthworm is made up of many rings joined end to end.

An earthworm does not have bones. It has muscles which help to extend and shorten the body. During movement, the earthworm first extends the front part of the body keeping the rear portion fixed to the ground. Then it fixes the front end and releases the rear end. It then shortens the body and pulls the rear end forward. This makes it move forward by a small distance.

Repeating such muscular expansion and contractions, the earthworm can move through soil. Its body secretes a slimy substance to facilitate the movement.

Under its body the earthworm has a large number of tiny bristles (hair like structures) protecting out. These bristles are connected with muscles. The bristles help to get a good grip on the ground.

The earthworm actually, eats its way through the soil. Its body then throws away the undigested part of the material that it eats. This activity of earthworm makes the soil more useful to plants.

Movement in Snail: The rounded structure seen on the back of snail is its shell. It is the outer skeleton of snail. But it does not have any bones. The shell is one piece and it is of no use to the snail in moving around. In fact it has to be dragged along.

A thick structure and the head of the snail come out through an opening is the shell when it has to move. The thick structure is its foot. It is made up of strong muscles.

Movement of Cockroach: Cockroaches belong to the insect family. They can walk, climb, and also fly in the air. They have 3 pairs of legs. These help in walking. The body is covered with a hard outer skeleton. This outer skeleton is made of various units joined together to permit movement.

There are two pairs of wings attached to the breast of a cockroach. The cockroaches have noticeably different muscles - those near the legs move the legs for walking. The breast muscles move the wings when the cockroach flies.

Movement in Birds: Birds fly in air and can walk on the ground also. Some birds like ducks and swans swim in the water.

Birds can fly because of certain adaptive features they have. They have hollow bones and their body is very light. Their forelimbs are modified to feathers (wings) for flight. The bones of hind limbs are typical for walking & perching. They have strong shoulder bones. Their breast bones are mofied to hold muscles for flight which are used to move wings up and down.

Movement in Fishes: Fishes have a streamlined body. Their head & tail are much smaller than their middle portion of the body. The body tapers at both ends. This shape is called streamlined.

The streamlined shape permits water to flow around it easily which helps the fish to move in water. The skeleton of the fish is covered with strong muscles.

During swimming muscles make the front part of the body curve to one side and the tail part wings towards the opposite side. Then quickly, the body and tail curve to the other side. This makes a jerk and pushes the body forward. A series of such jerks make the fish swim ahead. This is helped by the fins of the tail.

Fish also have other fins on their body which help in maintaining the body balance and to keep direction while swimming.

Movement in Snakes: Snakes have a long backbone. They have many thin muscles. They are connected to each other even though they are far from one another. Muscles also interconnected the backbone, ribs & skin.

A snake's body curves into many loops. Each loop of the snake gives it a forward push by pressing against the ground. Since its long body makes many loops, each loop gives it this push. The snake moves forward very fast and not in a straight line.

Multiple Choice Questions

1. _____ gives a frame and shape to the body and also protects the inner organs.
   (a) Cartilage   (b) Bones
   (c) Skeleton   (d) Muscles

2. Fish swim by forming _____ on two sides of the body.
   (a) Loop   (b) Gait
   (c) Gills   (d) Streamline

3. Snails move with the help of _____.
   (a) Shell   (b) Muscular foot
   (c) Bristles   (d) Spikes

4. The _____ on the underside of the body of an earthworm help in gripping the ground.
   (a) Muscular foot
   (b) Shell on its back
   (c) Slimy skin
   (d) Bristles

5. Hinges in doors allow movement in
   (a) all directions
   (b) one direction
   (c) only forward direction
   (d) only backward direction

6. Body and legs of cockroaches have an outer skeleton which is very hard and called as
   (a) Endoskeleton   (b) Exoskeleton
   (c) Mesoskeleton   (d) Chitin

7. The only movable joint in the skull is
   (a) Upper jaw   (b) Neck
   (c) Lower jaw   (d) Brain

8. Rib cage is formed due to the joining of
   (a) Backbone & ribs
   (b) Backbone & chestbone
   (c) Chestbone & shoulder
   (d) Shoulder & backbone

9. An example of ball & socket joint is
   (i) Shoulder joint
   (ii) Neck joint
   (iii) Hip joint
   (iv) Elbow joint
   (a) (i) & (ii)   (b) only (ii)
   (c) (i) & (iv)   (d) only (iii)

10. _____ work in pairs to allow movement.
    (a) Cartilage   (b) Bones
    (c) Muscles   (d) Ribs

11. _____ is not as hard as bones and is seen in ears and nose.
    (a) Muscles   (b) Tendons
    (c) Ligaments   (d) Cartilage

12. Body of fishes is _____ shaped
    (a) Kite   (b) Streamlined
    (c) Boat shaped   (d) Snake shaped

13. Locomotory organs in starfish are _____.
    (a) Tube feet
    (b) Tentacles
    (c) Cilia
    (d) Appendages

14. The only movable bone in the skull is _____.
    (a) Maxilla
    (b) Frontoparietal
    (c) Mandible
    (d) Nasal

15. Cartilaginous joints _____.
    (a) Permit slight movements
    (b) Are found in symphysis
    (c) Are found in the bodies of vertebrae
    (d) All of these

16. Hinge joints _____.
    (a) Are synovial joints
    (b) Permit movements in one direction
    (c) Are found in knee
    (d) All of these

17. Longest bone in lower arm is _____.
    (a) Ulna
    (b) Radius
    (c) Tibia
    (d) Femur

18. Movable joints are called _____.
    (a) Fibrous joints
    (b) Symphyses
    (c) Synovial joints
    (d) Cartilaginous joints

Body Movements in Animals

19. The number of pair false ribs is _____.
    (a) 2 (b) 3
    (c) 4 (d) 7
20. The floating ribs are _____.
    (a) 11 and 12
    (b) 9 and 10
    (c) 7 and 8
    (d) 1 and 2
21. Long neck of camel or Giraffe has _____.
    (a) Numerous cervical vertebrae
    (b) Development of extra-large intervertebral pads
    (c) Longer vertebrae
    (d) Development of extra bony plates between adjacent cervical vertebrae
22. Six of the 206 bones of human skeleton occur in _____.
    (a) Skull
    (b) Middle ear
    (c) Pectoral girdle
    (d) Pelvic girdle
23. The region of the body on which we sit is the _____.
    (a) pectoral region
    (b) pelvic region
    (c) pivotal region
    (d) scapula region
24. Muscles are connected to bones by _____.
    (a) tendons
    (b) ligaments
    (c) cartilage
    (d) bones
25. Elbow joint is an example of _____.
    (a) Saddle joint
    (b) Hinge joint
    (c) Pivot joint
    (d) Ball and socket joint
26. Which of the following is composed of cartilage?
    (a) Arms
    (b) Legs
    (c) Skull
    (d) External ear
27. Which part of the body of a snake is used in locomotion?
    (a) Legs
    (b) Fins
    (c) Feet
    (d) Whole body
28. Which of the following bones protect the lungs and heart?
    (a) Cranium
    (b) Pectoral girdle
    (c) Pelvic girdle
    (d) Ribcage
29. The aquatic animal whose skeleton is made up of cartilage is _____.
    (a) Shark   (b) Dolphin
    (c) Whale   (d) Tuna
30. Vertebral column of man has _____. (vertebrae) bones.
    (a) 28   (b) 30
    (c) 33   (d) 42

SECTION 2
LOGICAL REASONING

Pattern

In these types of questions, a set of figures and arrangement or a matrix in given, each of which has a certain characters, be it numbers, letters or a group or combination of letters or numbers, follow a certain pattern. The candidate is required to analyse the pattern and find the missing number in the figure.

In pattern, the missing number is obtained by adding, subtracting, multiplying, or dividing by some number after going through the pattern. In the figure type, the middle term is the addition of all the given terms or addition of squares of each term or square of addition of all given terms.

Sometimes the left part of figure has exactly the same relation as the right part of the figure. The candidate is required to find the certain rule to find the missing number. He/she should know various mathematical operations, squares, cubes etc. and relate them accordingly.

Example 1: Choose the correct option to replace the question mark.

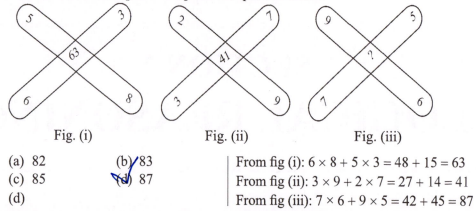

(a) 82   (b) 83
(c) 85   (d) 87

Solution: (d)

From fig (i): $6 \times 8 + 5 \times 3 = 48 + 15 = 63$
From fig (ii): $3 \times 9 + 2 \times 7 = 27 + 14 = 41$
From fig (iii): $7 \times 6 + 9 \times 5 = 42 + 45 = 87$

Example 2: Choose the correct option to replace the question mark.

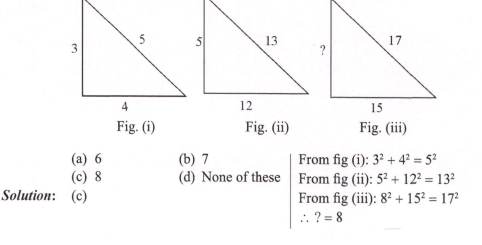

(a) 6   (b) 7
(c) 8   (d) None of these

Solution: (c)

From fig (i): $3^2 + 4^2 = 5^2$
From fig (ii): $5^2 + 12^2 = 13^2$
From fig (iii): $8^2 + 15^2 = 17^2$
$\therefore\ ? = 8$

Example 3: Choose the correct option to replace the question mark.

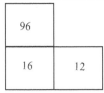
Fig. (i)

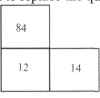
Fig. (ii)

Fig. (iii)

(a) 15 (b) 16
(c) 18 (d) None of these

Solution: (c)

From fig (i): $(16) \times \left(\dfrac{12}{2}\right)$

From fig (ii): $\left(12 \times \dfrac{14}{2}\right)$

From fig (iii): $? \times \dfrac{17}{2}$

$\Rightarrow \quad ? = 2 \times 9 \Rightarrow 18$

Example 4: Choose the correct option to replace the question mark.

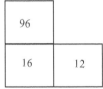
Fig. (i)

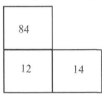
Fig. (ii)

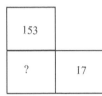
Fig. (iii)

(a) 14 (b) 16
(c) 17 (d) 18

Solution: (d)

From fig (i): $(96 \div 12) \times 2 = 8 \times 2 = 16$
From fig (ii): $(84 \div 14) \times 2 = 6 \times 2 = 12$
From fig (iii): $(153 \div 17) \times 2 = 9 \times 2 = 18$

(a) 81 (b) 216
(c) 343 (d) 729

Solution: (b) From fig

$1^3 = 1$
$2^3 = 8$
$3^3 = 27$
$4^3 = 64$
$5^3 = 125$
$6^3 = 216$

Example 5:

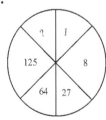

Pattern

Multiple Choice Questions

Study the pattern and find the missing number.

1.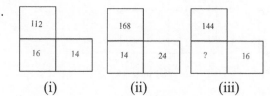
   (a) 14 (b) 16
   (c) 18 (d) 21

2.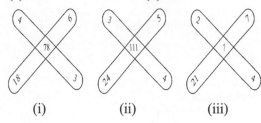
   (a) 98 (b) 96
   (c) 99 (d) 108

3.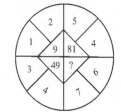
   (a) 121 (b) 149
   (c) 169 (d) 196

4.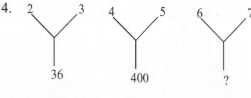
   (a) 1594 (b) 1764
   (c) 1664 (d) 1784

5.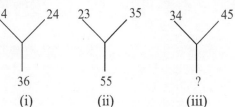

6.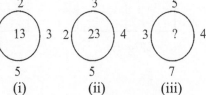
   (a) 75 (b) 76
   (c) 77 (d) 78

   (a) 43 (b) 45
   (c) 46 (d) 47

7.
   7—(13)—4   9—(33)—6   8—(?)—9
   5 above, 3 below; 7 above, 3 below; 5 above, 7 below
   (a) 35 (b) 36
   (c) 37 (d) 38

8.
   7(169)2 5(225)7 7(?)9
   1/3   1/2   2/3
   (a) 361 (b) 324
   (c) 441 (d) 484

9.
   4(384)6 5(630)7 8(?)9
   2/8   3/6   3/7
   (a) 1512 (b) 1412
   (c) 1212 (d) 1312

10.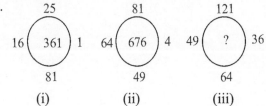

National Science Olympiad – 6

(a) 961 (b) 964
(c) 1024 (d) 1044

11.
```
       49              81              121
   81 [30] 64    25 [25] 49    81 [ ? ] 49
       36              16              25
      (i)             (ii)            (iii)
```
(a) 31 (b) 36
(c) 29 (d) 32

12.
```
   ( 7 | 2 )    ( 8 | 3 )    ( 7 | 6 )
   (42 | 3 )    (48 | 2 )    ( ? | 4 )
     (i)          (ii)         (iii)
```
(a) 148 (b) 168
(c) 158 (d) 178

13.
```
        3              4              7
   1 (17) 5      1 (31) 7      4 ( ? ) 6
        4              6              8
      (i)            (ii)           (iii)
```
(a) 68 (b) 72
(c) 78 (d) 80

14.
188	300	263
893	?	915

(a) 96 (b) 500
(c) 238 (d) 88

15.
16	210	14
14	156	12
12	?	10

(a) 100 (b) 110
(c) 120 (d) 90

16.
A	D	G
D	I	N
I	P	?

(a) X (b) Y
(c) W (d) V

17.
8	17	33
12	5	29
10	13	?

(a) 23 (b) 43
(c) 33 (d) 9

18.
2	2	256
3	2	?
4	2	46656

(a) 3125 (b) 2765
(c) 8796 (d) 30008

19.
6	11	25
8	6	16
12	5	?

(a) 10 (b) 12
(c) 16 (d) 18

20.
85	20	5
126	24	6
175	?	7

(a) 24 (b) 28
(c) 26 (d) 22

21.
?	13	49
9	17	69
13	11	59

(a) 21 (b) 10
(c) 9 (d) 5

22.
12	(47)	21
10	(52)	4
64	?	24

(a) 83 (b) 40
(c) 62 (d) 16

Pattern

23.
42	44	38
23	55	28
37	?	39

(a) 77 (b) 22
(c) 33 (d) 66

24.
963	2	844
464	?	903

(a) 4 (b) 2
(c) 1 (d) 3

25.
3	4	5
3	7	12
3	?	22

(a) 9 (b) 11
(c) 10 (d) 8

Analogy

2

Analogy means similarity. In this type of questions, two objects related in some way are given and third object is also given with four or five alternatives. The student has to find out the alternative that bears the same relation with the third object as the first and second objects have.

This type of questions covers all types of relationship that one can think of. There are many ways of establishing a relationship; some common are given here.

Example 1: See the analogy and find the correct option.

Curd : Milk :: Shoe : ?
(a) Leather (b) Cloth
(c) Jute (d) Silver

Solution: As curd is made from milk similarly shoe is made from leather.

Option (a) is correct.

Example 2: See the analogy and find the correct option.

Calf : Piglet :: Shed : ?
(a) Prison (b) Nest
(c) Pigsty (d) Den

Solution: Calf is young one of the cow and piglet is the young of Pig. Shed is the dwelling place of cow. Similarly Pigsty is the dwelling place of pig.

Option (c) is correct.

Example 3: See the analogy and find the correct option.

Malaria : Mosquito :: ? : ?
(a) Poison : Death
(b) Cholera : Water
(c) Rat : Plague
(d) Medicine : Disease

Solution: As malaria is caused due to mosquito, similarly cholera is caused due to water.

Option (b) is correct.

Example 4: See the analogy and find the correct option.

ABC : ZYX :: CBA : ?
(a) XYZ (b) BCA
(c) YZX (d) ZXY

Solution: CBA is the reverse of ABC, similarly XYZ is the reverse of ZYX.

Option (a) is correct.

Example 5: See the analogy and find the correct option.

4 : 18 :: 6 : ?
(a) 32 (b) 38
(c) 11 (d) 37

Solution: As, $(4)^2 + 2 = 18$

Similarly, $(6)^2 + 2 = 38$

Option (b) is correct.

Multiple Choice Questions

Complete the Analogous Pair

Directions (1 – 10): In each of the following questions, there is a certain relationship between two given words on one side of : : and one word is given on the other side of : : Find out the word from the given alternatives, having the same relation with this word as the words of the given pair bear.

1. Physician : Treatment :: Judge : ?
   (a) Punishment
   (b) Judgement
   (c) Lawyer
   (d) Court

2. Ice : Coldness :: Earth : ?
   (a) Weight   (b) Jungle
   (c) Gravity   (d) Sea

3. Race : Fatigue :: Fast : ?
   (a) Food   (b) Laziness
   (c) Hunger   (d) Race

4. Peace : Chaos :: Creation : ?
   (a) Build
   (b) Construction
   (c) Destruction
   (d) Manufacture

5. Tiger : Forest :: Otter : ?
   (a) Cage   (b) Sky
   (c) Nest   (d) Water

6. Poles : Magnet :: ? : Battery
   (a) Cells   (b) Power
   (c) Terminals   (d) Energy

7. Cassock : Priest :: ? : Graduate
   (a) Cap   (b) Tie
   (c) Coat   (d) Gown

8. Country : President :: State : ?
   (a) Governor
   (b) M.P
   (c) Legislator
   (d) Minister

9. Cloth : Mill :: Newspaper : ?
   (a) Editor   (b) Reader
   (c) Paper   (d) Press

10. South : North-West :: West : ?
    (a) North   (b) South-West
    (c) North-East   (d) East

11. 24 : 60 :: 120 : ?
    (a) 160   (b) 220
    (c) 300   (d) 108

12. 335 : 216 :: 987 : ?
    (a) 868   (b) 867
    (c) 872   (d) 888

13. 8 : 24 :: ? : 32
    (a) 5   (b) 6
    (c) 10   (d) 8

14. 9 : 8 :: 16 : ?
    (a) 27   (b) 17
    (c) 16   (d) 18

15. K/T : 11/20 :: J/R : ?
    (a) 10/18   (b) 11/19
    (c) 10/8   (d) 9/10

Choosing the Analogous Pair

Directions (16 – 30): Each of the following questions consists of two words that have a certain relationship with each other, followed by four lettered pairs of words. Select the lettered pair which has the same relationship as the original pair of words.

16. AERIE : EAGLE
    (a) capital : government
    (b) bridge : architect
    (c) unit : apartment
    (d) house : person

17. PROFESSOR : ERUDITE
    (a) aviator : licensed
    (b) inventor : imaginative
    (c) procrastinator : conscientious
    (d) overseer : wealthy

18. DELTOID : MUSCLE
    (a) radius : bone
    (b) brain : nerve
    (c) tissue : organ
    (d) blood : vein

19. JAUNDICE : LIVER
    (a) rash : skin
    (b) dialysis : kidney
    (c) smog : lung
    (d) valentine : heart
20. CONVICTION : INCARCERATION
    (a) reduction : diminution
    (b) induction : amelioration
    (c) radicalization : estimation
    (d) marginalization : intimidation
21. DEPENDABLE : CAPRICIOUS
    (a) fallible : cantankerous
    (b) erasable : obtuse
    (c) malleable : limpid
    (d) capable : inept
22. METAPHOR : SYMBOL
    (a) pentameter : poem
    (b) rhythm : melody
    (c) nuance : song
    (d) analogy : comparison
23. INTEREST : OBSESSION
    (a) mood : feeling
    (b) weeping : sadness
    (c) dream : fantasy
    (d) plan : negation
24. CONDUCTOR : ORCHESTRA
    (a) jockey : mount
    (b) thrasher : hay
    (c) driver : tractor
    (d) skipper : crew
25. FROND : PALM
    (a) quill : porcupine
    (b) blade : evergreen
    (c) scale : wallaby
    (d) tusk : alligator
26. SOUND : CACOPHONY
    (a) taste : style
    (b) touch : massage
    (c) smell : stench
    (d) sight : panorama
27. UMBRAGE : OFFENSE
    (a) confusion : penance
    (b) infinity : meaning
    (c) decorum : decoration
    (d) elation : jubilance
28. DIRGE : FUNERAL
    (a) chain : letter
    (b) bell : church
    (c) telephone : call
    (d) jingle : commercial
29. PHOBIC : FEARFUL
    (a) cautious : emotional
    (b) envious : desiring
    (c) shy : familiar
    (d) asinine : silly
30. FERAL : TAME
    (a) repetitive : recurrent
    (b) nettlesome : annoying
    (c) repentant : honourable
    (d) ephemeral : immortal

Simple Analogy

Directions (31 – 30): In each of the following questions, the first two words have definite relationship. Choose one word out of the given four alternatives which will show the same relationship with the third word as between the first two.

31. Artist is to painting as senator is to _____.
    (a) Attorney   (b) Law
    (c) Politician   (d) Constituents
32. Exercise is to gym as eating is to _____.
    (a) Food   (b) Dieting
    (c) Fitness   (d) Restaurant
33. Candid is to indirect as honest is to _____.
    (a) Frank   (b) Wicked
    (c) Truthful   (d) Untruthful
34. Guide is to direct as reduce is to _____.
    (a) Decrease   (b) Maintain
    (c) Increase   (d) Preserve
35. Careful is to cautious as boastful is to _____.
    (a) Arrogant   (b) Humble
    (c) Joyful   (d) Suspicious

Group Analogy

Directions (36 – 40): Each of the following questions has a group. Find out which one of the given alternatives will be another member of the group or of that class.

36. Pathology, Cardiology, Radiology, Ophthalmology
    (a) Biology   (b) Haematology
    (c) Zoology   (d) Geology

37. Wheat, Barley, Rice
    (a) Food   (b) Agriculture
    (c) Farm   (d) Gram

38. Lock, Shut, Fasten
    (a) Window   (b) Door
    (c) Iron   (d) Block

39. Lucknow, Patna, Bhopal, Jaipur
    (a) Shimla   (b) Mysore
    (c) Pune   (d) Indore

40. Tamilian, Gujarati, Punjabi
    (a) Aryan   (b) Dravidan
    (c) Indian   (d) Barbarian

Directions (41 – 50): In each of the following questions, two sets of figures are given. The first two problem figures bear a certain relationship. Based on the same relationship (analogy), select from answer figures an appropriate figure to replace the question mark in problem figures:

41.
Problem Figures

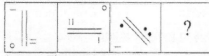

Answer Figures

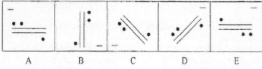

(a) A   (b) B
(c) C   (d) D
(e) E

42.
Problem Figures

Answer Figures

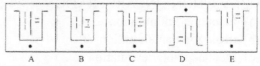

(a) A   (b) B
(c) C   (d) D
(e) E

43.
Problem Figures

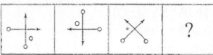

Answer Figures

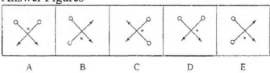

(a) A   (b) B
(c) C   (d) D
(e) E

44.
Problem Figures

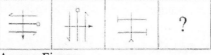

Answer Figures

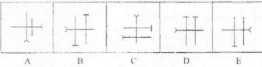

(a) A   (b) B
(c) C   (d) D
(e) E

45.
Problem Figures

Answer Figures

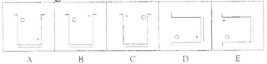

(a) A (b) B
(c) C (d) D
(e) E

46.
Problem Figures

Answer Figures

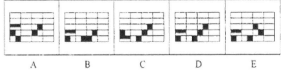

(a) A (b) B
(c) C (d) D
(e) E

47.
Problem Figures

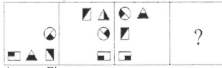

Answer Figures

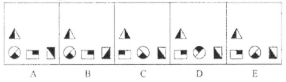

(a) A (b) B
(c) C (d) D
(e) E

48.
Problem Figures

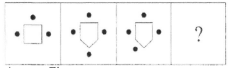

Answer Figures

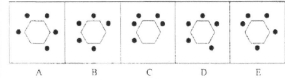

(a) A (b) B
(c) C (d) D
(e) E

49.
Problem Figures

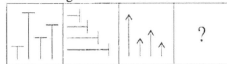

Answer Figures

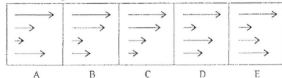

(a) A (b) B
(c) C (d) D
(e) E

50.
Problem Figures

Answer Figures

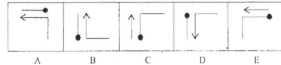

(a) A (b) B
(c) C (d) D
(e) E

Analogy

Series Completion

In Series Completion, a series of numbers or alphabet letters or combination of both numbers and letters is given. Each of the number or letter is called as term of the series. The terms of the series follow a particular pattern through the series. The candidate has to analyse the series and find out the certain pattern which is applied for whole of the series. Basically series completion is based on numbers. Each succeeding term of the series may be obtained by adding, subtracting multiplying or dividing by some number, which is same for whole of the series. Sometimes the alternate terms of the series obeys the certain pattern.

So, we have to analyse the terms of the series and then find out the missing term or wrong term in the given series. The candidate should study the given series, identify the pattern followed in the series and either complete the given series with most suitable alternative or find the wrong in the given series.

Example 1: 53, 65, 77, 89, ?

Solution: 53 65 77 89 101
             +12 +12 +12 +12

The next number = 101

Example 2: 0, 3, 8, 15, 24, 35, 48, 63, ?

Solution: 0, 3, 8, 15, 24, 35, 48, 63, 80

$1^2 - 1$, $2^2 - 1$, $3^2 - 1$, $4^2 - 1$, $5^2 - 1$, $6^2 - 1$, $7^2 - 1$, $8^2 - 1$, $9^2 - 1$

∴ Next number = 80

Example 3: –17, –7, 3, 13, 23, 33, ?

Solution: –17 + 10 = –7
 –7 + 10 = 3
 3 + 10 = 13
 13 + 10 = 23
 ∴ Next number = 33 + 10 = 43

Example 4: 7, 14, 28, 56, 112, 224, ?

Solution: $7 \times 2 = 14$
 $14 \times 2 = 28$
 ∴ Next term = $224 \times 2 = 448$

Example 5: 47, 52, 49, 54, 51, 56, 53, ?

Solution: 47 52 49 54 51 56 53 58
      +5 –3 +5 –3 +5 –3 +5

∴ ? = 58

Example 6: 331, 553, 775, 997, ?

Solution: 331 + 222 = 553
 553 + 222 = 775
 ∴ Next term = 997 + 222 = 1219

Example 7: 17, 85, 340, 1020, 2040, ?

Solution: $17 \times 5 = 85$
 $85 \times 4 = 340$
 $340 \times 3 = 1020$
 $1020 \times 2 = 2040$
 $2040 \times 1 = 2040$
 ∴ ? = 2040

Multiple Choice Questions

Direction (1–20): Identify the pattern in the given series and choose the correct option to replace the question mark.

1. 67, 74, 81, 88, 95, ?
   (a) 101   (b) 102
   (c) 103   (d) 104

2. 109, 101, 94, 88, 83, ?
   (a) 78   (b) 79
   (c) 80   (d) 81

3. 9, 25, 49, 81, 121, ?
   (a) 141   (b) 144
   (c) 161   (d) 169

4. 3, 8, 15, 24, 35, 48, ?
   (a) 61   (b) 62
   (c) 63   (d) 64

5. 6, 12, 24, 48, 96, 192, ?
   (a) 384   (b) 386
   (c) 388   (d) 392

6. 4, 3, 4, 9, 32, 155, ?
   (a) 924   (b) 926
   (c) 928   (d) 932

7. 85, 88, 91, 94, 97, 100, 103, 106, ?
   (a) 109   (b) 110
   (c) 111   (d) 112

8. 5, 10, 40, 80, 320, 640, ?
   (a) 2520   (b) 2540
   (c) 2560   (d) 2580

9. 1, 5, 9, 17, 25, 37, 49, ?
   (a) 64   (b) 63
   (c) 65   (d) 67

10. 6, 15, 35, 77, 143, ?
    (a) 221   (b) 223
    (c) 225   (d) 227

11. 16, 22, 30, 40, 52, 66, 82, ?
    (a) 100   (b) 98
    (c) 102   (d) 104

12. 225, 205, 180, 150, 115, ?
    (a) 55   (b) 65
    (c) 75   (d) 85

13. 10, 14, 28, 32, 64, 68, ?
    (a) 136   (b) 72
    (c) 126   (d) 82

14. 3, 4, 10, 33, 136, ?
    (a) 682   (b) 684
    (c) 685   (d) 687'

15. 1326, 2436, 3546, 4656, ?
    (a) 5760   (b) 5766
    (c) 5667   (d) 5768

16. 598, 505, 412, 319, 226, ?
    (a) 131   (b) 132
    (c) 133   (d) 134

17. 702, 773, 844, 915, 986, ?
    (a) 1052   (b) 1053
    (c) 1056   (d) 1057

18. 15, 45, 42, 126, 123, 369, 366, ?
    (a) 1094   (b) 1095
    (c) 1096   (d) 1098

19. 27, 56, 114, 230, 462, 926, ?
    (a) 1852   (b) 1854
    (c) 1848   (d) 1856

20. 2, 21, 154, 1085, 7602, ?
    (a) 53214   (b) 53216
    (c) 53221   (d) 53223

Series Completion

Odd One Out

In the questions based on odd one out a group of words are given, in which one word is completely different from the other words. Some words have a common quality and have same characteristics. In this type of problems, generally there are fours words or numbers or pair of words in which three are same in some particular manner but one word, number or pair of words is different from the other three.

For example, in a group of words three words belong to vegetables and one word is a type of fruit, then the word which is fruit is odd from the others.

Find the odd one out:

(a) Coward : Brave (b) Beginning : End
(c) White : Dirty (c) Easy : Difficult

In the above pairs of words option (c) is odd, as all others are antonyms of each other.

Find the odd one out:

(a) 121 (b) 169
(c) 256 (d) 145

In these numbers (a) (b) (c) are perfect squares but (d) is not a perfect square. So, 145 is odd.

Thus, 'Odd one out' means to assort items of a given group on the basis of a certain common property they have possess and then spot the stranger or 'odd one out'.

Example 1: Choose the odd one out from the following:
(a) Tiger (b) Horse
(c) Lion (d) Giraffe

Solution: (b) All except Horse, are wild animals, while Horse can be domesticated.

Example 2:
(a) January (b) May
(c) November (d) July

Solution: (c) All except November are months having 31 days, while November has 30 days.

Example 3:
(a) Sword (b) Gun
(c) Rifle (d) Cannon

Solution: (a) All except Sword are fire arms, and can be used from a distance.

Example 4:
(a) Mercury (b) Petrol
(c) Kerosene (d) Acetone

Solution: (a) Mercury is the only metal in the group.

Example 5:
(a) Soda water (b) Beer
(c) Cold drink (d) Milk

Solution: (d) All except milk are artificially prepared drinks.

Example 6:
(a) Day (b) Calendar
(c) Month (d) Fortnight

Solution: (b) All others are parts of a calendar.

Example 7:
(a) Rhea (b) Lamprey
(c) Salmon (d) Trout

Solution: (a) All except Rhea are kinds of fishes.

Example 8:
(a) Bars (b) Lagoons
(c) Beaches (d) Moraines

Solution: (d) All except Moraines are structures formed by the sea, while moraines are formed by glaciers.

Example 9:
(a) Accumulate (b) Congregate
(c) Aggregate (d) Disperse

Solution: (d) All except Disperse are synonyms of 'collect'.

Example 10:
(a) Insulin (b) Iodine
(c) Adrenaline (d) Thyroxine

Solution: (b) All except Iodine are hormones.

Multiple Choice Questions

Direction: Choose the odd one out from the following.

1. (a) History (b) Physics (c) Civics (d) Geography
2. (a) Mosque (b) Temple (c) Mantery (d) Church
3. (a) Operating system (b) Hard disk (c) Printer (d) Pendrive
4. (a) Ruby (b) Marble (c) Sapphire (d) Diamond
5. (a) Peel (b) Fry (c) Roast (d) Bake
6. (a) Silicon (b) Potassium (c) Gallium (d) Germanium
7. (a) Kiwi (b) Emu (c) Eagle (d) Penguin
8. (a) Tomato (b) Carrot (c) Brinjal (d) Gourd
9. (a) India (b) Japan (c) Sri Lanka (d) Malagasy
10. (a) Spectacles (b) Goggles (c) Microphone (d) Telescope
11. (a) Hammer (b) Dagger (c) Sword (d) Knife
12. (a) Trunk (b) Tree (c) Leaf (d) Flower
13. (a) Dog (b) Horse (c) Fox (d) Cat
14. (a) Cap (b) Helmet (c) Veil (d) Hat
15. (a) Write (b) Read (c) Learn (d) Knowledge
16. (a) Radio (b) X-ray (c) Computer (d) Television
17. (a) Earth (b) Venus (c) Saturn (d) Mercury
18. (a) Cabbage (b) Cauliflower (c) Radish (d) Lady finger
19. (a) Delicious (b) Sour (c) Bitter (d) Sweet
20. (a) Cotton (b) Nylon (c) Silk (d) Wool
21. (a) Nail (b) Feather (c) Fir (d) Trunk
22. (a) Arhar (b) Jower (c) Moong (d) Gram
23. (a) Blood (b) Bones (c) Muscles (d) Tendons
24. (a) Cool (b) Warm (c) Hot (d) Humid
25. (a) Leh (b) Aizwal (c) Shimla (d) Panaji
26. (a) Yak (b) Leopard (c) Silver fox (d) Reindeer
27. (a) Pineapple (b) Malta (c) Banana (d) Lemon
28. (a) Faraday (b) Newton (c) Marconi (d) Beethovan
29. (a) Indigo (b) Green (c) Pink (d) Yellow
30. (a) Whale (b) Cod (c) Starfish (d) Shark
31. (a) Father (b) Cousin (c) Uncle (d) Aunt
32. (a) Cancel (b) Repeat (c) Change (d) Revoke
33. (a) Mamba (b) Cobra (c) Viper (d) Python
34. (a) Medium (b) Average (c) Terrible (d) Mediocre
35. (a) Yeast (b) Mould (c) Smut (d) Mushroom
36. (a) Wood (b) Stone (c) Cork (d) Paper

37. (a) Beam (b) Wall
    (c) Roof (d) House
38. (a) Cry (b) Sad
    (c) Laugh (d) Weep
39. (a) Nymph (b) Caterpillar
    (c) Pupa (d) Larva
40. (a) Oil (b) Glue
    (c) Paste (d) Cement

★★★

Coding–Decoding

Coding is a method of transmitting a message between the sender and receiver without a third person knowing it. A code is nothing but a system of signals. There are various types of coding namely letter coding, direct letter coding, number and symbol, coding, substitution, deciphering message word codes etc.

In letter coding, the letters in a word are replaced by certain words according to a particular rule to form its code. The candidate is required to detect the coding pattern and answer the question according to the pattern.

In direct letter coding particular, letters are made code for particular letters without any set patterns. In direct coding, the code letters occur in the same sequence as the corresponding letters occur in the words.

In number/symbol coding, numerical code values are assigned in a word or alphabetical code. Letters are assigned to the numbers, then the candidate is required to analyse the rule as per the question.

Now, we will learn different types of Coding and Decoding methods.

Letter Coding

The letters in a word are replaced by certain other letters according to a specific rule to form its code.

Example 1: If BOMBAY is written as MYMYMY, how will TAMILNADU be written in that code?
 (a) MNUMNUMNU
 (b) IATIATIAT
 (c) ALDALDALD
 (d) TIATIATIA

Solution: (a) The letters at the third and sixth places are repeated thrice to code BOMBAY as MYMYMY. Similarly, the letters at the third, sixth and ninth places are repeated thrice to code TAMILNADU as MNUMNUMNU.

Example 2: In a certain code language, THANKS is written as SKNTHA. HOW is STUPID written in that code language?
 (a) DIPUTS (b) DISPUT
 (c) DIPUST (d) DPISTU

Solution: (d) The code is formed by just writing the last three letters of the word in a reverse order, followed by the first three letters in the same order. So, the code for STUPID should be DIPSTU.

Direct Letter Coding

Letters were assigned codes according to a set pattern or rule concerning the movement or recordering of letters and one needs to detect this hidden rule to decode a message.

Such type of coding is called direct – coding. The code letters occurs in the same sequence as the corresponding letters occur in the words.

Example 3: If TEACHER is coded as LMKJMMP, then how will HEART be coded?
 (a) NMKPL (b) NPKML
 (c) MMPKL (d) MMAPL

Solution: (a)

Letter: T E A C H R
Code: L M K J N P

The code for HEART is NMKPL.

Number/Symbol Coding

Numerical code values are assigned to a word or alphabetical code letters are assigned to the numbers.

Letters and numbers are correlated to each other in no other way except in relation to the position of the letters in the English alphabet.

Example 4: If MOBILITY is coded as 46293927, then EXAMINATION is coded as.
 (a) 67250623076 (b) 57159413955
 (c) 56149512965 (d) 45038401

Solution: **(c)** Let A = 1, B = 2, C = 3, ..., X = 24, Y = 25, Z = 26.

M = 13 = 1 + 3 = 4; O = 15 = 1 + 5 = 6; B = 2; I = 9; L = 12 = 1 + 2 = 3

T = 20 = 2 + 0 = 2; Y = 25 = 2 + 5 = 7

So, MOBILITY = 46293927

X = 24 = 2 + 4 = 6; N = 14 = 1 + 4 = 5

So, EXAMINATION = 56149512965.

Example 5: If REASON is coded as 5 and BELIEVED as 7, then what is the code for GOVERNMENT?

(a) 10   (b) 9
(c) 8   (d) 6

Solution: **(b)** Clearly, each word is coded by the numeral which is 1 less than the number of letters in the word.

Substitution

In this type of question, some particular words are assigned certain substituted names.

Example 6: If 'rain' is 'water', 'water' is 'road', 'road' is 'cloud', 'cloud' is 'sky', 'sky' is 'sea' and 'sea' is 'path' where do aeroplanes fly?

(a) Sea   (b) Water
(c) Cloud   (d) Road

Solution: **(a)**

Multiple Choice Questions

1. If TRUTH is coded as SUQSTVSUGI, then the code for FALSE will be _____.
   (a) FGZBKNRTDF
   (b) EGZBKMRDE
   (c) EGZKMRTDF
   (d) EGZBKMRTDF

2. In a certain code, INACTIVE is written as VITCANIE. How is COMPUTER written in the same code?
   (a) UTEPMOCR
   (b) MOCPETUR
   (c) ETUPMOCR
   (d) PMOCRETU

3. In a certain code, COVALENT, is written as BWPDUOFM and FORM is written as PGNS. How will SILVER be written in that code?
   (a) MJTSFW
   (b) MJTWFS
   (c) KHRSFW
   (d) None of these

4. In a certain code, VISHWANATHAN is written as NAAWTHHSANIV. How is KARUMAKARAMA written in that code?
   (a) KAAMRAURMAAK
   (b) NKKRAMKRAUK
   (c) RURNKAAUNAK
   (d) AKNUARRAANKA

5. In a certain code, MOTHER is written as ONHURF. How will ANSWER be written in that code?
   (a) NBWRRF   (b) MAVSPE
   (c) NBWTRF   (d) NBXSSE

6. In a certain code, the words COME AT ONCE, were written as XLNVZGLMXV. In the same code, which of the following would code OK?
   (a) LP   (b) KM
   (c) LM   (d) KL

7. In a certain code, RAIL is written as KCTN and SPEAK is written as CGRUM. How will AVOID be written in that code?
   (a) FKQXC   (b) KQVCB
   (c) KQXCF   (d) KRXCF

8. If CONTRIBUTE is written as ETBUIRNTOC, then which letter will be in the sixth place when counted from the left if POPULARISE is written in the same way?
   (a) L   (b) A
   (c) R   (d) I

9. If in a certain code, GRASP is coded as BMVMK, which word would be coded as CRANE?
   (a) BQZMD   (b) HWFSJ
   (c) GVERJ   (d) XMVIZ

10. If NARGRUED is the code for GRANDEUR, which word is coded as SERPEVRE?
    (a) PRESEVER
    (b) PERSERVE
    (c) PERSEVER
    (d) PRESERVE

11. If CONCEPT is written as unmulqr and FRIEND is written as ysglmt, then how is PREDICT written in that code?
    (a) qsltgur   (b) qgmnltr
    (c) slmgtur   (d) USXgmnl

12. In a certain code, FIRE is written as QHOE and MOVE as ZMWE. Following the same rule of coding what should be the code for the word OVER?
    (a) MWZO   (b) MWED
    (c) MWEO   (d) MWOE

13. If WORK is coded as 4 – 12 – 9 – 16, then how will you code WOMAN?
    (a) 23 – 12 – 26 – 14 – 13
    (b) 4 – 12 – 14 – 26 – 13
    (c) 4 – 26 – 14 – 13 – 12
    (d) 23 – 15 – 13 – 1 – 14

14. If GO = 32, SHE = 49, then SOME will be equal to
    (a) 64   (b) 62
    (c) 56   (d) 58

15. If ZIP = 198 and ZAP = 246, then how will you code VIP ?
    (a) 888   (b) 990
    (c) 222   (d) 174

Coding–Decoding 125

16. If MASTER is coded as $\overline{411259}$, then POWDER will be coded as.
    (a) $\overline{765549}$ (b) $\overline{765459}$
    (c) $\overline{765439}$ (d) $\overline{765439}$

17. In a certain code, BRAIN is written as * % ÷ # × and TIER is written as $ # + %. How is RENT written in that code?
    (a) % × # $ (b) % # × $
    (c) + × % $ (d) % + × $

18. If DELHI is coded as 73541 and CALCUTTA as 82589662, how can CALICUT be coded?
    (a) 8251896 (b) 8543691
    (c) 5978213 (d) 5279431

19. If NOIDA is written as 39658, how will INDIA be written?
    (a) 36568 (b) 65368
    (c) 63568 (d) 63569

20. If ENGLAND is written as 1234526 and FRANCE is written as 785291, how is GREECE coded?
    (a) 835545 (b) 381191
    (c) 832252 (d) 381171

21. If REQUEST is written as S2R52TU, then how will ACID be written?
    (a) 1D3E (b) IC94
    (c) B3J4 (d) 1394

22. In a certain code, DESK is written as #. 52, RIDE is written as % 7# . how is RISK written in that code?
    (a) % 7 $ # (b) % 752
    (c) % 7 # 2 (d) % 725

23. In a certain code, EAT is written as 318 and CHAIR is written as 24156. What will TEACHER be written as?
    (a) 8313426 (b) 8321436
    (c) 8312346 (d) 8312436

24. In a certain code, DEAF is written as 3587 and FILE is written as 7465. How is IDEAL written in that code?
    (a) 63548 (b) 43568
    (c) 43586 (d) 48536

25. If DRIVER = 12, PEDESTRIAN = 20, ACCIDENT = 16, then CAR = ?
    (a) 6 (b) 8
    (c) 10 (d) 3

26. If 'oranges' are 'apples', 'bananas' are 'apricots', 'apples' are 'chillies', 'apricots' are 'oranges' and chillies are 'bananas', then which of the following are green in colour?
    (a) Chillies (b) Oranges
    (c) Apples (d) Bananas

27. If 'sky' is 'star', 'star' is 'cloud', 'cloud' is earth, 'earth' is 'tree' and 'tree' is 'book', then where do the birds fly?
    (a) Sky (b) Cloud
    (c) Star (d) None of these

28. If 'blue' means 'green', 'green' means 'white', 'white' means 'yellow' means 'black', 'black' means 'red' and 'red' means 'brown', then what is the colour of milk?
    (a) Green (b) Yellow
    (c) Blue (d) Black

29. If 'eraser' is called 'box', 'box' is called 'pencil', 'pencil' is called 'sharpener' and 'sharpener' is called 'bag', what will a child write with?
    (a) Box (b) Sharpener
    (c) Bag (d) Pencil

30. If 'dust' is called 'air', 'air' is called 'fire', 'fire' is called 'water', 'water' is called 'colour', 'colour' is called 'rain' and 'rain' is called 'dust', then where do fish live?
    (a) Dust (b) Water
    (c) Colour (d) Fire

★★★

Alphabet Test

Alphabetical order means arrangement of words as they appear in the English dictionary. This is the order in which the beginning letters of these words appear in the English alphabet.

First, consider the first letter of each word, then second and so on and then arrange the words in the order in which the letters appear in English alphabet.

Direction: Arrange the given words in alphabetical order.

Example 1: Moment, Artist, Cricket, Patient, Worship, Neck.

The order of words as per English dictionary is as follows:

Artist, Cricket, Moment, Patient, Worship.

In some cases, two or more than two words begin with the same letter. Each word should be arranged in the order of second letters in the alphabet.

Example 2: Bucket, Parrot, Mirror, Memory, Crocon, Crowd, Cancel, Work, Nose.

The alphabetical order of the given words is as follows.

Bucket, Cancel, Crowd, Crown, Memory, Mirror, Nose, Parrot, Work.

If both the first and second letters of two or more words are the same, then arrange the words considering the third letters and so on. If first, second, and third letters of two or more words are the same, then arrange these words considering their fourth, letter and so on. In this way the words are arranged.

Alphabetical Order

Arranging words in alphabetical order implies 'to arrange them in the order as they appear in a dictionary' i.e., as per the order in which the beginning letters of these words appear in the English alphabet.

Directions (1 – 5): Arrange the given words in alphabetical order and choose the one that comes first.

Example 1:
    (a) Lesson   (b) Leopard
    (c) Language   (d) Lessen

Solution: **(c)** Language, Leopard, Lessen, Lesson.

Example 2:
    (a) Rubber   (b) Rumple
    (c) Ruby   (d) Rumour

Solution: **(a)** Rubber, Ruby, Rumour, Rumple.

Example 3:
    (a) Minority   (b) Miniature
    (c) Minister   (d) Minimalis

Solution: **(b)** Miniature, Minimalis, Minister, Minority.

First consider the first letter of each word. Arrange the words in the order in which these letters appear in the English alphabet.

Example 4:
    (a) Demand   (b) Diamond
    (c) Destroy   (d) Damage

Solution: **(d)** Damage, Demand, Destroy, Diamond.

Example 5:
    (a) School   (b) Science
    (c) Scissors   (d) Scorpion

Solution: **(a)** School, Science, Scissors, Scorpion.

Rule–Detection

Example 1: Number of letters skipped in between the adjacent letters in the series are multiples of 3.
    (a) AELPZ   (b) LORUX
    (c) GKOTZ   (d) DHLPU

Solution: (a) A̠ B C D E̠ F G H I J K L̠ M N O P̠ Q R S T U V W X Y Z̠
                    3   6   3   9

3, 6, 9 are multiples of 3.

Example 2: Number of letters skipped in between adjacent letters in the series is in the order of 1^2, 2^2, 3^2.

    (a) RTWZ   (b) CEJT
    (c) EGLP   (d) EGLO

Solution: (b)

    C D E F G H I J K L M N O P Q R S T
       1   4   9

Example 3: Number of letters skipped in between the adjacent letters in the series is equal.

    (a) SUXADF   (b) RVZDHL
    (c) HKNGSH   (d) RVZDFG

Solution: (b)

    R S T U V W X Y Z A B C D E F G H I J K L
      3   3   3   3   3

Alphabetical Quibble

A letter series is given, be it the English alphabets from A to Z or a randomized sequence of letters. The candidate is then required to trace the letters satisfy certain given conditions as regards their position in the given sequence.

Example 1: How many D's are there in the following series which are immediately followed by W but not immediately proceded by k?

    K D C W K D W N K G D W W D H K V D W Z D W

    (a) Four   (b) Three
    (c) Two   (d) One

Solution: (b) Clearly, D's satisfying the given conditions can be marked as under:

K D C W K D W N K G D W W D H K V D W Z D W.

We observe that such D' are three in number.

Example 2: Which letter will be sixth to the left of the nineteenth letter from the right end of the alphabet?

    (a) X   (b) Y
    (c) M   (d) None of these

Solution: (d) Counting right, i.e., from Z in the given alphabet series, the nineteenth letter is H.

Counting from H towards the left, the sixth letter is B.

Multiple Choice Questions

Directions (1 – 6): Arrange the given words in alphabetical order and choose the one that comes first.

1. (a) Guarantee (b) Group
   (c) Groan (d) Grotesque
2. (a) Necessary (b) Nature
   (c) Naval (d) Nautical
3. (a) Foment (b) Foetus
   (c) Foliage (d) Forceps
4. (a) Deuce (b) Dew
   (c) Devise (d) Dexterity
5. (a) Quarter (b) Quarrel
   (c) Quarry (d) Qualify
6. (a) Probe (b) Probate
   (c) Proceed (d) Proclaim

Directions (7 – 13): Arrange the given words in the alphabetical order and choose the one that comes last.

7. (a) Fault (b) Finger
   (c) Floor (d) Forget
8. (a) Evolution (b) Extra
   (c) Extreme (d) Extraction
9. (a) Transport (b) Transist
   (c) Transmit (d) Translate
10. (a) Romance (b) Roman
    (c) Rose (d) Repeat
11. (a) Different (b) Distance
    (c) Dialogue (d) Diagonal
12. (a) Temperature (b) Transition
    (c) Transmit (d) Temple
13. (a) Warring (b) Waving
    (c) Watching (d) Waiting

Directions (14 – 20): In each of the following questions find out which of the letter series follows the given rule.

14. Number of letters skipped in between adjacent letters in the series is odd.
    (a) MPRUX (b) FIMRX
    (c) EIMQV (d) BDHLR
15. Number of letters skipped in between adjacent letters in the series is in the order of 2, 5, 7, 10.
    (a) QTZHS (b) SYBEP
    (c) FNKOT (d) CEGLT
16. Number of letters skipped in between adjacent letters in the series decreases by three.
    (a) HVDKP (b) HUELP
    (c) HUELD (d) DMSXA
17. Number of letters skipped in between adjacent letters in the series decreases by one each time.
    (a) BHNSV (b) TZEIL
    (c) MSYBG (d) IMTXB
18. Number of letters skipped in between adjacent letters in the series doubles every time.
    (a) BDGLU (b) EGJOF
    (c) GJNSY (d) ADIPY
19. Number of letters skipped in between adjacent letters of the series starting from behind increases by one.
    (a) ONLKJ (b) OMKIG
    (c) OIGDC (d) OMJFA
20. Number of letters skipped in between adjacent letters decrease in order.
    (a) SYDHK (b) HNSWA
    (c) AGMRV (d) NSXCH

Directions (21 – 30): Each of the following questions is based on the following alphabet – series:

A B C D E F G H I J K L M N O P Q R S T U V W X Y Z

21. Which letter is seventh to the right of the thirteenth letter from the left end?
    (a) S (b) U
    (c) T (d) None of these
22. Which letter in the alphabet is as far from G as T is from M?
    (a) P (b) O (c) M (d) N
23. Which letter is sixteenth to the right of the letter which is fourth to the left of I?
    (a) U (b) V (c) T (d) S

Alphabet Test

24. If the order of the English alphabet is reversed, then which letter would be exactly in the middle?
    (a) M (b) N
    (c) L (d) None of these

25. If only the first half of the given alphabet is reversed, how many letters will be there between K and R?
    (a) 14 (b) 16
    (c) 10 (d) 6

26. If the last ten letters of the alphabet are written in the reverse order, which of the following will be the sixth to the right of the thirteenth letter from the left end?
    (a) Y (b) X (c) W (d) V

27. A B C D E F G H I J K L M N O P Q R S T U V W X Y Z.
    Which letter is exactly midway between G and Q in the given alphabet?
    (a) K (b) L (c) N (d) M

28. If 1st and 26th, 2nd and 25th, 3rd and 24th and so on, letters of the English alphabet are paired, then which of the following pair is correct?
    (a) EV (b) IP
    (c) GR (d) CW

29. If in the English alphabet every fourth letter is replaced by the symbol (*), which of the following would be seventh to the left of the fourteenth element from the left?
    (a) * (b) T
    (c) H (d) G

30. In the following alphabets, which letter is eighth to the right of the fourteenth letter from the right end?
    Z A B C D E F G H I J K L M N O P Q R S T U V W X Y
    (a) H (b) R
    (c) S (d) T

Number and Ranking Test

The problems based on Number Ranking consist of a set, group or series of numerals. The candidate has to trace out the numerals following some certain given conditions or lying at particular specified position according to a certain given pattern. For this, he/she has to analyse the given series of numerals or number sequence and study the pattern to answer the appropriate option.

In the number sequence a number which comes after a given number is said to follow it while the number which comes before the given number precedes it.

The problems such as a number in between two odd numbers or two even numbers or a number in between two of its factors are based on the number test.

Number Test

In this type of questions, a series of numbers is given. The students to study the series and answer the given questions according to the given conditions.

Ranking Test

In this test the rank of a person from the top and from the bottom is mentioned and the candidate has to find out total number of persons.

In some problems, the test is in the form of puzzle of interchanging positions by two persons. In the ranking problems, the student has to find out the total number of persons, position of particular person from left end or right end.

Example 1: In the given series, how many 7's are there which is preceded by 5 and followed by 3?

4 2 7 6 5 7 3 8 9 5 7 3 4 6 7 5 3 4 6

(a) 1 (b) 2
(c) 3 (d) 4

Solution: (b) 4 2 7 6 5 7 3 8 9 5 7 3 4 6 7 5 3 4 6

Example 2: How many 8's are there which is exactly divisible by its immediate preceding as well as successing numbers?

2 8 3 8 2 4 8 6 4 8 6 8 2 8 2 4 8 3 8 2 8 6

(a) 1 (b) 2
(c) 3 (d) 4

Solution: (a)
2 8 3 8 2 4 8 6 4 8 6 8 2 8 2 4 8 3 8 2 8 6

Example 3: How many 5's are there which is exactly preceding by 1 and followed by 2?

6 4 2 3 1 5 2 6 8 9 5 4 3 1 5 2 7 8 9 5 4 3 6

(a) 1 (b) 2
(c) 3 (d) 4

Solution: (b) 6 4 2 3 1 5 2 6 8 9 5 4 3 1 5 2 7 8 9 5 4 3 6

Example 4: Mohit is 14th from the right end in a row of 40 students. What is his position from the left end?

(a) 1 (b) 2
(c) 3 (d) 4

Solution: (c) Number of students towards the left of Mohit = 40 – 14 = 26.

So, his position is (26 + 1)th = 27th from left.

Example 5: Mohan ranks 8th from the top and 32th from the bottom in a class. How many students are there in class?

(a) 41 (b) 39
(c) 38 (d) 40

Solution: (b) No. of students in the class
= 8 + 32 – 1 = 39

Multiple Choice Questions

1. In the series given below, how many 8's are there each of which is exactly divisible by its immediate preceding as well as succeeding numbers?

   2 8 4 3 8 5 4 8 2 6 7 8 4 6 2 8 4 1 7 ?
   (a) 1   (b) 2
   (c) 3   (d) 4

2. How many 5's are there in the following number sequence which are immediately preceded by 7 and immediately followed by 8?

   7 5 5 8 4 5 7 8 4 5 9 8 7 5 8 7 8 4 3 2 5 8 7 6 ?
   (a) 1   (b) 2
   (c) 3   (d) None of these

3. In the given series 7 4 5 7 6 8 4 2 1 3 5 1 7 6 8 9 2 how many pairs of alternate numbers have a difference of 2?
   (a) 1   (b) 2
   (c) 3   (d) 4

4. How many 4's are there preceded by 7 but not followed by 5?

   5 9 3 1 7 4 5 8 4 6 7 4 3 1 4 7 4 2 8 7 4 1 ?
   (a) 1   (b) 2
   (c) 3   (d) 4

5. How many 5's are there which are in between two even numbers.

   4 3 5 6 4 5 2 3 4 5 8 5 4 6 7 5 2 6 9 8 5 1 2 4 5
   (a) 1   (b) 2
   (c) 3   (d) 4

6. How many 3's are there preceded by 2 but not followed by 7?

   1 2 3 7 4 3 2 5 6 7 2 8 9 6 4 3 2 5 6 8 4 6 8 2 3 4
   (a) 1   (b) 2
   (c) 3   (d) 4

7. In how many terms, the difference between two consecutive terms is 3?

   8 5 2 4 1 6 2 7 6 4 1 3 5 2 5 7 4 1 8 9 6 2 5 6 9 4 1
   (a) 8   (b) 9
   (c) 10   (d) 11

8. In how many times, between two odd numbers, there is an even number?

   4 6 3 4 7 2 5 4 1 2 3 4 5 6 7 8 9 6 4 7 5 2 ?
   (a) 5   (b) 6
   (c) 7   (d) 8

9. In how many times, the sum of two consecutive terms is 7?

   4 2 5 1 6 4 3 8 1 9 4 5 2 3 4 1 6 7 4 5 3 4 5 6 2
   (a) 4   (b) 5
   (c) 6   (d) 7

10. How many times the difference between two consecutive terms is 5?

    1 3 4 6 9 8 4 2 7 6 4 9 6 3 8 2 6 4 1 6 7 4
    (a) 3   (b) 4
    (c) 5   (d) 6

11. Ranjan ranks 18th in a class of 49 students. What is his rank from last?
    (a) 28   (b) 29
    (c) 31   (d) 32

12. If Aman finds that he is 12th from the right in a line of boys and 4th from the left. How many boys should be added to the line such that there are 35 students in the line?
    (a) 18   (b) 19
    (c) 20   (d) 21

13. In a queue, Ravi is 13th from the back Amar is 12th from the front. Hari is standing between the two. What should be the minimum number of boys standing in queue?
    (a) 14   (b) 15
    (c) 16   (d) 17

14. In a row of boys Raja is 10th from the left and Pramod, who is 9th from the right interchange their positions, Raja becomes 15th from the left. How many boys are there in the row?
    (a) 23   (b) 24
    (c) 25   (d) 26

15. Shankar ranked 7th from the top and 34th from the bottom in a class. How many students are there in a class?
    (a) 38   (b) 39
    (c) 40   (d) 41

16. Saket is 7 ranks ahead of Manoj in a class of 50. If Manoj's rank is 17th from the last, what is Saket's rank from the start?
    (a) 25 (b) 26
    (c) 27 (d) 28
17. If in a single line, Mohan is 23rd from both the ends. How many boys are there in the class?
    (a) 44 (b) 45
    (c) 46 (d) 47
18. Naresh ranks 5th in a class, Vikas is 8th from the last. If Raju is 6th after Naresh and Just in the middle of Naresh and Vikas. How many students are there in the class?
    (a) 23 (b) 24
    (c) 25 (d) 26
19. Ashok is 8th from the left and Sanjay is 14th from the right end in a row of boys. If there are 12 boys between Ashok and Sanjay, how many boys are there in the row?
    (a) 32 (b) 33
    (c) 34 (d) 35
20. If the numbers from 1 to 100, which are exactly divisible by 5 are arranged in descending order, which would come at the 11th position from the bottom?
    (a) 50 (b) 55
    (c) 60 (d) 65

Direction Sense Test

The questions on Directions Sense are based on various directions called direction puzzles. The figure given below shows four main directions namely North, South, East and West. There are four cardinal directions namely North – East (NE), North – West (NW), South – East (SE) and South – West (SW).

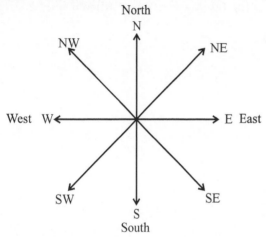

In this type of questions, a successive follow up of directions is formulated. The candidate is required to decide the final direction or distance between starting and end points. Direction Sense Test is basically hold to check the candidate's ability to trace and follow the direction correctly.

The candidate is required to trace the diagram and find out the distance between initial point and final point. He/she has to analyse directions carefully and answer the questions. The diagram is very essential in direction sense problems.

Example 1: Mohan faces towards north. Turning to his right, he walks 25m. He then turns to his left and walks 30m. Next he moves 25m to his right. He then turns to his right again and walks 55m. At last, he turns to his right and moves 40m. In which direction is he now from his starting point?

(a) SE (b) NE
(c) South (d) East

Solution: **(a)** The movements of the Mohan are as shown below:

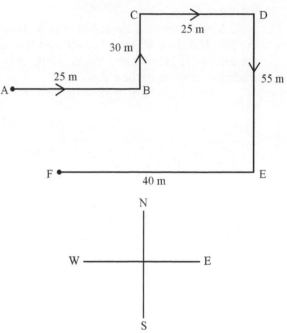

Here, A is the starting position and F is the final position.
Clearly, F is towards south east from A.

Example 2: Geeta is facing North – West. She turns 90° in the clock wise direction and then 135° in the anti clock wise direction. Which direction is she facing now?

(a) East (b) West
(c) North (d) None of these

Solution: **(b)** The movements of Geeta are as shown in figure:

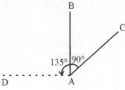

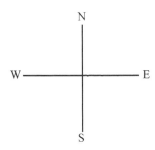

Starting point is A. Initially she is facing AB. Finally the position is AD, which is west from starting position.

Example 3: Sohan walks 30 m towards south then turning to his right he walks 30 m, then turning to his left he walks 20 m, Again he turns to his left and walks 30 m. How far is he from his starting position?

(a) 30 m (b) 40 m
(c) 50 m (d) 60 m

Solution: **(c)** The movements of Sohan are as shown below:

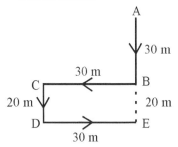

Starting point A, Final Point E.
AE = AB + BE = AB + CD
= 30 + 20 = 50m

Direction Sense Test

Multiple Choice Questions

1. One morning after sunrise, Mohan was standing facing a pole. The shadow of the pole falls exactly to his right. Which direction was he facing?
   (a) North   (b) South
   (c) East   (d) West

2. If south – east is called east, north – west is called west, south – west is called south and so on what will north be called?
   (a) South
   (b) North East
   (c) East
   (d) North West

3. A, B, C and D are playing a game of carom. A & C and B & D are partners. D is to the right of C, who is facing west, then in which direction B is facing?
   (a) East   (b) West
   (c) North   (d) South

4. Rajesh is 40m south – west of Rohit. Rakesh is 40m south-east of Rohit. Then Rakesh is in which direction of Rajesh?
   (a) East   (b) West
   (c) South   (d) North

5. Pravin wants to go to the college. He starts from his home which is in the east and comes to a crossing. The road to the left ends in a theatre, straight ahead in the hospital. In which direction is the college?
   (a) North   (b) South
   (c) East   (d) West

6. Naresh walks 30m towards south. Then turning to his right, he walks 30m then turning to his left, he walks 20m. Again he turns to his left and walked 30m. How far is he from his initial position?
   (a) 30m   (b) 40m
   (c) 50m   (d) 60m

7. Manoj walks 10m in front end 10m to the right then every time turning to his left. He walks 5m, 15m and 15m respectively. How far is he now from his starting point?
   (a) 5m   (b) 10m
   (c) 15m   (d) 20m

8. Nilesh went 15 km to the west from my house then turned left and walked 20 km. Then turned east and walked 25 km and finally turning left covered 20 km. How far was he from his house?
   (a) 5 km   (b) 10 km
   (c) 60 km   (d) 40 km

9. Geeta walks Northwards. After a while, she turns to her right and a little further to her left. Finally after walking a distance of 0.5km, she turns to her left again. In which direction is she moving now?
   (a) East   (b) West
   (c) North   (d) South

10. Kishan walked 40m towards East, took a right turn and walked 50m. then he took a left turn and walked 40m. in which direction is he now from the starting point?
    (a) East   (b) South
    (c) North-east   (d) South-east

11. Mahesh goes 30m North then turns right and walks 40m then again turns right and walks 20m then again turns right and walks 40m. How many metres is he from his starting position.
    (a) 10 m   (b) 15 m
    (c) 20 m   (d) 30 m

12. A, B, C, D, E, F, G, H are sitting around a round table in the same order at equal distance for group discussion. Their positions are clockwise. If G sits in the north then what will be the position of D?
    (a) South east   (b) South west
    (c) South   (d) East

13. If P is to south of Q and R is to the east of Q. In which direction is P with respect to R?
    (a) North-East   (b) North-West
    (c) South-East   (d) South-West

14. Ramesh is performing yoga with his head down and legs up. His face is towards the west. In which direction will his left hand be?
    (a) East   (b) West
    (c) South   (d) North

15. A clock is so placed that at 12 noon its minute hand points towards north-east. In what direction does its hour hand point at 1.30 P.M.?
    (a) East   (b) West
    (c) North   (d) South

16. Rohan is facing North. He turns 135° in the anticlockwise direction and then 180° in the clockwise direction. Which direction is he facing now?
    (a) NE   (b) NW
    (c) SW   (d) SE

17. Ritesh went to meet his cousin to another village situated 5 km away in north-east direction of Ritesh's village. From there he came to meet his friend living in a village situated 4km in the south of his cousin's village. How far away and in which direction is he now?
    (a) 3km, East   (b) 4km, East
    (c) 3km, North   (d) 4km, West

18. Karim goes 30m North then turns right and walks 40m then again turns right and walks 20m, then again turns right and walks 40m. How far is he from his original position?
    (a) 10m   (b) 20m
    (c) 25m   (d) 40m

19. Ankur walked 30m towards east, took a right turn and walked 40m. then took a left turn and walked 30m. In which direction is he now from the starting point?
    (a) South   (b) South-east
    (c) East   (d) North-east

20. Rohit went 15km to the west from my house then turned left and walked 20km. he then turned east and walked 25km and finally turning left covered 20km. How far was he from his house?
    (a) 10km   (b) 15km
    (c) 20km   (d) 40km

Direction Sense Test

Essential Element

9

In the questions based on Essential Element the student will find an essential part of something. Each question has an underlined word followed by four answer choices. The student is required to choose the word that is a necessary part of the underlined word. A good approach could be to say the following sentence: "A _____ could not exist without _____." Put the underlined word in the first blank. Try each of the answer choices in the second blank to see which choice is most logical.

Directions (1 – 3):
Find the word that names a necessary part of the underlined word.

1. <u>Vibration</u>
   (a) motion
   (b) electricity
   (c) science
   (d) sound

Solution: Option (a) is correct.

Explanation:
Anything cannot vibrate without creating motion, so motion is essential to vibration.

2. <u>Vertebrate</u>
   (a) backbone
   (b) reptile
   (c) mammal
   (d) animal

Solution: Option (a) is correct.

Explanation:
All vertebrates have a backbone. Reptiles (choice b) are vertebrates, but so are many other animals. Mammals (choice c) are vertebrates, but so are birds and reptiles. All vertebrates (choice d) are animals, but not all animals are vertebrates.

3. <u>Itinerary</u>
   (a) map
   (b) route
   (c) travel
   (d) guidebook

Solution: Option (b) is correct.

Explanation:
An itinerary is a proposed route of a journey. A map (choice a) is not necessary to have a planned route. Travel (choice c) is usually the outcome of an itinerary, but not always. A guidebook (choice d) may be used to plan the journey but is not essential.

Multiple Choice Questions

Directions (1 to 30): Find the word that names a necessary part of the underlined word.

1. Knowledge
   - (a) School
   - (b) Teacher
   - (c) Textbook
   - (d) Learning
2. Culture
   - (a) Civility
   - (b) Education
   - (c) Agriculture
   - (d) Customs
3. Antique
   - (a) Rarity
   - (b) Artefact
   - (c) Aged
   - (d) Prehistoric
4. Dimension
   - (a) Compass
   - (b) Ruler
   - (c) Inch
   - (d) Measure
5. Purchase
   - (a) Trade
   - (b) Money
   - (c) Bank
   - (d) Acquisition
6. Infirmary
   - (a) Surgery
   - (b) Disease
   - (c) Patient
   - (d) Receptionist
7. Sustenance
   - (a) Nourishment
   - (b) Water
   - (c) Grains
   - (d) Menu
8. Provisions
   - (a) Groceries
   - (b) Supplies
   - (c) Gear
   - (d) Caterers
9. School
   - (a) Student
   - (b) Report card
   - (c) Test
   - (d) Learning
10. Language
    - (a) Tongue
    - (b) Slang
    - (c) Writing
    - (d) Words
11. Book
    - (a) Fiction
    - (b) Pages
    - (c) Pictures
    - (d) Learning
12. Desert
    - (a) Cactus
    - (b) Arid
    - (c) Oasis
    - (d) Flat
13. Lightning
    - (a) Electricity
    - (b) Thunder
    - (c) Brightness
    - (d) Rain
14. Swimming
    - (a) Pool
    - (b) Bathing suit
    - (c) Water
    - (d) Life jacket
15. Shoe
    - (a) Sole
    - (b) Leather
    - (c) Laces
    - (d) Walking
16. Ovation
    - (a) Outburst
    - (b) Bravo
    - (c) Applause
    - (d) Encore
17. Bonus
    - (a) Reward
    - (b) Raise
    - (c) Cash
    - (d) Employer
18. Cage
    - (a) Enclosure
    - (b) Prisoner
    - (c) Animal
    - (d) Zoo
19. Wedding
    - (a) Love
    - (b) Church
    - (c) Ring
    - (d) Marriage
20. Faculty
    - (a) Buildings
    - (b) Textbooks
    - (c) Teachers
    - (d) Meetings
21. Recipe
    - (a) Desserts
    - (b) Directions
    - (c) Cookbook
    - (d) Utensils
22. Autograph
    - (a) Athlete
    - (b) Actor
    - (c) Signature
    - (d) Pen
23. Champion
    - (a) Running
    - (b) Swimming
    - (c) Winning
    - (d) Speaking
24. Saddle
    - (a) Horse
    - (b) Seat
    - (c) Stirrups
    - (d) Horn
25. Dome
    - (a) Rounded
    - (b) Geodesic
    - (c) Governmental
    - (d) Coppery

Essential Element

26. Glacier
    (a) Mountain   (b) Winter
    (c) Prehistory   (d) Ice
27. Directory
    (a) Telephone   (b) Listing
    (c) Computer   (d) Names
28. Contract
    (a) Agreement   (b) Document
    (c) Written   (d) Attorney
29. Hurricane
    (a) Beach   (b) Cyclone
    (c) Damage   (d) Wind
30. Town
    (a) Residents   (b) Skyscrapers
    (c) Parks   (d) Libraries

★★★

Mirror Images

Mirror Image
The image of an object, as seen in a mirror, is called its mirror reflection or mirror image.
In such an image, the right side of the object appears on the left side and vice – versa. A mirror – image is therefore said to be laterally inverted and the phenomenon is called lateral inversion.

Mirror Image of Capital Letters

Letter	Mirror Image	Letter	Mirror Image	Letter	Mirror Image
A	A	J	↲	S	Ƨ
B	ᙠ	K	ꓘ	T	T
C	Ɔ	L	⅃	U	U
D	ᗡ	M	M	V	V
E	Ǝ	N	И	W	W
F	ꟻ	O	O	X	X
G	ꓱ	P	ꟼ	Y	Y
H	H	Q	Ọ	Z	Ƹ
I	I	R	Я	–	–

Remark: The letters which have their mirror images identical to the letter itself are:
A, H, I, M, O, T, U, V, W, X, Y

Examples: Mirror images of certain words are given below:

1. FUN : ᴎUꟻ
2. STOP : ꟼOTƧ
3. ZEBRA : ARBEƸ
4. GOLKONDA : AᗡИOꓘ⅃OG
5. XYLOPHONE : ƎИOHꟼO⅃YX

Mirror Image of Small Letters

Letter	Mirror Image	Letter	Mirror Image	Letter	Mirror Image
a	ɒ	j	ᴊ	s	ꙅ
b	d	k	ʞ	t	ʇ
c	ɔ	l	l	u	u
d	b	m	m	v	v
e	ɘ	n	n	w	w
f	ʇ	o	o	x	x
g	ǫ	p	q	y	ʏ
h	ʜ	q	p	z	ꙅ
i	i	r	ꞅ		

Mirror Images

Examples: Mirror images of certain words are given below:
1. arpit : tiqra
2. blade : ǝbald
3. determine : ǝnimrǝtǝb

Mirror Image of Numbers

Number	Mirror Image	Number	Mirror Image	Number	Mirror Image
1	1	4	ᔭ	7	⅂
2	ς	5	₹	8	8
3	ε	6	ϱ	9	ϱ

Examples: Mirror-images of certain combinations of alphabets and numbers are given below:
1. alpha348mz1 : 1zm84εahqla
2. BMC49JN2317 : ⁊lεςИⱢϱᔭƆMᙠ
3. 15bg82XQh : hQX28gdζl

Multiple Choice Questions

Directions (1 – 16): In each of the following questions, there is combination of alphabet or number followed by four alternatives. Choose the alternative which most clearly resembles the mirror image of the given combination.

1. TERMINATE
    (a) TARMINET (mirror) (b) ETANIMRET (mirror)
    (c) TERMINATE (mirror) (d) ETANIMRET (mirror)
2. 1965INDOPAK
    (a) KAPODNI5691 (mirror) (b) KAPINDO5691 (mirror)
    (c) KAPODNI5691 (mirror) (d) KAPODNI5691 (mirror)
3. NATIONAL
    (a) LANOITAN (mirror) (b) LANOITAN (mirror)
    (c) LANOITAN (mirror) (d) LANOITAN (mirror)
4. UTZFY6KH
    (a) HK6YFZTU (mirror) (b) UTZFY6KH (mirror)
    (c) HK6YFZTU (mirror) (d) HK6YFZTU (mirror)
5. SUPERVISOR
    (a) ROSIVREPUS (mirror) (b) SUPERVISOR (mirror)
    (c) ROSIVREPUS (mirror) (d) SUPERVISOR (mirror)
6. JUDGEMENT
    (a) TNEMEGDUJ (mirror) (b) JUDGEMENT (mirror)
    (c) TNEMEGDUJ (mirror) (d) JUDGEMENT (mirror)
7. ANS43Q12
    (a) ANS43Q12 (mirror) (b) ANS43Q12 (mirror)
    (c) ANS43Q12 (mirror) (d) ANS43Q12 (mirror)
8. BRISK
    (a) BRISK (mirror) (b) BRISK (mirror)
    (c) BRISK (mirror) (d) BRISK (mirror)
9. EFFECTIVE
    (a) EFFECTIVE (mirror) (b) EVITCEFFE
    (c) EVITCEFFE (d) EFFECTIVE (mirror)
10. TARAIN1014A
    (a) TARAIN1014A (mirror) (b) TARAIN1014A (mirror)
    (c) TARAIN1014A (mirror) (d) TARAIN1014A (mirror)
11. MAGAZINE
    (a) MAGAZINE (mirror) (b) MAGAZINE (mirror)
    (c) MAGAZINE (d) MAGAZINE (mirror)
12. BR4AQ16HI
    (a) BR4AQ16HI (mirror) (b) BR4AQ16HI (mirror)
    (c) BR4AQ16HI (mirror) (d) BR4AQ16HI (mirror)
13. DL9CG4728
    (a) DL9CG4728 (mirror) (b) DL9CG4728 (mirror)
    (c) DL9CG4728 (mirror) (d) DL9CG4728 (mirror)
14. IMFORMATIONS
    (a) INFORMATIONS (mirror) (b) INFORMATIONS (mirror)
    (c) INFORMATIONS (mirror) (d) INFORMATIONS (mirror)
15. REASONING
    (a) REASONING (mirror) (b) REASONING (mirror)
    (c) REASONING (mirror) (d) REASONING (mirror)
16. AN54WMG3
    (a) AN54WMG3 (mirror) (b) AN54WMG3 (mirror)
    (c) AN54WMG3 (mirror) (d) AN54WMG3 (mirror)

Directions (17 – 30): In each of the following questions, choose the correct mirror image of the figure (X) from amongst the four alternatives (a), (b), (c) and (d) given along with Fig. (X).

17.
    (X)   (a)   (b)   (c)   (d)

Mirror Images

18.

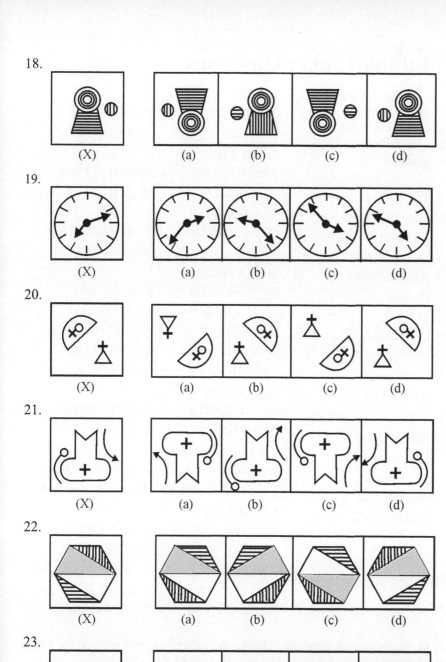

24.

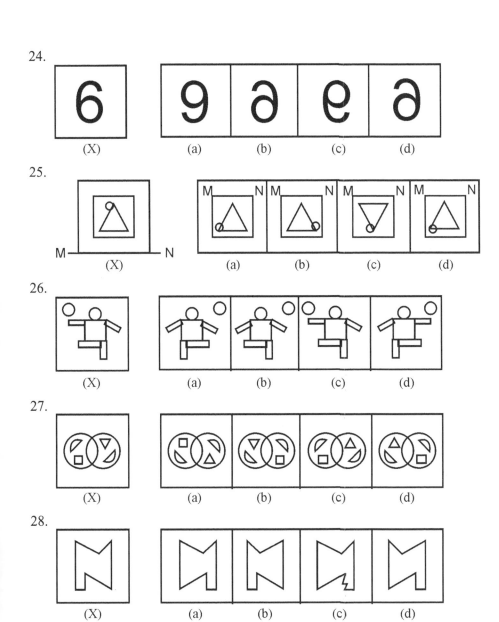

Mirror Images

29.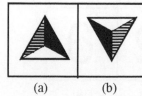

(X)　　　　(a)　　　(b)　　　(c)　　　(d)

30.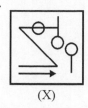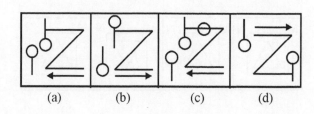

(X)　　　　(a)　　　(b)　　　(c)　　　(d)

Embedded Figure

A figure (A) is said to be embedded in figure (B) if figure (B) contains figure A as its parts. In such problems a figure (A) is given, followed by four complex figures in such a way that figure (A) is embedded in one and only one of them.

In these questions, the candidate has to analyze the figures and select the figure in which figure (X) is embedded.

Example 1:

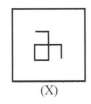 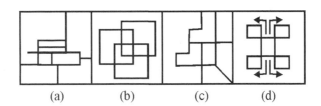

(X)   (a)   (b)   (c)   (d)

Solution: (b)

Multiple Choice Questions

Directions (1 - 30): Analyze the set of figures and choose the correct option that contains figure X.

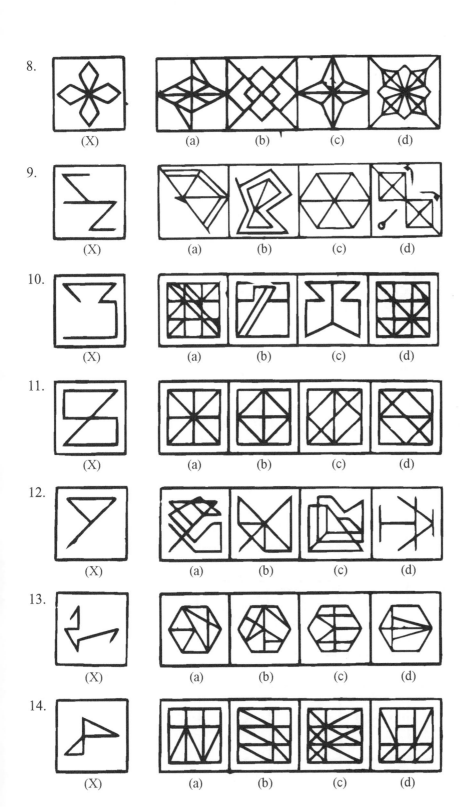

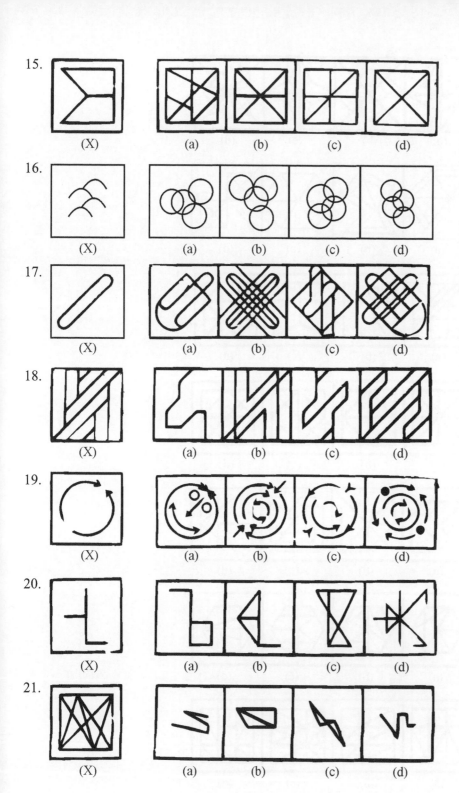

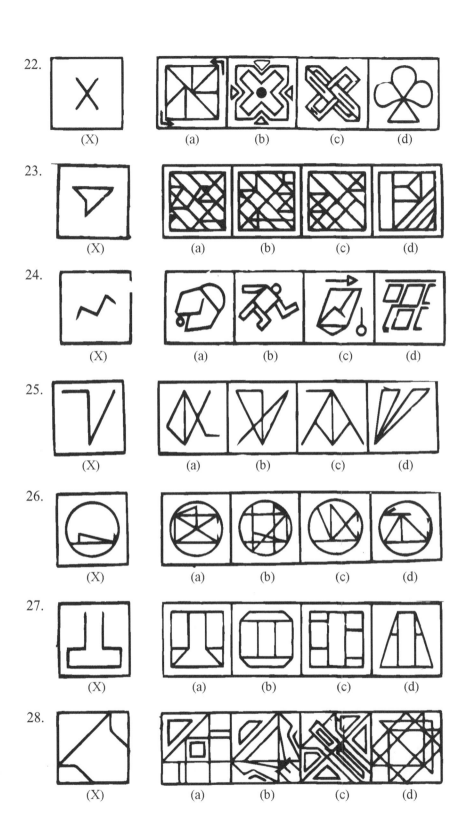

Embedded Figure

29.

30.

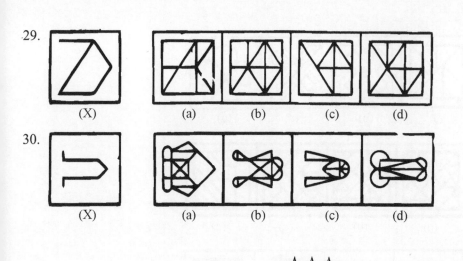

★★★

Figure Puzzles

The questions based on Figure Puzzles are designed to test candidate's skills in sowing mathematical operations and numbers. In mathematical operations, usual mathematical symbols are converted into another form by either interchanging the symbols or using different symbols in place of original symbols in order to make simple calculation tedious. On the other hand, in the questions asked on number puzzles, a few numbers are inserted into a figure which follows a particular rule for the placement of different numbers at different places. Students are asked to select the missing number, following the rule of placement of numbers, from the given options.

Example 1:
Which number will replace the question mark?

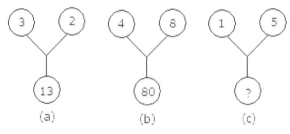

Solution:
From fig. a: $(3)^2 + (2)^2 = 13$
From fig. b: $(4)^2 + (8)^2 = 80$
From fig. c: $? = (1)^2 + (5)^2$
$= 1 + 25$
$= 26$

Hence, the number 26 will replace the question mark.

Example 2:
Which number will replace the question mark?

9	17	16
5	4	?
5	4	8
9	17	8

Solution:
From column I: $(9 \times 5) \div 5 = 9$
From column II: $(17 \times 4) \div 4 = 17$
From column III: $(16 \times ?) \div 8 = 8$
$16 \times ? = 64$
$\Rightarrow \quad ? = 4$

Hence, the number 4 will replace the question mark.

Example 3:
Which number will replace the question mark?

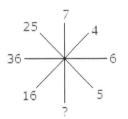

Solution: Here,
$(5)^2 = 25$
$(6)^2 = 36$
$(4)^2 = 16$
$\therefore (7)^2 = 49$

Hence, the number 49 will replace the question mark.

Multiple Choice Questions

Directions (1 – 25): In this type of questions, a figure or a matrix is given in which some numbers are filled according to a rule. A place is left blank or a question mark put. You have to find out a character (a number or a letter) from the given possible answers which may be filled in the blank space or may replace the question mark.

1. Which option will replace the question mark?

   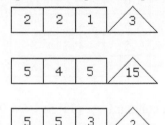

   (a) 11 (b) 19
   (c) 15 (d) 22

2. Which option will replace the question mark?

   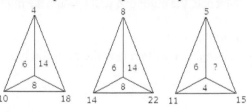

   (a) 8   (b) 14
   (c) 10 (d) 6

3. Which option will replace the question mark?

   (a) 80   (b) 114
   (c) 108 (d) None of these

4. Which option will replace the question mark?

   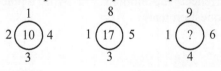

   (a) 18 (b) 20
   (c) 21 (d) 19

5. Which option will replace the question mark?

   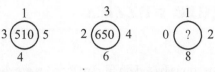

   (a) 660 (b) 670
   (c) 610 (d) 690

6. Which option will replace the question mark?

   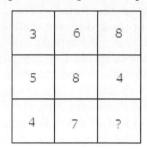

   (a) 6 (b) 7
   (c) 8 (d) 9

7. Which option will replace the question mark?

   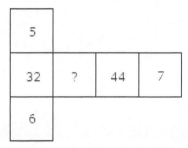

   (a) 33 (b) 38
   (c) 32 (d) 37

8. Which option will replace the question mark?

   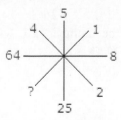

   (a) 1 (b) 2
   (c) 3 (d) 4

9. Which option will replace the question mark?

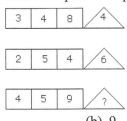

(a) 8 (b) 9
(c) 10 (d) 11

10. Which option will replace the question mark?

13 15   36   54   45   63

28   90   ?

(a) 18 (b) 90
(c) 108 (d) 28

11. Which option will replace the question mark?

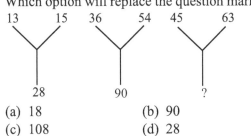

(a) 14 (b) 22
(c) 32 (d) 320

12. Which option will replace the question mark?

4	7	5
33	78	46
8	?	9

(a) 12 (b) 13
(c) 11 (d) 10

13. Which option will replace the question mark?

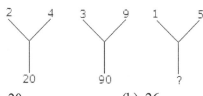

(a) 20 (b) 26
(c) 25 (d) 75

14. Which option will replace the question mark?

3	?	5
5	4	7
4	4	4
60	96	140

(a) 4 (b) 6
(c) 9 (d) 8

15. Which option will replace the question mark?

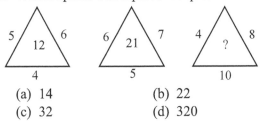

(a) 2 (b) 4
(c) 6 (d) 8

16. Which option will replace the question mark?

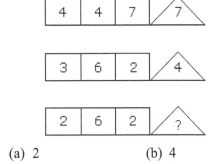

(a) 25 (b) 625
(c) 125 (d) 50

17. Which option will replace the question mark?

4	9	2
3	5	7
8	1	?

(a) 9 (b) 6
(c) 15 (d) 14

Figure Puzzles

18. Which option will replace the question mark?

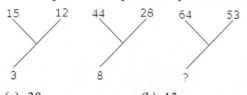

(a) 30 (b) 13
(c) 70 (d) 118

19. Which option will replace the question mark?

(a) 40 (b) 38
(c) 44 (d) 39

20. Which option will replace the question mark?

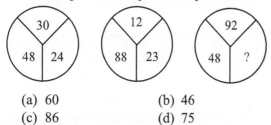

(a) 60 (b) 46
(c) 86 (d) 75

21. Which option will replace the question mark?

(a) 3 (b) 2
(c) 7 (d) 6

22. Which option will replace the question mark?

5	6	5
8	9	7
10	7	?
400	378	315

(a) 9 (b) 5
(c) 7 (d) 3

23. Which option will replace the question mark?

1	$\frac{1}{2}$	$\frac{3}{2}$
2	$\frac{2}{3}$	$\frac{8}{3}$
3	?	$\frac{19}{5}$

(a) 1/2 (b) 2/3
(c) 3/4 (d) 4/5

24. Which option will replace the question mark?

7	4	5
8	7	6
3	3	?
29	19	31

(a) 3 (b) 5
(c) 4 (d) 6

25. Which option will replace the question mark?

4	5	6
2	3	7
1	8	3
21	98	?

(a) 94 (b) 76
(c) 16 (d) 73

SECTION 3
ACHIEVERS' SECTION

Higher Order Thinking Skills (HOTS)

Read the following paragraph and answer the questions that follow.

Shobhit performed the following activities at home. He soaked green gram (moong) seeds in water overnight in a bowl. Next morning, he drained out the excess water and kept the wet seeds in the folds of a muslin cloth. (We should keep the cloth moist all the time by sprinkling the water at regular intervals [once or twice every day]).After another 24 hours, he checked them again. He saw that the seeds began to sprout.

1. Choose the correct option and answer the following questions.
   I. Which part of the plant is used in the previous activity?
   II. What makes the nutrient contents increase in the seeds?

	I	II
(a)	Seeds	Germination
(b)	Grains	Germination
(c)	Seeds	Sprouting
(d)	Seeds	Soaking

2. Take small amount of food sample in a test tube. Put a few drops of iodine on it. Note down the change in colour. Bluish black colour indicates the presence of (a). The food product (b) can be used for this experiment.

   Choose the correct option from 'a' and 'b' and answer the question.

	a	b
(a)	Calcium	Bread
(b)	Starch	Potato
(c)	Proteins	Dals
(d)	Vitamin C	Orange

3. The thin strand of _____ that we see, are made up of still thinner strand called _____.
   (a) Fiber, yarn
   (b) Fiber fabrics
   (c) Fabrics, fiber
   (d) Yarn, fibers

4. Swati, Sanchit, Surbhi and Sakshi were talking about the difference between the weaving and knitting.

   Who among them correctly made the difference between weaving and knitting?
   (a) Swati: The process of making a yarn from fibers is called knitting. And weaving is interlacing of two sets of yarns at right angles to make a fabric
   (b) Sanchit: The process of making a yarn from fibers is called weaving. And knitting is interlacing of two sets of yarns at right angles to make a fabric. Weaving is done on looms
   (c) Surbhi: Weaving is interlacing of two sets of yarns at right angles to make a fabric. In the knitting process, the thread or yarn is used to create a cloth
   (d) Sakshi: Weaving is done for silk only while knitting is done for wool only

5. Somya poured hot water into two cups made of same material as shown in the figures below.

   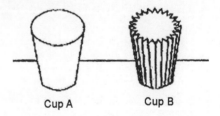

   She then realized that she could hold cup B for a longer time as compared to cup A. Which one of the following best explains this activity?

(a) Cup A is a better conductor of heat than cup B
(b) Cup B is a better conductor of heat than cup A
(c) Somya's hand was in contact with a larger surface area for cup B than A
(d) Somya's hand was in contact with a smaller surface area for cup B than A

6. Salt cultivator Shyam made sea water confined by making a dam. Salt is deposited in his land after a few days. After the purification, he sells the salt in the market.
   Choose the correct option to answer the following questions:
   I. By which process does Shyam produce salt?
   II. By which process does Shyam purify salt?

	I	II
(a)	Evaporation	Filtration
(b)	Vapourisation	Filtration and thickening
(c)	Sublimation	Filtration and distillation
(d)	Filtration	Filtration, thickening and distillation

7. Which of the following statement(s) is true for formation of compost from vegetable waste:
   i. It is a physical change.
   ii. An irreversible change and a slow change
   iii. A chemical and non-desirable change.
   iv. A chemical and desirable change
   (a) i and ii
   (b) ii and iii
   (c) iii and iv
   (d) iv only

8. If bread is baked, the observational changes which support it being a chemical change are:
   i. Change in odour
   ii. Change in texture
   iii. Change in taste
   iv. Bread remains bread
   (a) i only
   (b) i and ii only
   (c) i, ii and iii
   (d) iv only

9. The following flow-chart shows the classification of micro-organisms.

```
                Micro-organisms
               /               \
   ◆ make yoghurt          ◆ cause flu
   ◆ make cheese           ◆ cause stomach ache
   ◆ helps in digestion    ◆ cause infection of wounds
     of food
```

Based on the above information, explain the uses of micro-organisms grouped.
i. Whether they are useful to man
ii. Whether they reproduce from spores
iii. According to the number of cells (single-celled or multi-celled)

(a) i only
(b) ii only
(c) i and ii only
(d) ii and iii only

Higher Order Thinking Skills (HOTS)

10. The diagrams below show the life-cycle of organisms X and Y.

Organism X	Organism Y

On the basis of the diagrams, which of the following statement(s) is/are true?

i. Both the adults of organisms X and Y are able to fly.
ii. The young of organism X does not look like its adult while the young of organism Y looks like its adult.
iii. Organism X has a 4-stage life cycle while organism Y has a 3-stage life cycle.

(a) iii only
(b) i and ii only
(c) ii and iii only
(d) i, ii and iii

11. Match column I with column II and choose the correct option:

Column I	Column II
a. Metre	i. Non-standard unit of length
b. Yard	ii. Unit to measure small distance
c. Millimetre	iii. S.I. Unit of length
d. Hand span	iv. Unit to measure long distances
e. Kilometre	v. Standard unit of length

(a) a-iv, b-v, c-ii, d-i, e-iii
(b) a-iii, b-v, c-ii, d-i, e-iv
(c) a-iv, b-ii, c-v, d-i, e-iii
(d) a-iv, b-i, c-v, d-ii, e-iii

12. Column I defines the kind of activity and column II defines the type of motion. Match column I with column II and choose the correct option.

Column I	Column II
1. Motion of a potter wheel	o. Random motion
2. A falling stone	p. Vibratory motion
3. A spinning top	q. Rectilinear motion
4. Motion of mosquito in flight	r. Circular motion
5. Plucking the string of a guitar	s. Rotatory motion

(a) 1-s, 2-q, 3-r, 4-o, 5-p
(b) 1-r, 2-q, 3-s, 4-o, 5-p
(c) 1-q, 2-p, 3-r, 4-o, 5-s
(d) 1-s, 2-o, 3-r, 4-q, 5-p

13. When a lit torchlight is shone on an object X, a shadow is formed on the screen.

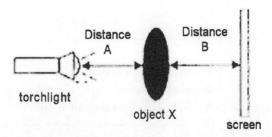

Which of the following options shows how the size of the shadow changes when the distance A and/or distance B changes?

	Size of shadow	Distance A	Distance B
(a)	Bigger	Decreases	Increases
(b)	Smaller	Stays the same	Increases
(c)	Stays the same	Increases	Decreases
(d)	Smaller	Decreases	Stays the same

14. Match column I with column II and choose the correct option:

Column I	Column II
a. Luminous body	i. Moon
b. A transparent object	ii. Brick
c. A translucent object	iii. Star
d. An opaque object	iv. Clear water
e. A non-luminous body	v. Thick window glass pan

    (a) a-v, b-iv, c-iii, d-ii, e-i
    (b) a-iii, b-ii, c-v, d-iv, e-i
    (c) a-i, b-iv, c-v, d-ii, e-iii
    (d) a-iii, b-iv, c-v, d-ii, e-i

15. John prepares an electric circuit. Study the circuit and find out the correct option.

    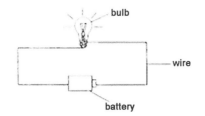

    In the circuit given above, electricity passes through the _____
    (a) Wire only
    (b) Battery and bulb only
    (c) Wire, battery and bulb
    (d) Wire and bulb only

16. The following picture shows two circuits with batteries and light bulbs.

    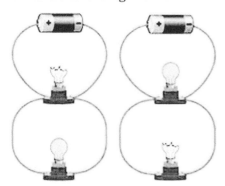

    Choose the option which explains the above figure correctly.
    (a) They are the parallel circuits with electricity flowing along one pathway
    (b) They are the series circuits with electricity flowing along one pathway
    (c) They are the parallel circuits with electricity flowing along more than one pathway
    (d) They are the series circuits with electricity flowing along more than one pathway

17. Shivani wanted to find out whether a nail was magnetized. She put the nail near a magnet, a compass and a paper clip. Then, she recorded the observations as follows:
    i. It could move the compass needle.
    ii. It attracted the paper clip.
    iii. It attracted the magnet.
    iv. It repelled the magnet.

    From which of the observations can she ensure that the nail was magnetized?
    (a) i only
    (b) i and ii only
    (c) ii and ii only
    (d) All of the above

18. Look the following compass carefully

    Now, observe the following arrangements of magnet and compass and find out which of the following shows the direction of compass when they are put near a bar magnet?

    (a)
    (b)
    (c)
    (d)

Higher Order Thinking Skills (HOTS)

19. The diagram below shows the water cycle.

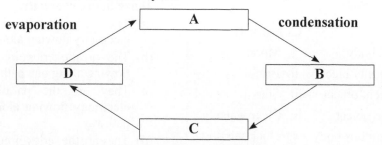

In the diagram above, what do A, B, C and D represent?

	A	B	C	D
(a)	Rain	Clouds	Water vapour	Water
(b)	Water vapour	Clouds	Rain	Water
(c)	Clouds	Rain	Water	Water vapour
(d)	Water vapour	Rain	Clouds	Water

20. Arav performed the following experiment.

He pasted a piece of paper onto the inner bottom surface of a glass. He turned the glass upside down and pushed it into a basin of water. He noticed that the paper remained dry.

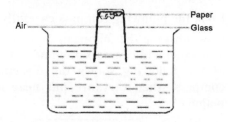

Which property of air does this experiment show? Choose the correct option.
(a) Air has mass
(b) Air occupies space
(c) Air cannot dissolve into water
(d) Air takes the volume of the container

Short Answer Questions

1. **Name the organ in your body which works in periodic motion.**

   Answer: Heart. The rate at which heart beats per minute is 60–100 beats per minute.

2. **Is there any difference between the movement of a child who rides on a merry-go round and that of a child who takes part in a 50 m race?**

   Answer: Yes, the first child is in a circular motion and the other child is in a linear motion.

3. **Can a body perform more than one type of motion at a time?**

   Answer: Yes, a body can perform two types of motion at a time. For example, while riding a bicycle: the motion of the wheels of a bicycle is rotational, whereas the motion of the bicycle is linear. The wheels of a bicycle perform rotational as well as linear motion simultaneously. Similarly, a rolling ball and a drilling machine perform more than one type of motion simultaneously.

4. **When an object is at rest, are any forces acting on it?**

   Answer: Yes. Even when an object is stationary, the force of gravity is pulling it towards the earth's centre. Friction is helping to hold it in place against a surface. At the same time, whatever the object is sitting on opposes the force of gravity and holds the object up. This force is called the normal force. In addition, other forces such as air movement could be acting on the object but are not strong enough to overcome the object's inertia.

5. **What is the meaning of perimeter?**

   Answer: Perimeter is the distance around a polygon.

   The four ends of the rectangle are A, B, C and D.

   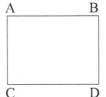

   A to B distance is 6 cm. A to C is 2.5 cm.
   The perimeter of this rectangle would be:
   Length from [A to B + B to C + C to D + D to A] cm = [6 + 2.5 + 6 + 2.5] cm = 17 cm.

   HOTS
   1. There is one big and one small clock. Do the second hands of both the clocks take same amount of time for one complete round?

6. **How can you see the things around yourself?**

   Answer: We can see the things around us when light from a luminous object (like the sun, a torch or an electric light) falls on these objects and then travels towards our eye after being reflected back.

7. **What is light?**

   Answer: Light is the part of the electromagnetic spectrum sensed by our eyes. The electromagnetic spectrum is the set of all waves that have simultaneously varying electric and magnetic fields associated with them and travel through space at 300,000 kilometres per second (a velocity commonly referred to as the speed of light).

8. **What are harmful light waves?**

   Answer: Waves that are a bit shorter and more energetic than violet are called ultraviolet. Prolonged exposure to ultraviolet rays can cause skin cancer and the formation of cataracts on the eyes. Unfortunately, we can't sense the presence of ultraviolet light. We can, however, detect infrared light—as heat.

9. **What is solar eclipse?**

   Answer: A solar eclipse occurs when the moon passes in a direct line between the earth and the sun. The moon's shadow travels over the earth's surface and blocks out the sun's light as seen from the earth.

10. How many types of reflection are there?

Answer: When you shine light from a laser pen or flashlight on the ceiling, everybody in the room can see the light spot on the ceiling. This means that the light rays of the flashlight coming from one direction, are reflected or "scattered" by the ceiling in all directions. This is called a diffuse reflection. **Diffuse reflection** occurs with all objects around us except for shiny objects like mirrors.

When you shine the light from a laser pen or a narrow and parallel beam of light from a flashlight onto a mirror, then you do not see a light spot on the mirror. The light beam is reflected in a particular direction and can only be seen in that direction. This is called specular reflection or mirror reflection.

HOTS
2. In a completely dark room, can you see your face in a mirror? Why?
3. What are X-rays?

11. What are different types of circuit symbols?

Answer:

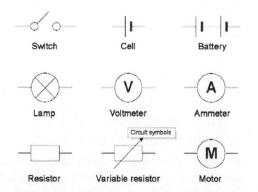

12. What is voltage?

Answer: Voltage is the name for the electric force that causes electrons to flow. It is the measure of the potential difference between two points in the circuit. Voltage may come from a battery or a power plant.

13. What are the major requirements to make a circuit?

Answer: To allow an electric current to flow, a circuit must be complete and to have a power source. All of the wires need to be properly connected and must both start and finish at the power source. Any other objects (e.g., buzzers, bulbs and switches must also be securely connected in order for the circuit to work). The cell or battery is the source of energy in a circuit. This energy can be transformed from electrical energy into other types of energy like sound energy (by a buzzer) or light energy (by a bulb). In a metal wire, the current is made of electrons (these are particles much smaller than atoms) pushed along the wire by the cell or the battery. Anything that stops these electrons from moving along the wire will cause the circuit to stop working.

14. Differentiate between a conductor and an insulator.

Answer: A conductor is any material that will allow an electric current to flow easily. Metals are good conductors: that is why electrical wires are made of copper.

An insulator is any material that does not allow electricity to flow easily. Plastic is a good insulator, as are air and glass. We use insulators to protect us from electrical currents, e.g. plastic around wires.

15. Electric charge originates in the atom. Is it correct? How?

Answer: Atoms are the building blocks of matter. They are composed of neutral particles with no electric charge and protons with a positive charge in the center or nucleus. On the outside of the nucleus, electrons with a negative charge encircle the positive charge of the protons within the nucleus. Opposite charges, positive and negative, are attracted to one another. When many like charges are near one another, they try to get far away from the same charge because charges that are alike tend to repel one another. This flow is the basis of the electric movement.

HOTS
4. How could you find out which metal is the best conductor of electricity?
5. Demonstrate and explain at least three ways you can get a bulb to light up.

16. **What is the difference between magnetism and magnetic field?**

    Answer: The property of magnets to attract certain other material, i.e., magnetic substances like iron, nickel, cobalt etc., is called magnetism, while the region around a magnet where its magnetic effect can be felt is called magnetic field.

17. **What do you understand by the term magnetic lines of force?**

    Answer: The magnetic lines of force are closed continuous curves in a magnetic field along which the North Pole will move if free to do so and its direction is given by the direction in which the free North Pole will point.

18. **Why does a freely suspended magnetic needle point in geographic north-south direction? Name a device which is based on the above phenomenon.**

    Answer: A freely suspended magnetic needle points in a geographic north-south direction because earth behaves like a giant magnet with its north pole near the geographic south and its south pole near geographic north. So, the North Pole of a suspended magnet turns towards geographic North Pole and South Pole of the magnet turns towards geographic South Pole.

19. **How can you increase the strength of a magnetic field around a conductor carrying current?**

    Answer: We can increase the strength of magnetic field around a conductor carrying current by increasing the strength of current; doing so will increases the number of magnetic lines of force around the conductor. This, in turn, increases the magnetic strength of the conductor.

20. **Define attractive and directive property of a magnet.**

    Answer: Attractive property: A magnet has the property to attract some substances like iron, cobalt and nickel when brought near it. This property of magnet is called its attractive property.

    Directive property: If we suspend a magnet freely in air then it always aligns itself in the geographic north-south direction. This is called the directive property of a magnet.

21. **Name the two methods of making magnets.**

    Answer: The two methods of making magnets are:
    A. Single-touch method
    B. Electrical method

    HOTS
    6. Why does the earth behave like a huge magnet?

22. **What is dry ice?**

    Answer: "Dry ice" refers to frozen carbon dioxide (CO_2). It's dry in the sense that it sublimates directly from a solid to a gas, without going through a liquid or "wet" phase.

23. **If you lived high in the mountains, and you wanted to make a hard-boiled egg, you would need to boil the egg longer than you would boil it at sea level. Why?**

    Answer: At sea level the boiling temperature of water is 212°F or 100°C. At higher altitudes, because there is less air pressure, water will boil at a lower temperature, depending on the elevation. As a general rule, the temperature decreases by 1 (one) degree for every 540 feet of altitude (0.56 degrees C for every 165 meters). So the egg may be boiling, but the water is cooler than at sea level, so it takes longer to cook it as much.

24. **What are wind farms?**

    Answer: A wind turbine changes the energy from moving air into electricity. When there are many wind turbines together, they are called a "wind farm". They are built in windy areas.

25. **Why does a water bottle kept in the freezer crack upon freezing?**

    Answer: It happens because the frozen water molecules arrange themselves into a crystal lattice form that has more space between molecules compared to liquid water molecules. Hence, the volume of the water actually expands as it changes from a liquid to a solid. This is a very unusual property of water as most substances decrease in volume when they become a solid.

Short Answer Questions

26. **What is groundwater recharge?**

    Answer: The groundwater recharge is the process through which water infiltrates from the surface down into the ground. The water table is the depth at which the soil and the rocks are fully saturated with water. The recharge maintains the supply of fresh water that flows through the underground water system to wells, streams, springs, and wetlands.

    > **HOTS**
    > 7. What is acid rain?
    > 8. At a molecular level, how does water freeze differently than other substances?

27. **Why do you cook food in utensils made of aluminium, copper or steel?**

    Answer: Aluminum, copper and steel are metals. Metals are good conductor of heat. Hence utensils made up of metals are used for cooking.

28. **Why does kerosene oil form a separate layer in water?**

    Answer: Oil is not soluble in water. They are immiscible liquids. Hence, kerosene oil makes a separate layer on water.

29. **When a substance is added to water, it disappears. What does it mean?**

    Answer: This means that the substance which is added in water is soluble in it and hence it gets dissolved in the water.

30. **What are the bases on which the materials can be grouped?**

    Answer: Materials can be grouped on the basis of various functions and properties:
    (i) Appearance
    (ii) Hardness
    (iii) Solubility
    (iv) Density (floating and sinking)
    (v) Transparency (transparent, translucent, opaque)

31. **How does filtration help in separating a mixture?**

    Answer: During filtration, the large particles of a substance cannot pass through the very tiny holes in the filter paper. These large particles are thus trapped on the filter paper, effectively separating the mixture.

    > **HOTS**
    > 9. Is it possible to separate sugar mixed with wheat flour? If yes, how will you do it?

32. **When water is mixed with plaster of Paris and allowed to dry, it sets into a hard mass. State whether the change is reversible or irreversible. Justify your answer.**

    Answer: The above change is an example of an irreversible change. This is because when water is added to the plaster of Paris, it sets as a hard mass and cannot be converted back into the original form.

33. **You must have seen that construction workers heat a black material called coal tar for repairing a road. State whether the change which has occurred in coal tar on being heated is reversible or irreversible.**

    Answer: When coal tar is heated, it melts to form a thick dark liquid. The melting of coal tar is a reversible change as it solidifies again on cooling.

34. **Why is shaping of wet clay into clay pot a reversible change whereas baking a clay pot an irreversible change?**

    Answer: The shaping of wet clay into a clay pot is a reversible change as wet clay can be converted back into the original clay. Whereas a baked clay pot cannot be changed back into the original form (baking hardens the clay pot due to heat effect), therefore it is an irreversible change.

35. **Give an example of a physical change that you observe in your everyday life.**

    Answer: Some common physical changes are: melting, freezing, boiling, condensation, dissolving, bending, evaporation, heating or cooling.

36. **Explain why breaking a piece of chalk is an example of a physical change and not a chemical change.**

    Answer: Breaking a piece of chalk doesn't change the actual molecules in the chalk, so it is not a chemical change. It merely changes

> **HOTS**
> 10. Can gases be a product of a chemical reaction? What is a chemical formula?

37. **What is photo respiration?**

    Answer: Photo respiration is the light-dependent release of CO_2 from photosynthetic organisms and is caused by O_2 substituting for CO_2 in the first step of photosynthetic CO_2 fixation.

38. **What do you mean by species?**

    Answer: Each kind of organisms (dog, cat, pig, goat) has many individuals which are similar to each other. These individuals may differ slightly but their form, habitat and behaviour are almost the same. Such a group of similar organisms is known as species.

39. **How do living organisms use energy and how is it a complex chemistry?**

    Answer: A flower has a complicated and beautiful structure. So does a crystal. But if you look closely at the crystal, you see no change. The flower, on the other hand, is transporting water through its petals, producing pigment molecules, breaking down sugar for energy, and undergoing a large number of other chemical reactions that are needed for living organisms to stay alive. We call the sum of the chemical reactions in a cell its metabolism. As another example, humans, eat to fuel their cells. The food they consume provides cells with chemical energy.

40. **Is a living thing the same as something that is alive?**

    Answer: No these terms are different. To say that something is alive means that it is currently living and it generally refers to a whole organism. Living thing makes up a broader category, that includes things that once were alive (but are now dead) as well as parts of things that are or once were alive.

41. **Which abiotic factor is required by plant which is not essentially required by animals?**

    Answer: Light. Plants need light for making food through the process of photosynthesis.

    > **HOTS**
    > 11. Do living things only consist of human beings, plants, animals, birds and fish?

42. **It is observed that constipation is common among people in the western countries than us. True or false?**

    Answer: It is true because they eat more processed food which does not contain roughage, and lack of roughage causes constipation because roughage is necessary for proper functioning of the digestive system.

43. **A food web is a diagram of 'who eats whom' for the organisms in a given area. Is this statement true?**

    Answer: Yes the statement is true because animals obtain the energy they need to live from food. Organisms are connected to other organisms through food webs. So, a food web is a diagram of 'who eats whom' for the organisms in a given area.

44. **Ananya's diet for whole day is only 2 glasses of milk and four rusks. Will she remains healthy?**

    Answer: No, she will not remain healthy, and if she continues to have same diet, she may be suffer from various deficiency diseases as milk and rusk can provide her little energy and proteins, but not micronutrients which are equally important to have a good health.

45. **Humans eat both plants and animals. Which teeth in humans are suitable for tearing flesh?**

    Answer: Humans have four canines, these are their sharpest teeth and are used for ripping and tearing food apart. Primary canines generally appear between 16 and 20 months of age, with the upper canines coming in just ahead of the lower canines. In permanent teeth, the order is reversed. Lower canines erupt around age 9 with the uppers arriving between 11 and 12 years of age.

Short Answer Questions

46. **In what way is a scavenger useful to the environment?**

   Answer: Scavengers are those organisms that feed on dead and decaying organic matter. They keep our environment clean from dead organic matter. In this way, they prevent the accumulation of waste in the environment and the spread of diseases caused due to such accumulation.

   HOTS
   12. Carnivores and parasites both depend on other animals for food. Then, How are they different from each other?
   13. A person who does more sedentary work should consume less energy. True or false? Why?

47. **What is linen?**

   Answer: Linen is a plant fibre made from the stalk of flax plants. It is one of the earliest fibres to be made into string and cloth and is the strongest of the vegetable fibres, with two to three times the strength of cotton.

48. **What is made up of what: a yarn is made up of fibre or a fibre is made up of yarn?**

   Answer: A yarn is a continuous strand made up of a number of fibres which are twisted together. Fibres are thin and small and cannot be made into a fabric directly. Hence, the first statement is true.

49. **Nylon ropes are used by mountaineers. Yes/ No and why?**

   Answer: Yes, nylon ropes are used in mountaineering. Consider a mountain climber who falls and is brought to a stop by a safety rope. Initially the falling climber has some momentum (mass x velocity). After the rope brings the climber to a stop, the climber's momentum is zero. As nylon ropes stretch, they exert a force over a greater time so that force will be smaller than with a hemp rope which exerts a force over a shorter time. The elasticity of nylon helps mountaineer to climb well and hence is used.

50. **What is coir?**

   Answer: Coir is the fibrous husk of the coconut shell. Being tough and naturally resistant to seawater, the coir protects the fruit enough to survive months of floating on ocean currents to be washed up on a sandy shore where it may sprout and grow into a tree. These characteristics make coir quite useful in making floor and outdoor mats, aquarium filters, cordage and rope, and garden mulch.

51. **Silk shirts get dirty easily. Yes/No and Why?**

   Answer: No; Silk is a delicate fabric and should be handled with care. However, it is fairly easy to clean. It has a naturally tendency to release dirt quickly and does not always require dry cleaning to keep its quality.

   HOTS
   14. Why does wool keep us warm?
   15. Silk has come under fire from animal rights activities. Why?

Model Test Paper - 1

In the following question, you are given a figure (X) followed by four alternative figures (1), (2), (3) and (4) such that figure (X) is embedded in one of them. Trace out the alternative figure which contains fig. (X) as its part.

1. Find out the alternative figure which contains figure (X) as its part.

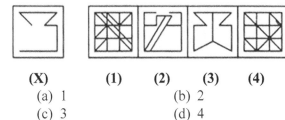

   (X)   (1)   (2)   (3)   (4)

   (a) 1   (b) 2
   (c) 3   (d) 4

2. Solve the given question based on Number Series.

   3 2 2 5 5 5 7 8 8 9 11 11 ?

   (a) 12   (b) 11
   (c) 9   (d) 14
   (e) 16

3. A man pointing to a photograph says, "The lady in the photograph is my nephew's maternal grandmother." How is the lady in the photograph related to the man's sister who has no other sister?
   (a) Mother   (b) Cousin
   (c) Mother–in–law (d) Sister–in–law

4. Siva Reddy walked 2 km west of his house and then turned south covering 4 km. Finally, he moved 3 km towards east and then again 1 km west. How far is he from his initial position?
   (a) 10 km   (b) 9 km
   (c) 2 km   (d) 4 km

5. Anil wants to go the university. He starts from his house which is in the East and comes to a crossing. The road to his left ends in a theatre, straight ahead is the hospital. In which direction is the University?
   (a) East   (b) North
   (c) South   (d) West

6. Choose the alternative that correctly represents the water image of the word N U C L E A R.

   (1) ᴙᴧⱻꞀᑌИ   (2) ᴎUCꞀEAᴙ
   (3) ᴎUCꞀEAᴙ   (4) ᴎUCꞀEAᴙ

   (a) 1   (b) 2
   (c) 3   (d) 4
   (e) None of these

7. Choose the alternative that correctly represents the water image of the word G R 9 8 A P 7 6 E S

   (1) GR68Ab19E2 (2) GR98Ap19E2
   (3) GR98Ab19E2 (4) GR98Ab19E2

   (a) 1   (b) 2
   (c) 3   (d) 4
   (e) None of these

8. Choose the alternative which is closely resembles the mirror image of the given combination.

   TARAIN1014A
   (1) A4101NIARAT (2) A1014NIARAT
   (3) A101ATARAIN (4) A4101NIARAT

   (a) 1   (b) 2
   (c) 3   (d) 4

9. In the following question find out the alternative which will replace the question mark.

   1. CUP : LIP :: BIRD : ?
   (a) BUSH   (b) GRASS
   (c) FOREST   (d) BEAK

10. Six friends are sitting in a circle and are facing the centre of the circle. Deepa is between Prakash and Pankaj. Priti is between Mukesh and Lalit. Prakash and Mukesh are opposite to each other.

    Who is sitting right to Prakash ?
    (a) Mukesh   (b) Deepa
    (c) Pankaj   (d) Lalit

11. A young plant is seen to grow from the underground stem as shown below.

    The young plant gets its food from _____.
    (a) Its roots
    (b) Its seeds
    (c) The buds of the underground stem
    (d) The food stored in the underground stem

12. Select the correct pair:
    (a) Vitamin B1 - Beriberi
    (b) Vitamin A - Rickets
    (c) Vitamin C - Goiter
    (d) Vitamin D - Anaemia

13. The following image shows:

    (a) Weaving
    (b) Looming
    (c) Spinning
    (d) Stitching

14. Identify the fiber:

    (a) Cotton
    (b) Linen
    (c) Jute
    (d) Synthetic

15. Because of the crimp, _____ fabrics have greater bulk than other textiles and retain air, which causes the product to retain heat.
    (a) Cotton
    (b) Silk
    (c) Wool
    (d) Synthetic

16. Study the picture below and answer the questions that follow.

    Which statement describes the picture correctly?
    (a) The process of the settling down of heavier, insoluble components in a mixture is called Sedimentation
    (b) The process of separation of soluble solids from their solutions using a filter is called filtration
    (c) Evaporation of solids and leaving behind the solids
    (d) A and C both

17. The classification chart below shows the properties of four different materials. Which materials is most suitable for making raincoat?

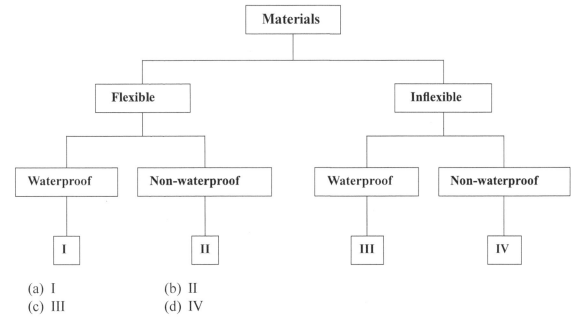

(a) I
(b) II
(c) III
(d) IV

18. The chart below shows how some objects are grouped into two groups, X and Y.

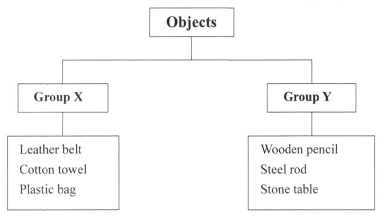

Which of the following headings best describe the two groups?

	Group X	Group Y
(a)	Hard	Soft
(b)	Fragile	Non-fragile
(c)	Flexible	Non-fragile
(d)	Made from natural materials	Made from man-made materials

Model Test Paper - 1

19. Choose the substance that shows sublimation:
    (a) Water (b) Kerosene
    (c) Naphthalene (d) Toluene
20. Cooking of rice is an example of _____.
    (a) Reversible change
    (b) Irreversible change
    (c) Irreversible and endothermic change
    (d) Reversible and endothermic change
21. Iron rusts because _____.
    (a) Iron reacts with the moisture present in the atmosphere
    (b) It is a weak material
    (c) Iron is an unstable material
    (d) It is an intrinsic property of iron
22. The reactions which are accompanied by production of heat are called _____.
    (a) Endothermic reactions
    (b) Exothermic reactions
    (c) Exothermic and reversible reactions
    (d) A and C both
23. Phyllotaxy is the best arrangement of leaves on the stem. Identify the three types of phyllotaxy shown in the figure given below:

X   Y   Z

    (a) X: Alternate, Y: Spiral, Z: Opposite
    (b) X: Whorled, Y: Spiral, Z: Alternate
    (c) X: Alternate, Y: Opposite, Z: Spiral
    (d) X: Opposite, Y: Spiral, Z: Alternate
24. Read the features of a plant as given below.
    1. Roots are much shorter in size.
    2. Stems are generally long and narrow.
    3. Stems possess air spaces.
    4. They have waxy upper surface.
    To which of these habitats does this plant belong?
    (a) Desert
    (b) Polar region
    (c) Tropical region
    (d) Aqvatic
25. The organisms which are smaller than bacteria are:
    (a) Fungus (b) Viruses
    (c) Frogs (d) Vallisnaria
26. One centimeter on a scale is divided into 20 equal divisions. The least count of this scales is:
    (a) 0.1 mm (b) 20 cm
    (c) 0.5 mm (d) 1 mm
27. The motion of the arm of a soldier marching along the road is:
    (a) Oscillatory (b) Non periodic
    (c) Rotatory (d) Circular
28. Which of the following statements should be followed while using a symbol for a unit of a physical quantity?
    (a) They can be written in full
    (b) The symbol named after scientist should have capital letter
    (c) They take plural forms
    (d) They should always be written in lowercase
29. A solid, transparent sphere has a small, opaque center. When observed from outside, the apparent position of the dot will be:
    (a) Farther away from the eye than its actual position
    (b) Closer to the eye than its actual position
    (c) The same as its actual position
    (d) None of these
30. At 8 a.m., the shadow of Ananya's flat was as shown below.

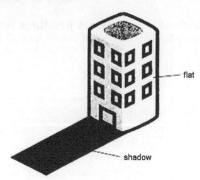

Which one of the following diagrams shows the shadow of her flat at 6.30 p.m.?

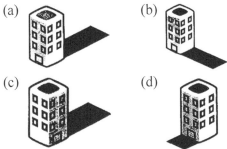

(a)   (b)   (c)   (d)

31. A piece of clear glass and an object were placed between a lighted torch and a screen as shown in the diagram below.

A shadow was formed on the screen.

How could the shadow on the screen be enlarged?
(a) By removing the clear glass
(b) By moving the object nearer to the screen
(c) By moving the object nearer to the clear glass
(d) By moving the torch further away from the clear glass

32. Which of the following parts of the bulb are made of conductors of electricity?

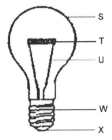

(a) W and X only
(b) S, T and U only
(c) T, W and X only
(d) T, U, W and X only

33. Study the circuit below.

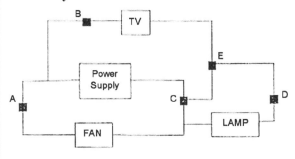

The switches at points A, B, C, D and E were closed and all 3 electrical appliances were working.

Opening the switch at point _____ would allow both the TV and the lamp to work.
(a) A   (b) B
(c) C   (d) E

34. What is the function of the components shown below?

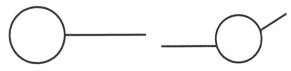

(a) It controls the flow of current in a circuit
(b) It measures the current in a circuit
(c) It is used to connect the bulb to the other components in the circuit
(d) It provides the energy for the bulb to glow

35. On which property of magnet does the design of the mariner's compass is based?
(a) A magnet attracts iron
(b) A magnet aligns itself east-west
(c) A magnet can be obtained from natural source
(d) A magnet rests in a north-south direction, always

Model Test Paper - 1

36. The diagram below shows a compass

Two compasses are placed near a bar magnet. Which one of the following diagrams shows the correct positions of the needles?

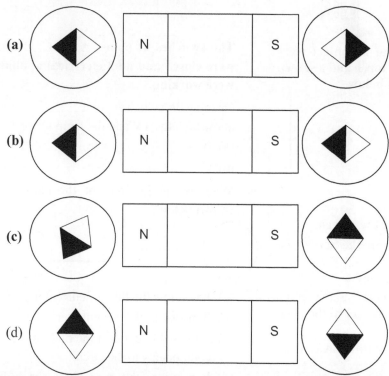

37. This set of elements produce strong magnets?
    (a) Steel and aluminum only
    (b) Steel and nickle only
    (c) Steel and pure iron only
    (d) Pure iron, steel and an alloy of Al, Co, Ni and Fe

38. Select the option the letters of which, on reshuffling, will give the term given to describe water seepage into the ground.
    (a) Ntciepirtaipo
    (b) Atooniaervp
    (c) Aitfinlronit
    (d) Tspratniaoinr

39. Which of the following actions will help in reducing pollution?
    (i) Restricting smoking in public areas
    (ii) Treatment of sewage to remove human waste
    (iii) Using unleaded petrol in cars
    (iv) Spraying pesticides on paints to kill pests
    (a) (i), (ii) and (iv) (b) (i), (ii) and (iii)
    (c) (i) and (ii)   (d) (i) and (iv)

40. Which of the following is not a form of precipitation?
    (a) Snow   (b) Rain
    (c) Hailstone   (d) None of them

41. Identify the experiment shown below and answer the question below.

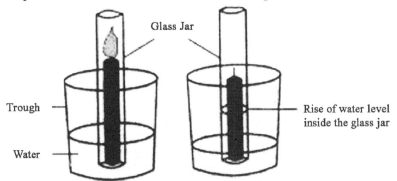

   Why is the candle in second figure not burning?
   (a) This happens because the supply of air for the burning process stopped due to a glass jar and as a result of that, the burning of a candle is also stopped.
   (b) Rising water has put off the candle.
   (c) There is excess of oxygen in the test tube because of which the candle does not burn.
   (d) Water has dissolved carbon dioxide which puts off the candle.

42. When a lump of cotton wool is dipped in water, why does it shrink?
   (a) Cotton is soft, so it shrinks.
   (b) Cotton can easily absorb water.
   (c) Cotton has a tendency to hold water.
   (d) Pores present in the cotton wool have air and water enters into the air space when dipped in water.

43. Ginger is used as a spice, and is an excellent remedy for digestive problems. When we eat ginger, we are actually eating a
   (a) Stem   (b) Root
   (c) Tuber   (d) leaf

44. Why is metal rim heated before fixing on to wooden cart wheel?
   (a) The metal is heated so that it contracts after heating
   (b) The metal rim gets its shine after heating.
   (c) The metal rim will stick better to the wooden cart if it is heated before fixing.
   (d) Metals have a property of expanding on heating, this makes the fixing on the wooden cart easy.

45 Direction: See the following flowchart which gives the technique a student adopted to separate the constituents of a mixture.

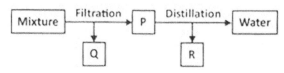

   What could the mixture be?
   (a) Water + sand + glass
   (b) Oxygen + hydrogen + salt
   (c) Stones + rice + water
   (d) Chalk powder + sugar + water

Model Test Paper - 1

46. The graph given below shows the change in the population of frogs near a pond.

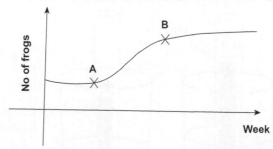

Observe the graph carefully and choose the correct statement(s).

Statements are based on the possible events which cause the change in the population of frogs from point A to B?

Sanchit: A significant decrease in the water level of the pond

Shivani: A significant decrease in the number of fish in the pond

Rahul: A significant increase in the number of dragonflies nymphs in the pond

Rohit: A significant decrease in the number of disease-causing organisms that kill the the frogs.

(a) Sanchit and Rahul
(b) Shivani and Rahul
(c) Rohit and Rahul
(d) Sanchit, Rahul and Rohit

47. The figure below shows a glass tank completely filled with a block of ice. After one hour, it was noticed that the block of ice had melted as shown in the diagram below.

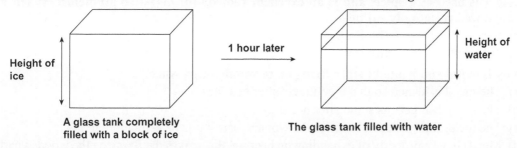

Which one of the following best explains the above observation?
(a) The melted ice has a smaller mass than the ice cube
(b) The melted ice has a smaller volume than the ice cube
(c) The melted ice can be compressed to fit the volume of the glass
(d) The melted ice has definite shape and takes the shape of the glass

48. The diagram below shows how animals can be classified.

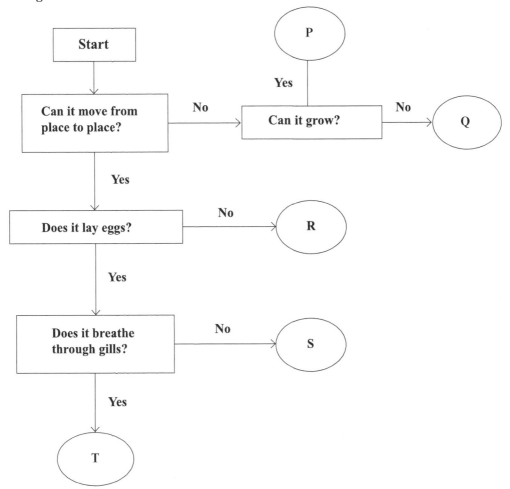

Which of the following statements can you infer from the flow chart above?
(i) P could be a mushroom.
(ii) R can be a mammal.
(iii) P and S require air to survive.
(iv) T have different method of reproduction.
(a) (i) only
(b) (i) and (iv) only
(c) (ii) and (iii) only
(d) (ii), (iii) and (iv) only

49. Smith classified some objects into two groups as shown in the chart below.

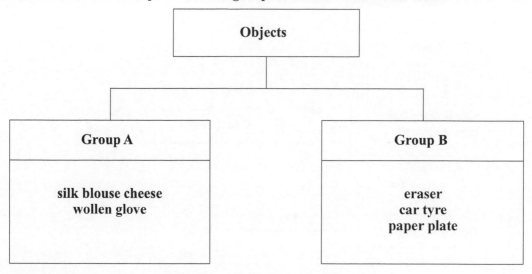

Which of the following is the correct heading for the two groups?

	Group A	Group B
(a)	Man-made materials	Natural materials
(b)	Biodegradable	Non-biodegradable
(c)	Not waterproof	Waterproof
(d)	Materials from animals	Materials from plants

50. The following diagram shows a light bulb.

Which of the following statements about the part labelled Z is/are true?
i. It determines the brightness of the bulb.
ii. It must be made of a material of a high melting point.
iii. It melts when there is too much electrical current passing through it.
iv. It gives off light energy only when an electric current passes through it.
(a) iv only
(b) i, ii and iii
(c) ii, iii and iv
(d) All of the above

Model Test Paper - 2

1. Find out the alternative figure which contains figure (X) as its part.

   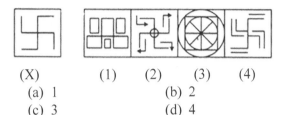

   (X)   (1)   (2)   (3)   (4)
   (a) 1   (b) 2
   (c) 3   (d) 4

2. Solve the given question based on the number series 17 16 14 12 11 8 8 ?
   (a) 4   (b) 7
   (c) 3   (d) 2
   (e) None of these

3. A woman introduces a man as the son of the brother of her mother. How is the man related to the woman?
   (a) Son   (b) Nephew
   (c) Grandson   (d) Uncle

4. Rajesh's school bus is facing North when reaches his school. After starting from Rajesh's house, it turning twice and then left before reaching the school. What direction the bus facing when it left the bus stop in front of Rajesh's house?
   (a) East   (b) North
   (c) South   (d) West

5. I am facing South. I turn right and walk 20 m .Then I turn right again and walk 10 m .Then I turn left and walk 10 m and then turning right walk 20 m.Then,I turn right again and walks 60 m. In which direction am I from the starting point?
   (a) North-East   (b) North-West
   (c) North   (d) West

6. Choose the option that represents the correct water image of b r i d g e

   (1) pɹiqǝ   (2) pliqǝ
   (3) pɹiqǝ   (4) plipǝ

   (a) 1   (b) 2
   (c) 3   (d) 4
   (e) None of these

7. Choose the alternative which closely resembles the mirror image of the given combination.

   ANS43Q12
   (1) ANƧ4ƐO1S   (2) SƖOE4ƧИA
   (3) ƧИAƐ4OS1   (4) 12O4ƐAИƧ

   (a) 1   (b) 2
   (c) 3   (d) 4

8. Choose the alternative which closely resembles the mirror image of the given combination.

   1965INDOPAK
   (1) ƘAPODИI5691   (2) S691ODИIKAP
   (3) ƘAPODИI5691   (4) 1965INDOPAK

   (a) 1   (b) 2
   (c) 3   (d) 4

9. See the analogy and find out the correct option.
   Flow : River :: Stagnant : ?
   (a) Rain   (b) Stream
   (c) Pool   (d) Canal

10. Six friends are sitting in a circle and are facing the centre of the circle. Deepa is between Prakash and Pankaj. Priti is between Mukesh and Lalit. Prakash and Mukesh are opposite to each other.

    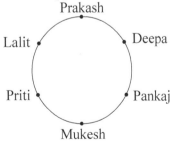

    Who is just right to Pankaj?
    (a) Deepa   (b) Lalit
    (c) Prakash   (d) Priti

11. Which of the following statement(s) about saliva is/are true?
    (a) Saliva helps to digest food
    (b) Saliva causes food to be rolled into a ball
    (c) Saliva moistens the food to make swallowing easier
    (d) Both (a) and (c)

12. Refer the given flowchart and select the correct option.

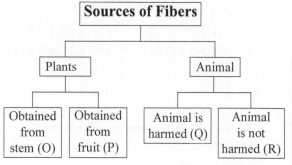

    (a) O: Cotton, P: Flax, Q: Silk, R: Wool
    (b) O: Cotton, P: Flax, Q: Wool, R: Silk
    (c) O: Flax, P: Cotton, Q: Silk, R: Wool
    (d) O: Cotton, P: Silk, Q: Flax, R: Wool

13. Which of these is a correct statement?
    (a) Cotton is also called *Gossypium hirsutum*
    (b) The process of making yarn from raw fibrous material is called spinning
    (c) Jute is a rainy season crop, which grows best in warm, humid climate
    (d) All of them

14. Identify X and Y in the given Venn diagram and select the correct option.

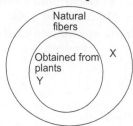

    (a) X is nylon   (b) Y is silk
    (c) X is rubber   (d) Y is cotton

15. Decantation process is used to separate:
    (a) Two immiscible liquids
    (b) Two miscible liquids
    (c) Two metals in an alloy
    (d) Solid-solid mixture

16. Crude oil is purified using fractional distillation process. This method is based on:
    (a) the difference of the volumes of the components
    (b) the difference of the boiling points of the components
    (c) the difference of the masses of the components
    (d) the difference in the solubility of the components

17. Winnowing is used only for:
    (a) Homogeneous solid-liquid mixture
    (b) Heterogeneous solid-solid mixture
    (c) Homogeneous solid-solid mixture
    (d) Heterogeneous solid-liquid mixture

18. When the temperature of the solid is increased, the _____ energy of the particles increases.
    (a) Heat   (b) Potential
    (c) Kinetic   (d) Chemical

19. Study this Venn diagram.

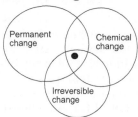

    The point at the center represents:
    (a) Rusting   (b) Condensation
    (c) Melting of ice   (d) Boiling of water

20. What is one common property among the following phenomena?
    1. the rotation of blades of a fan
    2. the blinking of traffic lights
    3. the swinging of a pendulum
    (a) All are periodic changes
    (b) All are irreversible and desirable changes
    (c) All are chemical changes
    (d) All are undesirable changes

21. Shiva covered one of the leaves of his green plant shown below with a piece of black pastel paper. He then kept the plant in a dark place for 2 days.

After 2 days of darkness, he kept the plant in a bright sunny place for a day. At the end of the day, Shiva conducted an iodine test on the leaf.

Which one of the diagrams below shows the result of the test?

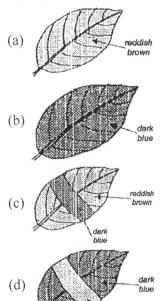

(a) reddish brown

(b) dark blue

(c) reddish brown / dark blue

(d) dark blue / reddish brown

22. Mary made the following statements about photosynthesis.

Which of the statements is/are INCORRECT?

(a) Oxygen production takes place during photosynthesis
(b) Only heat energy is needed for plants to carry out photosynthesis
(c) Photosynthesis can only take place in cells that contain chloroplasts
(d) During respiration, the excess food made during photosynthesis is used up for energy

23. Plants lose gases through _____.

(a) Flowers (b) Seeds
(c) Small porous roots (d) Leaves

24. The smallest time measured by a wrist watch accurately is:
(a) 60 seconds (b) 1 second
(c) 1 hour (d) 1 millisecond

25. When a drill bores a hole in a piece of wood, it demonstrates:
(a) Translatory motion
(b) Rotatory motion
(c) Translatory and rotatory motion
(d) Curvilinear motion

26. Two identical metal balls A and B moving in opposite directions hit each other at points X as shown in the figure. Changes are most likely to appear in their:
(a) Shapes
(b) Volumes
(c) Speed
(d) Speed and direction

27. Adam shone a beam of light from a torch at two objects, X and Y, as shown in the diagram below.

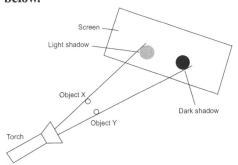

The shadow formed by object X was much lighter than the one formed by object Y.

Which of the following materials are X and Y likely to be made of?

	Object X	Object Y
(a)	Iron	Glass
(b)	Mirror	Paper
(c)	Frosted glass	Copper
(d)	Styrofoam	Tracing paper

Model Test Paper - 2

28. A plane mirror reflects a pencil of light to form a real image. Then the pencil of light incident on the mirror is _____.
    (a) Divergent   (b) Convergent
    (c) Parallel   (d) None of them

29. Kara performed an experiment. She positioned a tennis ball between a screen and a torch as shown below.

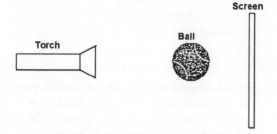

    She wrote down the steps she followed:
    1. Switch on the torch.
    2. Measure the height of the shadow of the tennis ball formed on the screen.
    3. Move the tennis ball 5 cm closer to the torch.
    4. Measure the height of the shadow again.
    5. Repeat steps (3) and (4) twice, moving the tennis ball 5 cm closer to the torch each time.

    Which of the following states the correct hypothesis for the above experiment?
    (a) The brightness of the torch will affect the size of the shadow
    (b) The strength of the battery will affect the darkness of the shadow
    (c) The distance between the torch and the tennis ball will affect the height of the shadow
    (d) The distance between the tennis ball and the screen will affect the shape of the shadow

30. Sameer's torch does not light up. This could be because of the following reason:
    (a) There is a gap between the batteries
    (b) The metal tip of the bulb is not connected to one of the batteries
    (c) The positive terminal of one battery is not connected to the negative terminal of the next battery
    (d) All are correct

31. Bulb will glow in:

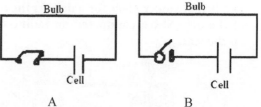

    (a) A   (b) B
    (c) Both (a) and (b)   (d) None of these

32. In which of the following a permanent magnet not used?
    (a) Loudspeakers
    (b) In magnetic door catches
    (c) In compasses
    (d) None of these

33. The diagram below shows what happens when two objects, X and Y, are placed very close to each other on a piece of paper laced with iron fillings.

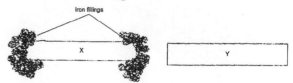

    Which one of the following statement(s) is/are definitely true?
    (i) Object X is a magnet
    (ii) Object X is made of copper
    (iii) Object Y is made of non-magnetic material
    (iv) Object Y is made of magnetic material
    (a) (i) only   (b) (i) and (iii)
    (c) (ii) and (iii)   (d) (i), (ii) and (iv)

34. Which of the following groups of items is needed to make an electromagnet?
    (a) An iron nail, copper wire and a light bulb
    (b) An iron nail, a battery and a light bulb
    (c) An iron nail, a battery and a copper wire
    (d) None of them

35. The needle of the compass is made of a magnet because it _____.
    (a) Attracts metal
    (b) Comes to rest in a north-south direction
    (c) Gets deflected when a magnet is brought closer
    (d) Both (b) and (c)

36. Four nails of different materials – iron, steel, copper, aluminum – were stroked with a magnet. Which of them will turn into a magnet?
    (a) Iron and steel nails
    (b) Iron and copper nails
    (c) Iron and aluminum nails
    (d) All of the above

37. Set-ups A and B below are placed on a table in the science room.

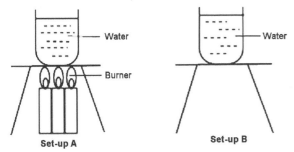

    What are the similarities that can be observed in both set-ups after 45 minutes?
    (a) The volume of water decreases
    (b) The temperature of the water increases
    (c) The water gains heat and evaporates
    (d) A and C both

38. Which of the following situations show(s) that heat is lost?
    (i) When ice melts
    (ii) When water vapour condenses
    (iii) When water changes to ice
    (iv) When a steel pot is left in the fridge
    (a) (i) and (ii)
    (b) (ii) only
    (c) (ii), (iii) and (iv)
    (d) (iii) and (iv)

39. Early in the morning, Ryan observed that there were water droplets on the outside of cars, even though it did not rain the night before.
    What is the correct explanation for Ryan observation?
    (a) Water vapour on the cool car condensed into the air
    (b) Water droplets from the warm air evaporated on the car
    (c) Water vapour from the air condensed on the cool car
    (d) Water droplets on the warm car evaporated to the air

40. Read the following statement about diseases.
    (i) They are caused by germs
    (ii) They are caused due to lack of nutrients in our diet
    (iii) They can be passed on to another person through contact
    (iv) They can be prevented by taking a balanced diet

    Which pair of statements best describes a deficiency disease?
    (a) (i) and (ii)
    (b) (ii) and (iv)
    (c) (i) only
    (d) (i), (ii) and (iii)

41. Direction: Questions 5 - 7 are based on the following flow chart which gives the techniques a student adopted to separate the constituents of a mixture.

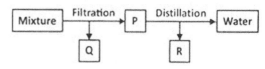

    What could substance R be?
    (a) Sugar   (b) Chalk powder
    (c) Glass   (d) Oxygen

42. Direction: Questions 5 - 7 are based on the following flow chart which gives the techniques a student adopted to separate the constituents of a mixture.

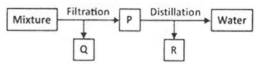

    What is substance Q?
    (a) Sugar   (b) Chalk powder
    (c) Alcohol   (d) Oxygen

43. Observe the given diagram carefully and fill in the blanks.

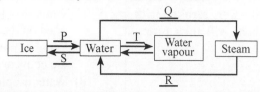

	P	Q	R	S	T
(a)	Freeaing	Boiling	Condensation	Melting	Evaporation
(b)	Freezing	Evaporation	Boiling	Melting	Condensation
(c)	Melting	Boiling	Condensation	Freezing	Evaporation
(d)	Melting	Evaporation	Condensation	Freezing	Boiling

44. Read the given passage.

Animals X, Y and Z are found in completely different habitats. Animal X is nocturnal and has developed many characters to conserve as much water as possible in the body. Animal Y has furry body with thick skin. It is large in size and has padded feet. Animal Z is adapted to live on trees, sticky pads on its feet help it to climb trees.

Which of the following can you conclude regarding the habitats of these animals?

(a) Animal X lives in a place with annual rainfall of about 80-100 cm.
(b) Animal Y lives in a place where days may be extremely hot and nights can be very cold.
(c) Animal Z lives in an area with annual rainfall of about 20-25 cm.
(d) Animal Y lives in an area where temperature sometimes reach 0°C or fall below it.

45. Which of the following graphs correctly shows the change in volume with temperature of water?

(a)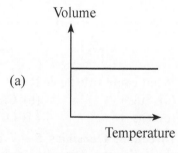

(b)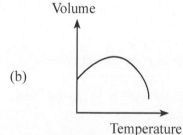

(c)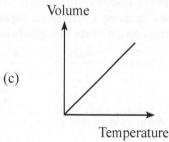

(d)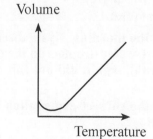

46. Understand the classification shown below and choose the correct option that follow.

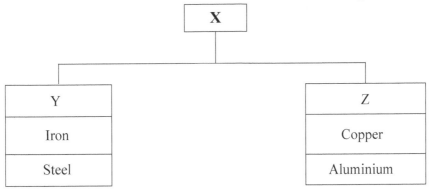

Which of the following correctly describes the X, Y and Z?

	X	Y	Z
(a)	Metals	Can sink	Can float
(b)	Metals	Can be magnetized	Cannot magnetized
(c)	Metals	Can be attached by magnets	Cannot be attached by magnets
(d)	Metals	Can allow electricity to pass through	Cannot allow electricity to pass through

47. The diagram below shows a floating plant, the water hyacinth, and its parts labelled A, B, C and D.

Sanya has started to point out the functions of the parts as follows.

Parts	Functions
P	Helps in photosynthesis
Q	Traps light to make food
R	Helps the plant to float on water
S	Holds the plant firmly to the soil

Which part(s) of the plant is wrongly matched to its functions?
(a) R only (b) P only
(c) P and Q only (d) Q and S only

48. When a drill bores a hole into a piece of wood, it describes:
(i) Oscillatory motion
(ii) Rotatory motion
(iii) Curvilinear motion
(iv) Translatory motion
(a) (i) and (ii) (b) (ii) and (iii)
(c) (i) and (iv) (d) ii and (iv)

Model Test Paper - 2

49. In an experiment, two set-ups are created. In the Set-up X, the salt has been added to the ice while in the Set-up Y, only ice cubes were added.

Which of the following statement(s) is correct for the experiment described above? Choose the correct option to answer the question.

(i) Salt decreases the melting temperature of ice below −20°C.
(ii) Ice in Set-up X melts slower than the ice in Set-up Y.
(iii) More water will be collected in Set-up X than that in Set-up Y.
(iv) The water collected from Set-up Y will take longer time to freeze than the water collected from Set-up X.

(a) (i) only
(b) (i) and (ii) only
(c) (i), (ii) and (iii) only
(d) (ii), (iii) and (iv) only

50. The diagram below shows four circuits with different arrangements of identical batteries and identical bulbs. The bulbs in all four circuits light up.

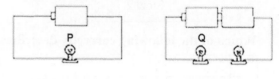
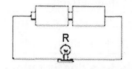
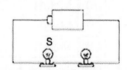

Which of the following pairs of bulbs have the same brightness? Choose the correct option.

(a) P and Q
(b) P and S
(c) Q and R
(d) R and S

Hints and Solutions

SECTION 1: SCIENCE

1. MOTION AND MEASUREMENT OF DISTANCES

Answer Key

1. (a)	2. (b)	3. (a)	4. (d)	5. (b)	6. (c)	7. (d)	8. (c)	9. (c)	10. (d)
11. (d)	12. (c)	13. (a)	14. (c)	15. (b)	16. (b)	17. (d)	18. (d)	19. (a)	20. (b)
21. (c)	22. (a)	23. (d)	24. (b)	25. (c)					

11. If Kavya takes 10 minutes to cover 2 km, then in 1 minute, she will cover 2 km ÷ 10 = 0.2 km (using the formula: speed = distance travelled ÷ time taken) Similarly, if Yamini takes 20 minutes to cover 5 km, then in 1 minute she will cover 5 km ÷ 20 = 0.25 km.

2. LIGHT, SHADOWS AND REFLECTION

Answer Key

1. (c)	2. (b)	3. (b)	4. (c)	5. (c)	6. (b)	7. (b)	8. (d)	9. (c)	10. (b)
11. (a)	12. (b)	13. (a)	14. (c)	15. (a)	16. (d)	17. (a)	18. (c)	19. (b)	20. (c)
21. (d)	22. (b)	23. (c)	24. (d)	25. (d)	26. (c)	27. (b)	28. (a)	29. (b)	30. (a)

3. ELECTRICITY AND CIRCUITS

Answer Key

1. (b)	2. (d)	3. (a)	4. (d)	5. (b)	6. (c)	7. (d)	8. (a)	9. (b)	10. (a)
11. (c)	12. (a)	13. (a)	14. (b)	15. (c)	16. (c)	17. (b)	18. (d)	19. (b)	20. (a)
21 (d)	22. (d)	23. (b)	24. (d)	25. (d)	26. (d)	27. (a)	28. (b)	29. (c)	30. (b)

4. FUN WITH MAGNETS

Answer Key

1. (c)	2. (a)	3. (b)	4. (d)	5. (d)	6. (c)	7. (a)	8. (d)	9. (a)	10. (c)
11. (a)	12. (c)	13. (b)	14. (a)	15. (b)	16. (c)	17. (a)	18. (b)	19. (b)	20. (c)
21. (b)	22. (c)	23. (c)	24. (d)	25. (c)	26. (d)	27. (c)	28. (c)	29. (d)	30. (c)

5. AIR AND WATER

Answer Key

1. (c)	2. (b)	3. (a)	4. (b)	5. (d)	6. (b)	7. (b)	8. (d)	9. (c)	10. (d)
11. (d)	12. (d)	13. (c)	14. (c)	15. (b)	16. (b)	17. (c)	18. (b)	19. (d)	20. (c)
21. (c)	22. (d)	23. (b)	24. (b)	25. (d)	26. (a)	27. (a)	28. (d)	29. (d)	30. (d)

6. SORTING AND SEPARATION OF MATERIALS

Answer Key

1. (c)	2. (b)	3. (d)	4. (b)	5. (c)	6. (d)	7. (b)	8. (b)	9. (d)	10. (b)
11. (a)	12. (b)	13. (d)	14. (b)	15. (d)	16. (b)	17. (b)	18. (b)	19. (d)	20. (b)
21. (c)	22. (d)	23. (d)	24. (c)	25. (c)	26. (b)	27. (c)	28. (a).	29. (b)	30. (a)

7. CHANGES AROUND US

Answer Key

1. (a)	2. (b)	3. (d)	4. (a)	5. (a)	6. (a)	7. (c)	8. (d)	9. (d)	10. (b)
11. (c)	12. (b)	13. (a)	14. (d)	15. (c)	16. (b)	17. (c)	18. (b)	19. (c)	20. (c)
21. (c)	22. (c)	23. (a)	24. (d)	25. (b)	26. (b)	27. (a)	28. (b)	29. (c)	30. (d)

8. LIVING ORGANISMS AND THEIR SURROUNDINGS

Answer Key

1. (a)	2. (c)	3. (d)	4. (d)	5. (d)	6. (c)	7. (d)	8. (d)	9. (b)	10. (c)
11. (a)	12. (c)	13. (c)	14. (c)	15. (b)	16. (b)	17. (b)	18. (b)	19. (b)	20. (a)
21. (b)	22. (d)	23. (a)	24. (b)	25. (d)	26. (d)	27. (c)	28. (c)	29. (a)	30. (c)

9. FOOD, HEALTH AND HYGIENE

Answer Key

1. (c)	2. (c)	3. (b)	4. (b)	5. (a)	6. (c)	7. (b)	8. (a)	9. (b)	10. (c)
11. (b)	12. (d)	13. (a)	14. (c)	15. (b)	16. (c)	17. (b)	18. (d)	19. (b)	20. (b)
21. (b)	22. (c)	23. (b)	24. (b)	25. (b)	26. (d)	27. (a)	28. (c)	29. (b)	30. (b)

10. FIBER TO FABRIC

Answer Key

1. (a)	2. (d)	3. (d)	4. (c)	5. (d)	6. (a)	7. (d)	8. (a)	9. (a)	10. (c)
11. (a)	12. (a)	13. (a)	14. (c)	15. (c)	16. (a)	17. (d)	18. (a)	19. (b)	20. (c)
21. (a)	22. (d)	23. (d)	24. (c)	25. (b)	26. (a)	27. (d)	28. (b)	29. (c)	30. (c)

11. BODY MOVEMENTS IN ANIMALS

Answer Key

1. (c)	2. (a)	3. (b)	4. (d)	5. (b)	6. (b)	7. (c)	8. (b)	9. (a)	10. (c)
11. (d)	12. (b)	13. (a)	14. (c)	15. (d)	16. (d)	17. (a)	18. (c)	19. (b)	20. (a)
21. (c)	22. (b)	23. (b)	24. (a)	25. (b)	26. (d)	27. (d)	28. (d)	29. (a)	30. (c)

Hints and Solutions

SECTION 2: LOGICAL REASONING

1. PATTERN

Answer Key

1. (c)	2. (a)	3. (c)	4. (b)	5. (a)	6. (d)	7. (c)	8. (c)	9. (a)	10 (c)
11. (d)	12. (b)	13. (d)	14. (c)	15. (b)	16. (a)	17. (c)	18. (a)	19. (c)	20. (b)
21. (d)	22. (a)	23. (b)	24. (b)	25. (c)					

1. **(c)** From fig (i) $(112 \div 14) \times 2 = 16$
   From fig (ii) $(168 \div 24) \times 2 = 14$
   From fig (iii) $(144 \div 16) \times 2 = 9 \times 2 = 18$

2. **(a)** From fig (i) $4 \times 6 + 18 \times 3 = 24 + 54 = 78$
   From fig (ii) $3 \times 5 + 24 \times 4 = 15 + 96 = 111$
   From fig (iii) $2 \times 7 + 21 \times 4 = 14 + 84 = 98$

3. **(c)** From fig (i) $1 + 2 = 3 \to 3^2 = 9$
   From fig (ii) $3 + 4 = 7 \to 7^2 = 49$
   $5 + 4 = 9 \to 9^2 = 81$
   $7 + 6 = 13 \to 13^2 = 169$

4. **(b)** From fig (i) $2^2 \times 3^2 = 4 \times 9 = 36$
   From fig (ii) $4^2 \times 5^2 = 16 \times 25 = 400$
   From fig (iii) $6^2 \times 7^2 = 36 \times 49 = 1764$

5. **(a)** From fig (i) $(14 + 24) - 2 = 38 - 2 = 36$
   From fig (ii) $(23 + 35) - 3 = 58 - 3 = 55$
   From fig (iii) $(34 + 45) - 4 = 79 - 4 = 75$

6. **(d)** From fig (i) $5 \times 2 + 1 \times 3 = 10 + 3 = 13$
   From fig (ii) $2 \times 4 + 5 \times 3 = 8 + 15 = 23$
   From fig (iii) $3 \times 4 + 5 \times 7 = 12 + 35 = 47$

7. **(c)** From fig (i) $7 \times 4 - 5 \times 3 = 28 - 15 = 13$
   From fig (ii) $9 \times 6 - 7 \times 3 = 54 - 21 = 33$
   From fig (iii) $8 \times 9 - 7 \times 5 = 72 - 35 = 37$

8. **(c)** From fig (i) $1 + 7 + 3 + 2 = 13 \to 13^2 = 169$
   From fig (ii) $1 + 5 + 2 + 7 = 15 \to 15^2 = 225$
   From fig (iii) $2 + 7 + 3 + 9 = 21 \to 21^2 = 441$

9. **(a)** $2 \times 4 \times 8 \times 6 = 384$
   $3 \times 5 \times 6 \times 7 = 630$
   $3 \times 8 \times 7 \times 9 = 1512$

10. **(c)** From fig (i) $\sqrt{25} + \sqrt{16} + \sqrt{81} + \sqrt{1}$
    $= 5 + 4 + 9 + 1 = 19 \to 19^2 = 361$
    From fig (ii) $\sqrt{81} + \sqrt{64} + \sqrt{49} + \sqrt{4}$
    $= 9 + 8 + 7 + 2 = 26 \to 26^2 = 676$
    From fig (iii) $\sqrt{121} + \sqrt{49} + \sqrt{64} + \sqrt{36}$
    $= 11 + 7 + 8 + 6 = 32 \to 32^2 = 1024$

11. **(d)** From fig (i) $\sqrt{49} + \sqrt{81} + \sqrt{36} + \sqrt{64}$
    $= 7 + 9 + 6 + 8 = 30$
    From fig (ii) $\sqrt{81} + \sqrt{25} + \sqrt{16} + \sqrt{49}$
    $= 9 + 5 + 4 + 7 = 25$
    From fig (iii) $\sqrt{121} + \sqrt{81} + \sqrt{25} + \sqrt{49}$
    $= 11 + 9 + 5 + 7 = 32$

12. **(b)** From fig (i) $7 \times 2 \times 3 = 42$
    From fig (ii) $8 \times 3 \times 2 = 48$
    From fig (iii) $7 \times 6 \times 4 = 168$

13. **(d)** From fig (i) $1 \times 5 + 3 \times 4 = 5 + 12 = 17$
    From fig (ii) $1 \times 7 + 4 \times 6 = 7 + 24 = 31$
    From fig (iii) $4 \times 6 + 7 \times 8 = 24 + 56 = 80$

14. **(c)** In the first row, $(263 - 188) \times 4 = 300$
    In the second row, missing number
    $= (915 - 893) \times 4 = 22 \times 4 = 88$

15. **(b)** In the first row, $16 \times 14 - 14 = 210$
    In the second row, $14 \times 12 - 12 = 156$
    $\therefore$ missing number $= 12 \times 10 - 10 = 110$

17. **(c)** In the first row, $8 \times 2 + 17 = 33$
    In the second row; $12 \times 2 + 5 = 29$
    $\therefore$ missing number $= 10 \times 2 + 13 = 33$

18. **(a)** In the first row, $2 + 2 = 4$ and $4^4 = 256$
In the third row, $4 + 2 = 6$ and $6^6 = 46656$
In the second row, $3 + 2 = 5$
So, missing number = $5^5 = 3125$

19. **(c)** In the first row, $11 \times 2 + (6 \div 2) = 25$
In the second row, $6 \times 2 + (8 \div 2) = 16$
∴ in the third row, missing number
$= 5 \times 2 + (12 \div 2) = 10 + 6 = 16$

20. **(b)** In the first row, $(85 \div 5) + 3 = 20$
In the second row, $(126 \div 6) + 3 = 24$
∴ In the third row, missing number
$= (175 \div 7) + 3$
$= (25 + 3) = 28$

21. **(d)** In the second row, $2 \times 9 + 3 \times 17 = 69$
In the third row, $2 \times 13 + 3 \times 11 = 59$.
Let the missing number in the first row be x.
Then, $2x + 3 \times 13 = 49 \Rightarrow 2x = 10 \Rightarrow x = 5$

22. **(a)** In the first row, $\dfrac{12}{4} - \dfrac{21}{7}$ in the second row, $\dfrac{10}{5} - \dfrac{4}{2}$
Clearly, in the third row we have $\dfrac{64}{8} - \dfrac{24}{3}$
∴ missing number = 83

23. **(b)** In the first row, $(42 - 38) \times 11 = 44$
In the second row, $(28 - 23) \times 11 = 55$
In the third row, missing number
$= (39 - 37) \times 11 = 22$

24. **(b)** In the first row, $(9 + 6 + 3) - (8 + 4 + 4) = 2$
∴ in the second row, missing number
$= (4 + 6 + 4) - (9 + 0 + 3) = 2$

25. **(c)** $3 + 4$ = number below $4 = 7$
$3 + 4 + 5$ = number below $5 = 12$
$3 + 7 + 12$ = number below $12 = 22$
∴ missing number = $3 + 7 = 10$

2. ANALOGY

Answer Key

1. (b)	2. (c)	3. (c)	4. (c)	5. (d)	6. (c)	7. (d)	8. (a)	9. (d)	10. (c)
11. (c)	12. (a).	13. (b)	14. (a)	15. (a)	16. (d)	17. (b)	18. (a)	19. (a)	20. (a)
21. (d)	22. (d)	23. (c)	24. (d)	25 (a)	26. (c)	27. (d)	28. (d)	29. (d)	30. (d)
31. (b)	32. (d)	33. (d)	34. (a)	35. (a)	36. (b)	37. (d)	38. (d)	30. (a)	40. (c)
41. (d)	42. (e)	43. (d)	44. (b)	45. (d)	46. (d)	47. (d)	48. (d)	49. (b)	50. (d)

1. **(b)** As Physician does the treatment, similarly Judge delivers the judgement.
2. **(c)** As effect of Ice is coldness, similarly the effect of Earth is gravitation.
3. **(c)** As the result of Race is Fatigue, similarly the result of Fast is Hunger.
4. **(c)** As opposite meaning of peace is chaos, similarly opposite meaning of creation is destruction.
5. **(d)** As Tiger is found in Forest, similarly Otter is found in the water.
6. **(c)** As magnet has poles, similarly battery has terminals.
7. **(d)** A Priest wears cassock while Graduate wears gown.
8. **(a)** As President is the nominal head of a country, similarly Governer is the nominal head of a State.

Hints and Solutions

9. **(d)** As Cloth is made in a mill, similarly Newspaper is printed in press.
10. **(c)** As North-West is 135° clockwise from South, in the same way North-East is 135° clockwise from the West.
11. **(c)** As 24:60 = (2/5)
    Similarly, (120/300) = (2/5)
12. **(a)** As 335 − 216 = 119
    Similarly, 987 − X = 119
    Therefore, X = 987 − 119 = 868
13. **(b)** As, 24 → 2 × 4 = 8
    Similarly, 32 → 3 × 2 = 6
14. **(a)** Here, $9 = (3)^2$
    $8 = (3 − 1)^3$
    and $16 = (4)^2$
    $? = (4 − 1)^3 = 27$
15. **(a)** In Eq. alphabets positions of K and T are 11 and 20 respectively.
    Similarly positions of J and R are 10 and 18.
16. **(d)** An aerie is where an eagle lives; a house is where a person lives.
17. **(b)** Being erudite is a trait of a professor; being imaginative is a trait of an inventor.
18. **(a)** The deltoid is a muscle; the radius is a bone.
19. **(a)** Jaundice is an indication of a liver problem; rash is an indication of a skin problem.
20. **(a)** A conviction results in incarceration; a reduction results in diminution.
21. **(d)** Dependable and capricious are antonyms; capable and inept are antonyms.
22. **(d)** A metaphor is a symbol; an analogy is a comparison.
23. **(c)** Obsession is a greater degree of interest; fantasy is a greater degree of dream.
24. **(d)** A conductor leads an orchestra; a skipper leads a crew.
25. **(a)** A palm (tree) has fronds; a porcupine has quills.
26. **(c)** A cacophony is an unpleasant sound; a stench is an unpleasant smell.
27. **(d)** Umbrage and offense are synonyms; elation and jubilance are synonyms.
28. **(d)** A dirge is a song used at a funeral; a jingle is a song used in commercial.
29. **(d)** To be phobic is to be extremely fearful; to be asinine is to be extremely silly.
30. **(d)** Feral and tame are antonyms; ephemeral and immortal are antonyms.
31. **(b)** An artist makes paintings; a senator makes laws. The answer is not choice (a) because an attorney does not make laws and a senator is not an attorney. Choice c is incorrect because a senator is not a politician. A constituent (choice d) is also incorrect because a senator serves his or her constituents.
32. **(d)** A gym is a place where people exercise. A restaurant is a place where people eat. Food (choice a) is not the answer because it is something people eat, not a place or location where they eat. The answer is not choice b or c because neither represents a place where people eat.
33. **(d)** Candid and indirect refer to opposite traits. Honest and untruthful refer to opposite traits. The answer is not choice (a) because frank means the same thing as candid. Wicked (choice b) is incorrect because even though it refers to a negative trait, it does not mean the opposite of honest. (Choice c) is incorrect because truthful and honest mean the same thing.
34. **(a)** Guide and direct are synonyms, and reduce and decrease are synonyms. The answer is not choice b or d because neither means the same as reduce. (Choice c) is incorrect because increase is the opposite of reduce.
35. **(a)** Careful and cautious are synonyms (they mean the same thing). Boastful and arrogant are also synonyms. The answer is not (choice b) because humble means the opposite of boastful. The answer is not choice c or d because neither means the same as boastful.

36. **(b)** As the all terms given in the question are medical terms and Haematology is also a medical term.
37. **(d)** All the terms given in the question are cereals and gram is also one of the cereals.
38. **(d)** The synonym of Lock, Shut and Fasten is Block.
39. **(a)** All the cities given in the question are state capitals, similarly Shimla is also a capital.
40. **(c)** All these words represent the inhabitants of India.
41. **(d)** As per pattern minus sign should be in right corner, parallel lines rotate through 90° and position of dots gets inverted.
42. **(e)** The inner figures are inverted. The number of lines and dots decrease by one.
43. **(d)** Two lines are get inverted. The position of dots is changed in order.
44. **(b)** The figure gets rotated through 90° ACW.
45. **(d)** The inner images are inverted. + sign changes to x.
46. **(d)** Shifting the shaded portion in opposite direction, we get the required image.
47. **(d)** All the figures get inverted.
48. **(d)** The number of dots is one less than the number of sides.
49. **(b)** The number of positions of arrow are changed in order.
50. **(d)** As per pattern the image includes arrow rotated through 90° and then inverts. The image with black dot should be in opposite direction with arrow.

3. SERIES COMPLETION

Answer Key

1. (b)	2. (b)	3. (d)	4. (c)	5. (a)	6. (a)	7. (a)	8. (c)	9. (c)	10 (a)
11. (a)	12. (c)	13. (a)	14. (c)	15. (b)	16. (c)	17. (d)	18. (d)	19. (b)	20. (c)

1. **(b)** The given series is

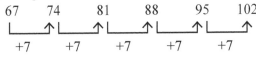

2. **(b)** The given series is

    109   101   94   88   83   79

    −8   −7   −6   −5   −4

3. **(d)** The given series is

    9   25   49   81   121   169

    3^2 5^2 7^2 9^2 11^2 13^2

4. **(c)** The given series is

    3   8   15   24   35   48   63   80

    (2^2-1) (3^2-1) (4^2-1) (5^2-1) (6^2-1) (7^2-1) (8^2-1) (9^2-1)

Hints and Solutions

5. **(a)** The given series is
   6, 12, 24, 48, 96, 192, 384 (×2 each step)

6. **(a)** The given series is
   4, 3, 4, 9, 32, 155, 924
   (×1 − 1, ×2 − 2, ×3 − 3, ×4 − 4, ×5 − 5, ×6 − 6)

7. **(a)** The given series is
   85, 88, 91, 94, 97, 100, 103, 106, 109 (+3 each step)

8. **(c)** The given series is
   5, 10, 40, 80, 320, 640, 2560 (×2, ×4, ×2, ×4, ×2, ×4)

9. **(c)** The given series is
   1, 5, 9, 17, 25, 37, 49, 65
   $(1^2), (2^2+1), (3^2), (4^2+1), (5^2), (6^2+1), (7^2), (8^2+1)$

10. **(a)** The given series is
    6, 15, 35, 77, 143, 221
    $(2\times3), (3\times5), (5\times7), (7\times11), (11\times13), (13\times17)$

11. **(a)** The given series is
    16, 22, 30, 40, 52, 66, 82, 100
    (+6, +8, +10, +12, +14, +16, +18)

12. **(c)** The given series is
    225, 205, 180, 150, 115, 75
    (−20, −25, −30, −35, −40)

13. **(a)** The given series is
    10, 14, 28, 32, 64, 68, 136
    (+4, ×2, +4, ×2, +4, ×2)

14. **(c)** The given series is
    3, 4, 10, 33, 136, 685
    (×1 + 1, ×2 + 2, ×3 + 3, ×4 + 4, ×5 + 5)

15. **(b)** The given series is

1326   2436   3546   4656   5766

+1110   +1110   +1110   +1110

16. **(c)** The given series is

598   505   412   319   226   133

−93   −93   −93   −93   −93

17. **(d)** The given series is

702   773   844   915   986   1057

+71   +71   +71   +71   +71

18. **(d)** The given series is

15   45   42   126   123   369   366   1098

×3   −3   ×3   −3   ×3   −3   ×3

19. **(b)** The given series is

27   56   114   230   462   926   1854

×2 + 2   ×2 + 2   ×2 + 2   ×2 + 2   ×2 + 2   ×2 + 2

20. **(c)** The given series is

2   21   154   1085   7602   53221

×7 + 7   ×7 + 7   ×7 + 7   ×7 + 7   ×7 + 7

4. ODD ONE OUT

Answer Key

1. (b)	2. (c)	3. (a)	4. (b)	5. (a)	6. (b)	7. (c)	8. (b)	9. (a)	10 (c)
11. (a)	12. (b)	13. (c)	14. (c)	15. (d)	16. (b)	17. (a)	18. (d)	19. (a)	20. (b)
21. (c)	22. (b)	23. (c)	24. (a)	25. (a)	26. (b)	27. (c)	28. (d)	29. (c)	30. (a)
31. (b)	32. (c)	33. (d)	34. (c)	35. (c)	36. (b)	37. (d)	38. (b)	39. (a)	40. (a)

Hints and Solutions

4. **(b)** All except marble are precious stones.
5. **(a)** All except peel are different form of cooking.
6. **(b)** All except potassium are metal used in semiconductor devices.
7. **(c)** All except Eagle are flightless birds.
9. **(a)** All except India are islands, while India is a Peninsula.
11. **(a)** All except Hammer are sharp edged and have a cutting action.
12. **(b)** All others are parts of tree.
17. **(a)** All except Earth denote Roman or Greek Gods.
20. **(b)** All except Nylon are natural fibres, while nylon is a synthetic fibre.
25. **(a)** All except Leh are capitals of Indian states, while Leh is a hill station.
26. **(b)** All except Leopard are found in Polar regions.
28. **(d)** All except Beethovan were Scientists, while Beethovan was a musician.
29. **(c)** All except Pink are the colours seen in a rainbow.
33. **(d)** All except Python are venomous snakes.
34. **(c)** All except Terrible are synonyms.
35. **(c)** All except Smut are forms of fungi.
36. **(b)** All except stone are obtained directly or indirectly from trees.
37. **(d)** All others are parts of house.
39. **(a)** All except Nymph are stages in the life cycle of a butterfly, while nymph is a young cockroack.

5. CODING – DECODING

Answer Key

1. (d)	2. (c)	3. (a)	4. (a)	5. (c)	6. (a)	7. (c)	8. (a)	9. (b)	10 (d)
11. (a)	12. (c)	13. (b)	14. (c)	15. (c)	16. (b)	17. (d)	18. (a)	19. (c)	20. (b)
21. (a)	22. (b)	23. (d)	24. (c)	25. (a)	26. (d)	27. (c)	28. (a)	29. (b)	30. (c)

1. **(d)** Each letter of the word 'TRUTH' is replaced by a set of two letters – one preceding it and the other following it – in the code. Thus, T is replaced by SU, R is replaced by QS and so on.

2. **(c)** All the letters of the word, except the last letter, are written in a reverse order to obtain the code.

3. **(a)** Here,
SILVER → SIL/VER $\xrightarrow{Reversing}$ LIS/REV $\xrightarrow{+1}$ MJT/SFW

4. **(a)** Divide the given word into six sets of two letters each and label these sets from 1 to 6. Then the code contains these sets in the order 4, 3, 5, 2, 6, 1 with the letters of sets 3, 2, 1 written in a reverse order. Thus, we have:

$\underset{1}{VI}\ \underset{2}{SH}\ \underset{3}{WA}\ \underset{4}{NA}\ \underset{5}{TH}\ \underset{6}{AN} \rightarrow \underset{4}{NA}\ \underset{3}{AW}\ \underset{5}{TH}\ \underset{2}{HS}\ \underset{6}{AN}\ \underset{1}{IV}$

5. **(c)** Divide the word into three groups of two letters each and write the letters of each group in the reverse order.

AN SW ER → NA WS RE → NBWTRF

6. **(a)** Each letter in the word is replaced by the letter which occupies the same position from the other end of the alphabet, to obtain the code.

7. **(c)** All the letters of the word, except the last letter, are written in the reverse order and in the group of letters so obtained each letter is moved into steps forward to get the code.

AVOID → IOVAD → KQXCF.

8. **(a)**

   $$\frac{\text{PO PU LA RI SE}}{1\ \ 2\ \ 3\ \ 4\ \ 5} \rightarrow \frac{\text{ES RI AL PU OP}}{5\ \ 4\ \ 3\ \ 2\ \ 1}$$

   Clearly, the sixth letter from the left in the code is L.

9. **(b)** Each letter of the word is five steps ahead the corresponding letter of the code.

10. **(d)** The code has been obtained by writing the first four and the last four letters of the word in the reverse order. Thus, we have.
    SERPEVRE → SERP/EVRE → PRES/ERVE → PRESERVE.

11. **(a)**
    Letter: C O N E P T F R I D
    Code: u n m l q r y s g t
    The code for PREDICT is qsltgur.

12. **(c)**
    Letter: F I R E M O V
    Code: Q H O E Z M W
    The code for OVER is MWEO.

13. **(b)** Each letter is coded by the numeral obtained by subtracting from 27 then numeral denoting the position of the letter in the English alphabet. W, O, M, A, N are 23rd, 15th, 13th, 1st and 14th letters. So their codes are (27 − 23), (27 − 15), (27 − 13), (27 − 1), (27 − 14) i.e. 4, 12, 14, 26, 13 respectively.

14. **(c)** In the given code, Z = 1, Y = 2, X = 3, ……. C = 24, B = 25, A = 26.
    So, GO = 20 + 12 = 32 and SHE = 8 + 19 + 22 = 49.
    Similarly, SOME = S + O + M + E = 8 + 12 + 14 + 22 = 56.

15. **(c)** Taking
    Z = 2, Y = 3, …., N = 14, ……, B = 26, A = 27
    ZIP = (Z + I + P) × 6 = (2 + 19 + 12) × 6
    = 33 × 6 = 198
    VIP = (V + I + P) × 6 = (6 + 19 + 12) × 6
    = 37 × 6 = 222

16. **(b)** Let A = 1, B = 2, C = 3, ……, Z = 26.
    Now, M = 13 = $\overline{4}$ (Remainder obtained after dividing by 9).

    S = 19 = 1 (Remainder obtained after dividing by 9 twice)
    T = 20 = 2 (Remainder obtained after dividing by 9 twice)
    R = 18 = $\overline{9}$ (Remainder obtained after dividing by 9)
    So, MASTER = $\overline{4}1125\overline{9}$, POWDER = $\overline{7}6545\overline{9}$

17. **(d)**
    Letter: B R A I N T E
    Code: * % ÷ # × $ +
    The code for RENT is % + × $

18. **(a)**
    Letter: D E L H I C A U T
    Code: 7 3 5 4 1 8 2 9 6
    The code for CALICUT is 8251896.

19. **(c)**
    Letter: N O I D A
    Code: 3 9 6 5 8
    The code for INDIA is 63568.

20. **(b)**
    Letter: E N G L A D F R C
    Code: 1 2 3 4 5 6 7 8 9
    The code for GREECE is 381191.

21. **(a)** Vowels A, E, I, O, U are coded as 1, 2, 3, 4, 5 respectively. Each of the consonants in the word is moved one step forward to give the corresponding letter of the code so, the code for ACID becomes ID3E.

22. **(b)**
    Letter: D E S K R I
    Code: #   5 2 % 7
    The code for RISK is % 752.

23. **(d)**
    Letter: E A T C H I R
    Code: 3 1 8 2 4 5 6
    The code for TEACHER is 8312436.

24. **(c)**
    Letter: D E A F I L
    Code: 3 5 8 7 4 6
    The code for IDEAL is 43586.

Hints and Solutions

25. **(a)** CAR = (Number of letters in CAR) × 2
   = 3 × 2 = 6
26. **(d)** 'Chillies' are green in colour and as given, 'chillies' are 'bananas'. So, 'bananas' are green in colour.
27. **(c)** Birds fly in the 'sky' and as given, 'sky' is 'star'. So, birds fly in the 'star'.
28. **(a)** The colour of milk is 'white'. But, as given 'green' means 'white'. So, the colour of milk is green.
29. **(b)** A child will write with a 'pencil' and 'pencil' is called sharpener. So, a child will write with a 'sharpener'.
30. **(c)** Fishes live in 'water' and as given, 'water' is called 'colour'. So, fishes live in 'colour'.

6. ALPHABET TEST

Answer Key

1. (c)	2. (b)	3. (b)	4. (a)	5. (d)	6. (b)	7. (d)	8. (c)	9. (b)	10. (c)
11. (b)	12. (c)	13. (b)	14. (d)	15. (a)	16. (b)	17. (b)	18. (a)	19. (d)	20. (a)
21. (c)	22. (d)	23. (a)	24. (d)	25. (a)	26. (b)	27. (b)	28. (a)	29. (d)	30. (d)

1. **(c)** Groan, Grotesque, Group, Guarantee.
2. **(b)** Nature, Nautical, Naval, Necessary.
3. **(b)** Foetus, Foliage, Foment, Forceps.
4. **(a)** Deuce, Devise, Dew, Dexterity.
5. **(d)** Qualify, Quarrel, Quarry, Quarter.
6. **(b)** Probate, Probe, Proceed, Proclaim.
7. **(d)** Fault, Finger, Floor, Forget.
8. **(c)** Evolution, Extra, Extraction, Extreme.
9. **(b)** Translate, Transmit, Transport, Transist.
10. **(c)** Repeat, Roman, Romance, Rose.
11. **(b)** Diagonal, Dialogue, Different, Distance.
12. **(d)** Temperature, Temple, Transition, Transmit.
13. **(b)** Waiting, Warring, Watching, Waving.
14. **(d)**
    B C D E F G H I J K L M N O P Q R
       1   3   3   5
    1, 3, 5 are all odd numbers.
15. **(a)**
    Q R S T U V W X Y Z A B C D E F G
       2   5   7
    H I J K L M N O P Q R S
              10
16. **(b)**
    H I J K L M N O P Q R S T U V W X Y Z
             12   9
    A B C D [E] F G H I J K [L] M N O [P]
            6   3
17. **(b)**
    [T] U V W X Y [Z] A B C D [E] F G H [I] J K [L]
      5   4   3   2
18. **(a)**
    [B] C [D] E F [G] H I J K [L] M N O P Q R S T [U]
     1   2   4   8

19. **(d)**
    O N M L K J I H G F E D C B A
    1   2   3   4

20. **(a)**
    S T U V W X Y Z A B C D E F G H I J K
              5   4   3   2

21. **(c)** Counting from the left, i.e. from A in the given alphabet series, the thirteenth letter is M. counting from M towards the right, the seventh letter is T.

22. **(d)** T is seventh letter to the right of M. Similarly, the seventh letter to the right of G is N.

23. **(a)** The fourth letter to the left of I is E. the sixteenth letter to the right of E is U.

24. **(d)** The new letter series obtained on reversing the order of the English alphabet is
    Z Y X W V U T S R Q P O N M L K J I H G F E D C B A.
    Since the series has an even number of letters there is no such letter which lies exactly in the middle.

25. **(a)** Reversing only the first 13 letters, we obtain the following letter series:
    M L K J I H G F E D C B A N O P Q R S T U V W X Y Z.
    Clearly, there are 14 letters between K and R in the above series.

26. **(b)** The new alphabet series is:
    A B C D E F G H I J K L M N O P Z Y X W V U T S R Q
    The thirteenth letter from the left is M. The sixth letter to the right of M is X.

27. **(b)** There are nine letters between G and Q – H, I, J, K, L, M, N, O, P. Clearly, the middle letter is L.

28. **(a)** The pairing up of letters may be done as shown.
    AZ, BY, CX, DW, EV, FU, GT, HS, IR, JQ, KP, LO, MN.

29. **(d)** The new series becomes
    A B C * E F G * I J K * M N O * Q R S * U V W * YZ.

30. **(d)** The fourteenth letter from the right is L. the eighth letter to the right of L is T.

7. NUMBER AND RANKING TEST

Answer Key

1. (c)	2. (a)	3. (c)	4. (c)	5. (c)	6. (a)	7. (d)	8. (c)	9. (d)	10. (b)
11. (d)	12. (c)	13. (a)	14. (a)	15. (c)	16. (c)	17. (b)	18. (b)	19. (c)	20. (b)

1. **(c)** The given series is
   2 8 4 3 8 5 4 8 2 6 7 8 4 6 2 8 4 1 7

3. **(c)** The given series is
   7 4 5 7 6 8 4 2 1 3 5 1 7 6 8 9 2

4. **(c)** The given series is
   5 9 3 1 7 4 5 8 4 6 7 4 3 1 4 7 4 2 8 7 4 1

5. **(c)** The given series is
   4 3 5 6 4 5 2 3 4 5 8 5 4 6 7 5 2 6 9 8 5 1 2 4 5

6. **(a)** The given series is
   1 2 3 7 4 3 2 5 6 7 2 8 9 6 4 3 2 5 6 8 4 6 8 2 3 4

11. **(d)** Here, 49 – 18 = 31
    So, Ranjan's rank = 31 + 1 = 32nd form the last.

12. **(c)** No. of boys in the line = 12 + 4 – 1 = 15
    No. of boys to be added = 35 – 15 = 20

Hints and Solutions

13. **(a)** 1 2 3 4 5 6 7 8 9 10 11 12 13
    ↑   ↑
    Ravi   Amar
    Minimum no. of boys = 13 + 1 = 14
14. **(a)** Raja's new position is 15th from the left and this is the same as 9th position from the right for Pramod.
    No. of boys = 15 + 9 − 1 = 23
15. **(c)** Total number of students = 6 + 1 + 33 = 40
16. **(c)** Manoj's rank is 17th from the last.

Saket's rank = 17 + 7 = 24th from the last.
No. of students ahead of Saket = 50 − 24 = 26
Saket's rank from start = 26 + 1 = 27th
17. **(b)** Required no. of boys = 22 + 1 + 22 = 45
18. **(b)** Total no. of students = 5 + 6 + 6 + 8 − 1 = 24
19. **(c)** Number of boys = 8 + 14 + 12 = 34
20. **(b)** 95, 90, 85, 80, 75, 70, 65, 60, **55**, 50, 45, 40, 35, 30, 25, 20, 15, 10, 5

8. DIRECTION SENSE TEST

Answer Key

1. (b)	2. (d)	3. (c)	4. (a)	5. (a)	6. (c)	7. (a)	8. (b)	9. (b)	10 (d)
11. (a)	12. (b)	13. (d)	14. (d)	15. (a)	16. (c)	17. (a)	18. (a)	19. (b)	20. (a)

1. **(b)** Sun rises in the east in the morning. So, in morning, the shadow falls towards the west. Now, Mohan's shadow falls to his right. So, he is standing, facing south.
2. **(d)** In diagram (A) the directions are shown as they actually are. Diagram (B) is as per the given data. So, comparing the direction of north in (A) with that in (B), north will be called north west.

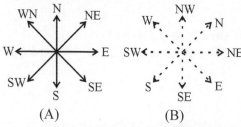

3. **(c)** As per the given data, C faces north. A faces towards west. D is to the right of C. So, D is facing towards south. Thus, B who is the partner of D will face towards north.

4. **(a)** It is clear from the adjoining diagram that Rakesh lies to the east of Rajesh.

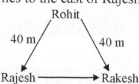

5. **(a)** Starting from his house in the East, Pravin moves west wards. Then, the theatre, which is the left, will be in the south. The hospital, which is straight ahead, will be to the west. So, the college will be to the north.

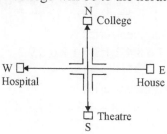

6. **(c)** The movments of the Naresh are as shown in fig.

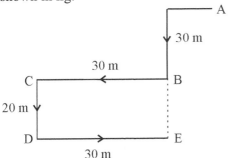

   ∴ Naresh's distance from initial position A
   = AE = (AB + BE) = (AB + CD)
   = (30 + 20) m
   = 50 m

7. **(a)** The movements of Manoj are as shown in figure (O to P, P to Q, Q to R, R to S and S to T).

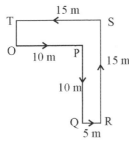

   Since TS = OP + QR, so T lies with O.
   ∴ Required distance
   OT = (RS − PQ)
   = (15 − 10) m
   = 5 m

8. **(b)** The movements of Nilesh are as shown in fig.

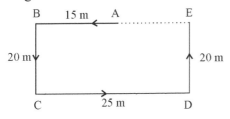

   ∴ Nilesh distance from his house at A.
   AE = (BE − BA)
   = (CD − BA)
   = (25 − 15) m
   = 10 m

9. **(b)** The movements of Geeta are as shown in figure. Clearly she is finally walking in the direction DE i.e, west.

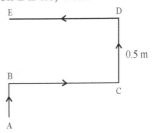

10. **(d)** The movements of Kishan are as shown in figure (A to B, B to C, C to D).

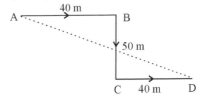

    Clearly his final position is D which is to south-east of starting point A.

11. **(a)** The movements of Mahesh are as shown in fig. (A to B, B to C, C to D, D to E).

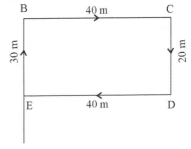

    ∴ Mahesh distance from his original position
    A = AE = (AB − BE)
    = (AB − CD)
    = (30 − 20)m = 10 m

12. **(b)** Clearly, the seating arrangement is as shown in the adjoining figure.

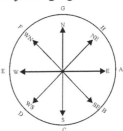

    So, D is at the south west position.

Hints and Solutions

13. **(d)** Clearly comparing the direction of P w.r.t. R in second diagram with that in the first diagram, P will be south – west of R.

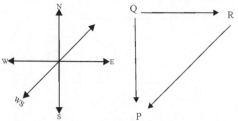

14. **(d)** The posture of the Ramesh is as shown. Clearly, the left hand points towards north.

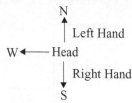

15. **(a)** Clearly, the positions of the minute and hour hands at 12 noon and 1.30 p.m. are as shown in the diagram. So, as shown, the hour hand at 1.30 p.m. points towards the east.

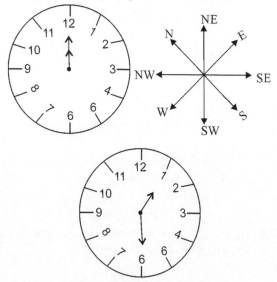

16. **(c)** Rohan initially faces in the direction OA. On moving 135° anti clockwise, he faces in the direction OB. On further moving 180° clockwise, he faces on the direction OC, which is south west, as shown in fig.

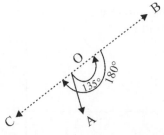

17. **(a)** Ritesh moves from his village at O to his uncle's village at A and thereon to his father in law village at B.

Clearly, ΔOBA is right-angled at B.

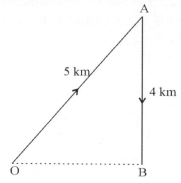

So, $OA^2 = OB^2 + AB^2$
$\Rightarrow OB^2 = OA^2 - AB^2$
$\Rightarrow OB = \sqrt{(25-16)}$ km = $\sqrt{(9)}$ km = 3km.

Thus B is 3km to the east of his initial position O.

18. **(a)** The movements of Karim are as shown in fig. (A to B, B to C, C to D, D to E).

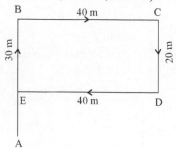

∴ Karim's distance from his original position A = AE = (AB − BE)
= (AB − CD)
= (30 − 20) m
= 10 m

19. **(b)** The movements of Ankur are as shown in fig. (P to Q, Q to R and R to S). Clearly, his final position is S which is to the south east of the starting point P.

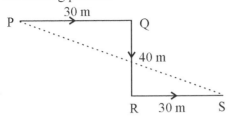

20. **(a)** The movements of Rohit are as shown in fig.

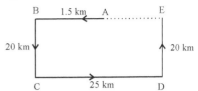

∴ Rohit's distance from his house at A
AE = (BE − BA)
= (CD − BA)
= (25 − 15)km = 10km

9. ESSENTIAL ELEMENT

Answer Key

1. (d)	2. (d)	3. (c)	4. (d)	5. (d)	6. (c)	7. (a)	8. (b)	9. (a)	10. (d)
11. (b)	12. (b)	13. (a)	14. (c)	15. (a)	16. (c)	17. (a)	18. (a)	19. (d)	20. (c)
21. (b)	22. (c)	23. (c)	24. (b)	25. (a)	26. (d)	27. (b)	28. (a)	29. (d)	30. (a)

1. **(d)** Knowledge is gained through experience or study, so learning is the essential element. A school (choice a) is not necessary for learning or knowledge to take place, nor is a teacher or a textbook (choices b and c).

2. **(d)** A culture is the behaviour pattern of a particular population, so customs are the essential element. A culture may or may not be civil or educated (choices a and b). A culture may be an agricultural society (choice c), but this is not the essential element.

3. **(c)** An antique is something that belongs to, or was made in, an earlier period. It may or may not be a rarity (choice a), and it cannot be an artifact, an object produced or shaped by human craft (choice b). An antique is old but does not have to be prehistoric (choice d).

4. **(d)** A dimension is a measure of spatial content. A compass (choice a) and ruler (choice b) may help determine the dimension, but other instruments may also be used, so these are not the essential element here. An inch (choice c) is only one way to determine a dimension.

5. **(d)** A purchase is an acquisition of something. A purchase may be made by trade (choice a) or with money (choice b), so those are not essential elements. A bank (choice c) may or may not be involved in a purchase.

6. **(c)** An infirmary is a place that takes care of the infirm, sick, or injured. Without patients, there is no infirmary. Surgery (choice a) may not be required for patients. A disease (choice b) is not necessary because the infirmary may only see patients with injuries. A receptionist (choice d) would be helpful but not essential.

7. **(a)** Sustenance is something, especially food, that sustains life or health, so nourishment is the essential element. Water and grains (choices b and c) are components of nourishment, but other things can be taken in as well. A menu (choice d) may present a list of foods, but it is not essential to sustenance.

8. **(b)** Provisions imply the general supplies needed, so choice b is the essential element. The other choices are by products, but they are not essential.
9. **(a)** Without students, a school cannot exist; therefore, students are the essential part of schools. The other choices may be related, but they are not essential.
10. **(d)** Words are a necessary part of language. Slang is not necessary to language (choice b). Not all languages are written (choice c). Words do not have to be spoken in order to be part of a language (choice a).
11. **(b)** The necessary part of a book is its pages; there is no book without pages. Not all books are fiction (choice a), and not all books have pictures (choice c). Learning (choice d) may or may not take place with a book.
12. **(b)** A desert is an arid tract of land. Not all deserts are flat (choice d). Not all deserts have cacti or oases (choices a and c).
13. **(a)** Lightning is produced from a discharge of electricity, so electricity is essential. Thunder and rain are not essential to the production of lightning (choices b and d). Brightness may be a by-product of lightning, but it is not essential (choice c).
14. **(c)** Water is essential for swimming; without water, there is no swimming. The other choices are things that may or may not be present.
15. **(a)** All shoes have a sole of some sort. Not all shoes are made of leather (choice b); nor do they all have laces (choice c). Walking (choice d) is not essential to a shoe.
16. **(c)** An ovation is prolonged, enthusiastic applause, so applause is necessary to an ovation. An outburst (choice a) may take place during an ovation; "bravo" (choice b) may or may not be uttered; and an encore (choice d) would take place after an ovation.
17. **(a)** A bonus is something given or paid beyond what is usual or expected, so reward is the essential element. A bonus may not involve a raise in pay or cash (choices b and c), and it may be received from someone other than an employer (choice d).
18. **(a)** A cage is meant to keep something surrounded, so enclosure is the essential element. A prisoner (choice b) or an animal (choice c) are two things that may be kept in cages, among many other things. A zoo (choice d) is only one place that has cages.
19. **(d)** A wedding results in a marriage, so choice d is the essential element. Love (choice a) usually precedes a wedding, but it is not essential. A wedding may take place anywhere, so a church (choice b) is not required. A ring (choice c) is often used in a wedding, but it is not necessary.
20. **(c)** A faculty consists of a group of teachers and cannot exist without them. The faculty may work in buildings (choice a), but the buildings aren't essential. They may use textbooks (choice b) and attend meetings (choice d), but these aren't essential.
21. **(b)** A recipe is a list of directions to make something. Recipes may be used to prepare desserts (choice a), among other things. One does not need a cookbook (choice c) to have a recipe, and utensils (choice d) may or may not be used to make a recipe.
22. **(c)** Without a signature, there is no autograph. Athletes and actors (choices a and b) may sign autographs, but they are not essential. An autograph can be signed with something other than a pen (choice d).
23. **(c)** Without a first-place win, there is no champion, so winning is essential. There may be champions in running, swimming, or speaking, but there are also champions in many other areas.
24. **(b)** A saddle is something one uses to sit on an animal, so it must have a seat (choice b). A saddle is often used on a horse (choice a), but it may be used on other animals. Stirrups (choice c) are often found on a saddle but can not be used. A horn (choice d) is found on

Western saddles, but not on English saddles, so it is not the essential element here.

25. **(a)** A dome is a large rounded roof or ceiling, so being rounded is essential to a dome. A geodesic dome (choice b) is only one type of dome. Some, but not all domes, have copper roofs (choice d). Domes are often found on government buildings (choice c), but domes exist at many other places.

26. **(d)** A glacier is a large mass of ice and cannot exist without it. A glacier can move down a mountain, but it can also move across a valley or a plain, which rules out choice a. Glaciers exist in all seasons, which rules out choice b. There are many glaciers in the world today, which rules out choice c.

27. **(b)** A directory is a listing of names or things, so (choice b) is the essential element. A telephone (choice a) often has a directory associated with it, but it is not essential. A computer (choice c) uses a directory format to list files, but it is not required. Names (choice d) are often listed in a directory, but many other things are listed in directories, so this is not the essential element.

28. **(a)** An agreement is necessary to have a contract. A contract may appear on a document (choice b), but it is not required. A contract may be oral as well as written, so choice c is not essential. A contract can be made without an attorney (choice d).

29. **(d)** A hurricane cannot exist without wind. A beach is not essential to a hurricane (choice a). A hurricane is a type of cyclone, which rules out (choice b). Not all hurricanes cause damage (choice c).

30. **(a)** Residents must be present in order to have a town. A town may be too small to have skyscrapers (choice b). A town may or may not have parks (choice c) and libraries (choice d), so they are not the essential elements.

10. MIRROR IMAGES

Answer Key

1. (c)	2. (d)	3. (b)	4. (d)	5. (a)	6. (c)	7. (b)	8. (d)	9. (a)	10. (d)
11. (d)	12. (a)	13. (c)	14. (c)	15. (b)	16. (b)	17. (b)	18. (d)	19. (d)	20. (b)
21. (d)	22. (d)	23. (c)	24. (b)	25. (c)	26. (d)	27. (b)	28. (d)	29. (a)	30. (c)

11. EMBEDDED FIGURE

Answer Key

1. (c)	2. (d)	3. (a)	4. (d)	5. (c)	6. (c)	7. (b)	8. (d)	9. (d)	10. (a)
11. (a)	12. (a)	13. (d)	14. (c)	15. (b)	16. (c)	17. (b)	18. (c)	19. (a)	20. (b)
21. (a)	22. (d)	23. (a)	24. (b)	25. (b)	26. (b)	27. (a)	28. (d)	29. (b)	30. (b)

Hints and Solutions

12. FIGURE PUZZLES

Answer Key

1. (d)	2. (c)	3. (c)	4. (b)	5. (d)	6. (a)	7. (d)	8. (a)	9. (d)	10. (c)
11.(c)	12. (c)	13. (b)	14. (b)	15. (c)	16. (c)	17. (b)	18. (b)	19. (b)	20. (c)
21. (b)	22. (a)	23. (d)	24. (b)	25. (a)					

1. **(d)**
    From figure I $(2 \times 2 - 1) = 3$
    and from figure II $(5 \times 4 - 5) = 15$
    From figure III $(5 \times 5 - 3) = 22$

2. **(c)**
    For first triangle,
    $10 - 4 = 6$
    $18 - 10 = 8$
    $18 - 4 = 14$
    For second triangle,
    $14 - 8 = 6$
    $22 - 14 = 8$
    $22 - 8 = 14$
    For third triangle,
    $11 - 5 = 6$
    $15 - 11 = 4$
    $\therefore\ ? = 15 - 5 = 10$

3. **(c)**
    From figure I $(4 + 8) \times 9 = 108$
    $\therefore\ ? = (5 + 4) \times 12 = 108$

4. **(b)**
    $1 + 2 + 3 + 4 = 10$
    and $1 + 3 + 5 + 8 = 17$
    Similarly, $? = 1 + 4 + 6 + 9 = 20$

5. **(d)**
    From figure I $(1)^2 + (5)^2 + (4)^2 + (3)^2$
    $= 51 \times 10 = 510$
    and from figure II $(3)^2 + (4)^2 + (6)^2 + (2)^2$
    $= 65 \times 10 = 650$
    Similarly, from figure III $(0)^2 + (1)^2 + (2)^2 + (8)^2 = 69 \times 10 = 690$

6. **(a)**
    From column I $(5 + 3)/2 = 4$
    and From column II $(6 + 8)/2 = 7$
    Therefore from column III $? = (8 + 4)/2 = 6$

7. **(d)** Here,
    $(5 \times 6) + 2 = 32$
    $(7 \times 6) + 2 = 44$
    $\therefore\ ? = (7 \times 5) + 2 = 37$

8. **(a)** Here,
    $(2)^2 = 4$
    $(8)^2 = 64$
    $(5)^2 = 25$
    $\therefore\ ? = (1)^2 = 1$

9. **(d)**
    From figure I $(3 \times 4 - 8) = 4$
    From figure II $(2 \times 5 - 4) = 6$
    and from figure III $(4 \times 5 - 9) = 11$

10. **(c)**
    From figure I $13 + 15 = 28$
    From figure II $36 + 54 = 90$
    Therefore, from figure III $45 + 63 = 108$

11. **(c)**
    From figure I $(5 \times 6 \times 4)/10 = 12$
    and from figure II $(6 \times 7 \times 5)/10 = 21$
    Therefore, from figure III $? = (4 \times 8 \times 10)/10 = 32$

12. **(c)**
    From column I $(4 \times 8) + 1 = 33$
    From column II $(5 \times 9) + 1 = 46$
    Similarly, from column III $(7 \times ?) + 1 = 78$
    $? = \dfrac{77}{7} = 11$

13. **(b)**
    $(2)^2 + (4)^2 = 20$
    $(3)^2 + (9)^2 = 90$
    Therefore, $? = (1)^2 + (5)^2 = 26$

14. **(b)**
    $3 \times 5 \times 4 = 60$
    and $5 \times 7 \times 4 = 140$
    Therefore, $4 \times 4 \times ? = 96$
    $\Rightarrow ? = (96/16) = 6$

15. **(c)**
    $(4 \times 7) \div 4 = 7$
    and $(6 \times 2) \div 3 = 4$
    Therefore, $(6 \times 2) \div 2 = 6$

16. **(c)**
    All numbers are cubes,
    $(7)^3 = 343$
    $(1)^3 = 1$
    $(3)^3 = 27$
    Similarly, $? = (5)^3 = 125$

17. **(b)** Here,
    $(4 + 9 + 2) = (3 + 5 + 7) = (8 + 1 + ?)$
    $\Rightarrow ? = 15 - 9 = 6$
    Total in each case = 15

18. **(b)**
    $(15 + 12)/9 = 3$
    and $(44 + 28)/9 = 8$
    Therefore, $? = (64 + 53)/9 = \dfrac{117}{9} = 13$

19. **(b)** Here,
    $9 + (2)^2 = 13$
    and $13 + (3)^2 = 22$
    and $? = 22 + (4)^2 = 38$

20. **(c)**
    $(30 - 24) \times 8 = 48$
    and $(23 - 12) \times 8 = 88$
    Therefore, $(92 - ?) \times 8 = 48$
    $\Rightarrow 92 - ? = 6$
    $\Rightarrow ? = 92 - 6 = 86$

21. **(b)**
    Putting the position of the letters in reverse order
    P = 11, S = 8, V = 5 and Y = 2

22. **(a)**
    From column I $5 \times 8 \times 10 = 400$
    and from column II $6 \times 9 \times 7 = 378$
    Therefore from column III $5 \times 7 \times ?$
    $= 315$
    $? = 9$

23. **(d)**
    From I row, $1 + (1/2) = 3/2$
    From II row, $2 + (2/3) = 8/3$
    From III row, $3 + ? = 19/5$
    $? = (19/5) - 3$
    $? = (4/5)$

24. **(b)**
    From column I $(7 \times 3) + 8 = 29$
    From column II $(4 \times 3) + 7 = 19$
    From column III $(5 \times ?) + 6 = 31$
    $? = 5$.

25. **(a)**
    From column I $(4)^2 + (2)^2 + (1)^2 = 21$
    and from column II $(5)^2 + (3)^2 + (8)^2 = 98$
    Therefore from column III
    $(6)^2 + (7)^2 + (3)^2 = 94$

SECTION 3: ACHIEVERS' SECTION

HIGHER ORDER THINKING SKILLS (HOTS)

Answer Key

1. (a)	2. (b)	3. (d)	4. (c)	5. (d)	6. (a)	7. (d)	8. (c)	9. (a)	10. (c)
11. (b)	12. (a)	13. (b)	14. (d)	15. (c)	16. (c)	17. (d)	18. (a)	19. (b)	20. (b)

MODEL TEST PAPER - 1

Answer Key

1. (a)	2. (2)	3. (a)	4. (d)	5. (b)	6. (d)	7. (c)	8. (d)	9. (d)	10. (d)
11. (d)	12. (a)	13. (a)	14. (c)	15. (c)	16. (a)	17. (a)	18. (c)	19. (c)	20. (c)
21. (a)	22. (b)	23. (b)	24. (d)	25. (b)	26. (c)	27. (a)	28. (b)	29. (c)	30. (a)
31. (c)	32. (d)	33. (a)	34. (c)	35. (d)	36. (b)	37. (d)	38. (c)	39. (b)	40. (d)
41. (a)	42. (d)	43. (a)	44. (d)	45. (d)	46. (c)	47. (b)	48. (d)	49. (d)	50. (b)

MODEL TEST PAPER - 2

Answer Key

1. (c)	2. (a)	3. (d)	4. (d)	5. (a)	6. (b)	7. (b)	8. (d)	9. (c)	10. (a)
11. (d)	12. (c)	13. (d)	14. (d)	15. (a)	16. (b)	17. (b)	18. (c)	19. (a)	20. (a)
21. (d)	22. (b)	23. (d)	24. (b)	25. (c)	26. (d)	27. (c)	28. (b)	29. (c)	30. (d)
31. (a)	32. (d)	33. (b)	34. (c)	35. (d)	36. (a)	37. (a)	38. (c)	39. (c)	40. (b)
41. (a)	42. (b)	43. (c)	44. (d)	45. (d)	46. (b)	47. (b)	48. (d)	49. (b)	50. (a)